'If you like *The Kite Runner*, you'll love *The Little Coffee Shop of Kabul*. This compelling story of a cafe in the heart of Afghanistan, and the men and women who meet there, is full of heart and intelligence'

Look magazine on *The Little Coffee Shop of Kabul*

'An eye-opening and uplifting tale about sisterhood and survival'

Grazia on *The Little Coffee Shop of Kabul*

'A brilliant story of strength and appreciation of difference that restores belief in humanity'

Daily Telegraph on *The Little Coffee Shop of Kabul*

'A novel of female friendship and support when East meets West, of magic and things we may not understand, of hope, of comfort, and in the background the enticing salty, fishy, spicy aromas of Zanzibar'

Dinah Jeffries on *The Zanzibar Wife*

'A compelling account of three very different women, each challenged by circumstances that reveal the inner conflict in their lives, and their refusal to conform. The book is also a glowing portrait of Oman, a country that for many in the west remains an enigma. The author uses her canvas to bring this unique culture to life, whilst crafting a deft and emotionally engaging tale'
Vaseem Khan on *The Zanzibar Wife*

Also by Deborah Rodriguez

DEBORAH
RODRIGUEZ

Island on the
Edge of the
World

sphere

SPHERE

First published in Australia in 2019 by Bantam,
a division of Penguin Random House Australia
First published in Great Britain in 2020 by Sphere

1 3 5 7 9 10 8 6 4 2

Copyright © Deborah Rodriguez 2019

Recipes © Georges H. Laguerre 2019

The moral right of the author has been asserted.

A CIP catalogue record for this book is available from the British Library.

ISBN 978-0-7515-7458-6

Printed and bound in Great Britain by Clays Ltd, Elcograf S.p.A.

Papers used by Sphere are from well-managed forests
and other responsible sources.

Sphere
An imprint of
Little, Brown Book Group
Carmelite House
50 Victoria Embankment
London EC4Y 0DZ

An Hachette UK Company
www.hachette.co.uk

www.littlebrown.co.uk

*For my two wonderful sons and
my tribe of fabulous grandchildren*

Prologue

Even at the center of the chaos surrounding her, she had never felt so completely alone. It was as though everyone who had ever been close to her had been driven away by a curse, disappearing to another place, a place where she was not allowed.

This was not how her life was supposed to be.

But loneliness was not new to her. She had been carrying it inside for years, missing those she had lost, yearning for things to be the way they had been. She had looked everywhere for hope, and thought she had finally found it. Yet, like everything else, that did not last.

The woman in the cot beside her would not stop moaning. Nobody came to help. She did not blame them. There was so much work to do, and so few of them to do it. It was nobody's fault she was still awake. As exhausted as she was, she did not want to sleep. She did not want to dream.

Tomorrow she would be told to leave. That was fine, as this was certainly not a place where anyone would want to stay long. Busy and cramped, with echoes of pain and grief that were far louder than any sounds of joy and healing. Even in the eyes of the doctors who had looked down on her early the previous morning, their faces half-covered with masks, she had seen only weariness and frustration. Then the electricity had gone out, and they were forced to finish their work by the light of their cell phones.

She turned onto her side and pulled the thin sheet she'd brought along with her around her aching body. The rusted iron cot squealed in protest. The night seemed to be lasting forever.

Finally, the morning sun began its slow climb into the skies over the city, peeking through the hospital's barred windows and streaming across the crowded room in thin white stripes. Roosters crowed, horns blared, motorbikes whirred, people shouted—a new day had begun in Port-au-Prince. As the women around her began to stir, Senzey took her pencils and pad from beneath her pillow, and started to draw.

1

"Voila!" Charlie spun the chair around and smiled into the mirror as she stood behind Meg. She could see her client's mouth turn down a little at the corners as the woman struggled to unsnap the leopard-skin-patterned cape draped across her torso. Charlie quickly turned the chair back toward herself. "It makes you look ten years younger. Maybe even twelve." She brushed stray hairs off Meg's shoulders and, not wanting to compound the doubt, guided her away from the mirror, following the number one rule that every smart hairdresser swore by: Never, ever let the client see their reflection without the cape, or all they'll see is fat.

"I don't know." Meg twisted her head around for another look. "Do you think it makes me look—"

"Trust me. Everyone's going to love it." Charlie helped her out of the cape and into her green quilted jacket.

A silvery voice drifted across the Bea's Hive salon. "You look magnificent, Meg." Charlie turned to see her grandmother seated in her favorite spot—the 1970s-era Naugahyde dryer chair that was stuffed into a corner, its translucent hood tilted back in permanent repose against the wall. She shot the old woman a look, knowing full well that her grandmother couldn't see the layering she'd added to Meg's usual severe bob. She could only hope that Meg would simply accept her grandmother's compliment and forget about just how blind Bea had become.

Charlie swiped Meg's credit card through the machine and scrounged around for a working pen among the dozens jammed into the chipped Wedgwood teapot next to the old cash register.

"Oh, did you raise your prices? I don't believe that's what *you* used to charge me, Bea," Meg snorted as she scrawled her signature across the slip of paper.

"I'd be happy to do your hair for you next time if you want, Meg," Charlie's grandmother said without looking up from her crocheting, the orange scarf she was making for Charlie now measuring at least twelve feet long. "Just hope you won't mind looking like a half-eaten hedgehog," she added, under her breath.

Charlie bit the inside of her cheek to keep from laughing. "Would you care for the receipt?"

After the brass shopkeeper's bell mounted on top of the salon door sounded Meg's exit, Charlie turned her attention to the client in the second chair, a tall woman whose scalp sprouted a garden of little foil packets.

"Jeez, how do you put up with people like that?" the woman said as the screen door banged shut.

"Oh," Charlie sighed, "Meg's all right, Sonja. You know how some people can be—never satisfied with anything, no matter what. We do this dance every time she comes in."

"Meg's all right," Bea echoed. "Just cheap. We all used to call her the Queen of the Alligators, her arms being so short she can never seem to reach her pockets to get out a tip."

After checking to make sure Sonja's color had taken, Charlie began to unwrap each lock of hair as if it were a precious square of artisanal chocolate.

"Do you want to know what *I* heard?" Sonja asked into the mirror.

Charlie paused, fighting an overwhelming urge to say no. Although listening to her clients talk—in fact, *getting* them to talk—was part of the fine art of being a hairdresser, sometimes it became just too much. Already that day she'd heard about two cheating husbands, one thieving housekeeper, and a scandal involving a city councilman. It all seemed so petty and, frankly, boring to her.

"A friend of a friend saw Meg's son at the rehab facility up in Monterey," Sonja continued. "You know, the one who caused that accident last year over at Ocean and Junipero?"

Charlie simply nodded. Often she wished she could un-hear the things she'd been told. It was sometimes hard keeping straight what you were and weren't supposed to know about the person in the chair, and even when you could, it could be challenging to deal with a client about whom you knew way too much. Sometimes she had to fight the urge to tell them to just shut up about their First World problems, and to share with them some of the real problems she'd witnessed growing up in a world so unlike the one they knew.

Charlie was finding Carmel-by-the-Sea to be a real hotbed for drama queens and small-town gossip. And being a hairdresser put her at the epicenter of it all. Of course, she couldn't help but feel sympathy for her clients and their problems, but what was she supposed to do about it? There was only so far lending an ear could go. She had read somewhere that psychiatrists suffered the highest rate of work-related stress of any occupation. Hairdressers, she thought, must come in a close second.

Her grandmother, Bea, had been born and bred in Carmel, and she loved it here. She was in her element hanging out with the artists and poets, the dreamers and drifters. The old woman was even at home among the wealthy of the town, many of whom still sought her out for those talents she possessed that had nothing whatsoever to do with hairdressing.

But Charlie, who had spent the past year helping out at her grandmother's salon, Bea's Hive, knew it was not for her. She hadn't lived here since she was five, when her mother had plucked her out of kindergarten and whisked her away to help her new stepfather bring the word of the Lord to the deepest corners of the Amazon rainforest—whether the people of the Amazon rainforest wanted it or not. When a teenage Charlie first arrived, alone, back on the doorstep of Bea's Hive, it was only to use Carmel as a hopping-off point, a place to crash temporarily, do her laundry and get her bearings before heading off to another semester at another school, another promising-sounding job in another city, another trial run in another country, and other attempts at finding a life for herself. She never intended to settle here. Apart from some ancient memories of Bea reading her bedtime stories and letting her lick cake batter off a spoon, Charlie felt no connection to this place. Nor to any place, for that matter. Her years as a third-culture kid living in a world that was not her own had left her with a rootlessness and restlessness that traveled around with her like extra baggage.

"Well," Sonja continued, "I know one thing. If it were me, I'd have kicked that kid out of the house a long time ago."

Charlie pointed Sonja toward the shampoo bowl.

"I'm sure you would have, Sonja," Bea chimed in. "The way you're dealing with your own son getting booted out of the community college over that cheating thing is proof of that."

Charlie watched the flush rise from Sonja's neck to her cheeks. She doubted the woman had shared that tidbit with Bea, and Charlie was well aware of how uncomfortable her grandmother's psychic abilities could make people feel—as though someone was reading their personal journal without their permission.

Of course, Charlie also knew plenty of things about her clients without them telling her. She could tell who'd had a facelift by the way their skin was folded into those little tucks behind the ears. Or who had a new boy toy, obvious from a sudden desire to cover their gray hairs. But her grandmother, well, she knew way, *way* more.

Once washed and towel-dried, Sonja plopped herself back down in the swivel chair for a blowout, sweeping the wet bangs off her face as she leaned in toward the gilt-framed mirror. "Why can't you give me color like yours, Charlie? And those curls!"

"Only Mother Nature can bless a person with hair like Charlie's," Bea said. "*Chestnut Filly*, I'd call it, if it were something that could be put in a bottle. Can I get you some coffee, Sonja?"

"Maybe Sonja would prefer some cucumber water, Bibi," Charlie said, using the name Bea had taught her to use when she first began to talk. She watched in the mirror as her grandmother stood and turned to the ring-stained mahogany night-stand, where the old percolator rested beside the new water dispenser Charlie had insisted upon in an attempt to bring the salon into the twenty-first century.

"Water? Nobody wants water with vegetables in it, honey."
Charlie's grandmother ran her spotted hands over the mismatched row of mugs, stopping at the one that would now proclaim Sonja—not Bea, not Charlie—to be the World's Best Hairdresser. She filled it to the brim without spilling a drop.

Charlie had just taken the cup from Bea and handed it to Sonja when the bell—which her grandmother swore "renewed the energy of the room" whenever someone entered or exited through the door—tinkled again. Charlie turned to see one of her regulars entering. "Oh shit, did we have an appointment?"

"Elaine, is that you?" Bea asked. "Elaine's here to see me, Charlie." The old woman pushed the purple frames of her thick, round glasses up onto the bridge of her nose, and began crossing the cluttered salon with the confidence of someone who'd walked those floors her entire life. Charlie managed, just in time, to wheel aside the plastic cart she'd snuck into the salon one day while her grandmother was napping. She'd been desperate for a proper spot to organize her tools amid the remnants of Bea's days behind the chair—the wig stands, the rollers, the ancient styling books. Charlie was not allowed to change a thing in the salon. Despite her attempts, she'd failed to convince her grandmother to part with any of the so-called treasures she'd accumulated over the years.

The room, with its trinkets and knickknacks, crystals and beads, felt claustrophobic to Charlie, who personally preferred to travel light. To Bea, everything told a story. The snow globe collection occupying the towel shelf? Gifts from her clients' travels. The pile of books blocking the window? A revolving lending library that spoke volumes about the tastes of her customers. The dingy white walls were jam-packed with photos of Bea and half the town's population—photos Bea could no longer see, yet refused to take down for a much-needed paint job. And the art! Carmel seemed to have more painters than residents, and none of them worth the paper they dribbled on, in Charlie's opinion at least.

Charlie let out a sigh as the two women disappeared through the door that led from the salon into the rest of the house. "Sorry for my grandmother's rudeness. She sometimes seems to lack a filter."

"Bea? Please." Sonja dismissed the apology with a wave of the hand. "She's a hoot. Honestly? I think she's got quite a gift. And I'm not the only one who thinks that."

Charlie's stepfather had always claimed that Bea was a witch. And he meant that literally, not in the bellyaching way that most sons-in-law toss the term around. Bea was doing the work of the devil, according to his beliefs—the same beliefs he twisted into a permanent wedge he drove straight between Charlie's mom and her own mother. As a child far away from home, Charlie had always been confused by his pronouncements and accusations, her own image of Bea as a fun-loving fairy godmother remaining vivid in her mind. Now, at twenty-seven years old, she knew better than to believe anything that man said.

The blow-dryer started up with a purr. As Charlie twirled and pulled the brush through Sonja's damp hair, her mind went back to the conversation she'd had with Bea over coffee that morning, as they prepared for the first client to arrive.

"Charlie," her grandmother had said, "I've had a dream."

Charlie rolled her eyes. She waited as Bea pulled her wavy gray hair away from her face, holding it in one blue-veined hand as she deftly wrapped a pink scarf around her forehead with the other. She finished it off with a fancy knot, tucked the edges into place, and continued.

"It was as if I were there. Right there in Haiti, with your mother."

"Huh." Charlie did not like thinking about her mother. She'd had word, secondhand, that her parents had been reassigned to Haiti, but knew little more than that. Her grandmother had been bringing up her mother's name a lot lately, as if dangling a piece of bait in front of Charlie's face. So far she'd managed not to bite.

"So what did you dream?" She placed a hand on Bea's arm, suddenly feeling a bit guilty for ignoring her grandmother's need to talk.

"It was strange, Charlie. She looked anxious, and worried."

"Well, who wouldn't be, living with a man like that?"

"That's not what I'm talking about. It was something more, something deeper, maybe something physical."

"You know how dicey those places can be. She'll be fine. She's used to that."

Bea shook her head. "I'm telling you, Charlie."

"So then what?"

"Then I woke up. I don't know. Maybe something's not right."

"I'm sure she's fine, Bibi." Charlie stood and gathered an armful of clean towels, still warm from the dryer. "It was only a dream. We all have dreams."

"Do you dream, Charlie?"

"Sometimes." Charlie had always kept her nightmares to herself, sparing her grandmother from the darker visions of what her life in the jungle had become.

"You should listen to your dreams."

"My dreams are just dreams." Charlie deposited the towels into her grandmother's lap to be folded.

"How do you know?"

"I just know."

Bea's bony fingers worked their magic, turning the pile of terrycloth into a tower of tidy little squares within minutes.

"You know, Charlie," she said once she was done, "I think you take after me more than you probably care to admit."

"Seriously? You mean I'm nosy and cranky and stubborn?" Charlie knew exactly what her grandmother meant, but that didn't mean it was true. "Bibi, I'm about as far from being psychic as I am from being an astronaut."

"Ha ha. Not funny. I'm serious. You are like me. We're not like other people."

Charlie had to laugh. She *never* felt as though she was like other people. She'd been a fish out of water for practically her entire life: at first in the jungle—before she learned to blend in like a chameleon, eventually becoming more Amazon than California—then later, after her exile back to the States, when the stress of trying to pass as just another normal, everyday American college kid took its toll. Life after that, spent couch-surfing and house-sitting, continent-hopping and driving cross-country back and forth like a criminal on the run, didn't allow Charlie enough time to fit in anywhere. And she definitely had nothing in common with anyone here in Carmel-by-the-Sea.

"So maybe we're not," Charlie said. "But I think it's best that you stick to your talents, and I'll stick to mine."

"Suit yourself. But I'm telling you, something's going on down there in Haiti."

Charlie turned her back on the old woman and busied herself cleaning the combs. "I don't want to hear it. If she wanted our help that badly, she would have found a way to let us know."

"You know how controlling that man is. You think he'd let her even get near a phone without him listening in?"

"So what do you want me to do about it?" Charlie turned around to face her grandmother, her hands coming to rest on her hips.

Bea swept her arm through the air as if swatting a fly, the heavy bangles stacked on her wrist clattering like a train on the tracks. "Never mind. What do I know? I'm just a silly old woman who only sees in her sleep. You go about your business. From now on I'll just keep my dreams to myself." She paused, then added: "Even if it means something terrible might happen."

"Cut it out, Bibi. I know what you're doing, and it's not going to work. Not this time." Charlie went to the door and flipped the sign around from *Closed* to *Open*.

"Even if—"

"I'm not listening."

"But let me just say—"

"Stop."

"If there's one—"

"Shush."

"Maybe—"

"*Enough*, Bibi, I am *not* going to Haiti!"

2

"Did you find the sunscreen? You know what happens to that fair skin of yours."

"I have it, Bibi."

"And don't forget the insect repellant. There's bound to be tons of mosquitos buzzing around down there."

"Got it."

"Hand wipes? Band-aids? Your hat?"

"Yep."

"You got all your shots, right?"

"Yes, Bibi. Remember I lived in the jungle? I know about shots."

"And make sure you grab some leaves from the aloe plant on the kitchen windowsill."

"I'll be fine. Stop worrying so much."

"I'm not worrying, Charlie. I'm just helping. Oh, and take my pashmina, the peachy one. It will go with everything."

"I'm not going on a cruise, Bibi. I hardly think what goes with what will matter."

"Well, a little color never hurts any situation, that's what I always say." Bea forced a smile in Charlie's direction. In truth, she was worried. After finally seeing success with her most recent attempt at convincing Charlie to try to reconnect with her mother, she didn't want it to backfire. It had taken a long couple of weeks, filled with Bea's increasingly vivid tales of nocturnal visions, underscored with a few tears, to get Charlie to cave in and agree to go down to Haiti herself to check on April. Bea had glowed with satisfaction at her victory, then had almost immediately become concerned about what Charlie might face once she got there. The last thing the girl needed was to be knocked off her feet, yet again.

For Bea, her granddaughter smoothing and folding her clothes on the bed between them brought back memories of the first time Charlie left her. That was the day her heart had truly broken in two.

"Why don't you leave the girl with me?" she had begged her daughter, during a standoff in this very room. The suitcases were already by the door. "At least let her finish out the school year here."

April had shaken her head firmly as she checked the empty bureau drawers one last time.

"It's your choice to go live in the godforsaken jungle with that man, not hers," Bea pleaded.

Still her daughter didn't answer.

"What, now you're not speaking to me?" Bea asked.

April spun toward her mother. "Charity is *my* daughter, not yours. And 'that man' is my husband. And it's my husband's calling that we go. And it's my duty to support him. And that's all I have to say about it. Done. Finished."

14

Bea hated the name Charity. The girl had been Charlie to her ever since she was born. And she'd cringed at the word "husband". April had been married to Jim for less than a month, and had known him for three, at most. He'd set his sights on her one afternoon at the coffee shop in town and never let go, reeling her in with sappy compliments, stopping by the salon with hot chocolate and flowers, the type of attention a single mother of a five-year-old wasn't used to. Next came an invitation to his church up in Seaside. April soon started attending two or three times a week, twice on Sundays. Bea had no objection to religion, though she leaned toward a more personally curated brand of spirituality herself. It would have been one thing if the guy had simply been one of those Jesus freaks who used to gather by the dozen down at the beach, with their puka-shell necklaces and ponytails and their charming thoughts about peace and love and living in harmony. But there was something that felt a bit dark about Jim's devotion, both to April and to the church. Something that made Bea worry her daughter was diving in way too deep, way too fast.

"You barely know the man, April. Take your time to sort things out. Don't drag the baby with you. It's not fair to her. He doesn't even know Charlie. Hell, he doesn't even know you! At least get to know each other on familiar ground."

April shook her head again. "This is bigger than Charity, Mom. It's bigger than me, and bigger than you. Jim has been called on by God." She shoved the last empty drawer shut.

"Since when did God become the one telling you how to raise your child? What the hell are you going to do when you're four thousand miles away in the middle of nowhere and have no one to turn to for support if things get rough? The girl needs her family, April. Charlie needs me."

What had she done, Bea thought, to make her daughter so vulnerable to this smooth-talker's bullshit? She'd always allowed April her freedom, but her past rebellions were never anything like this. A missionary's wife? In the jungle? God help us all.

"Despite what you so obviously think, Mom, Jim is a good man. God spoke to him and told him we were to be a family, that I was to be Jim's wife. Just like you have your crazy dreams, God speaks to Jim. You'd never understand." She turned her back on her mother and began to check the closet.

"I understand that you've gone nuts, is what I understand. Why else would you want to drop that innocent baby down in the middle of a jungle, in a place you know nothing of, with a man you've barely spent ten minutes with?"

April slammed the closet door with a force that seemed to rattle the whole old wooden house. "You can't stop me, Mom! It's God's will."

"So it's His will that you take this child away from her own grandmother, the woman who's practically raised her? All of a sudden you're hearing what God has to say so clearly? Or is that Jim's voice in your ears?"

"What don't you get?" her daughter yelled. "For the first time in my life I have a chance to do something that matters, to be part of something bigger than myself. And all you can do is try to manipulate me into staying here in this stupid salon, on my feet all day, making nice to women who whine about stupid little problems that no one in their right mind would give a damn about. You want me stuck here, clipping and curling and sweeping for the rest of my life, just like you? Well, you know what? I don't want to be like you. I want to do something *important* with my life."

April's words had hurt. Of course Bea had dreamed of something more for her daughter, but she was also proud of her profession, and enjoyed her life behind the chair. But it was April who got herself pregnant right out of high school, with a boy from up north who, shortly after, wrapped his motorcycle around a telephone pole. It had given the town plenty to gossip about at the time. But Bea hadn't given a damn about any of that, because then there was Charlie. The only thing she did regret was that her daughter hadn't had more of a chance, early on, to find herself, to become the person she wanted to be, before becoming a mother.

That last conversation had not ended well. More slammed doors, both of them yelling and crying. They never did have a proper goodbye. And Bea regretted the row every single day of her life.

The sound of a zipper closing brought her back to the present. "You're done?" She wagged a spindly finger toward the spot where Charlie's bag rested on the bed. "Open it back up. I want to make sure you've packed enough."

Charlie sighed and did as her grandmother asked. "I don't need that much, Bibi. I'm only staying for a couple of days."

"You never know."

"Yes, I do know. I promised you I'd do some snooping around, find out whatever I can find out. That's it."

Bea shrugged her shoulders.

"You know he won't let me see her, Bibi. What am I supposed to do then?"

"You'll find a way, dear. Trust me."

"Well, even if I do manage to see her, I'm in and out. That's it. I'll be back for my Friday appointments."

Bea kept quiet.

"I'm only doing this for you, you know. She didn't exactly barricade the door when I left. My own mother practically handed me my suitcase."

Bea knew very little about what had happened in the jungle during those years before Charlie left. She'd seen her daughter and granddaughter less than a handful of times after their move, while the family was back in the States on hiatus, traveling up and down the West Coast raising funds for their mission. Even in those early days of their marriage, Jim was keeping April on a short leash, allowing visits with her mother to take place only under his supervision, and only for an hour at a time. Those visits were torture for Bea, sitting there muzzled by his steely glare, bursting with questions she didn't dare ask.

And Charlie! The feeling of that girl rushing into her arms never failed to bring tears to her eyes. Even though each time they met the child's legs were a bit longer, her body a tad heavier, her words more skilled, it was always as though she'd never left. The two of them would escape into the salon and spin around in the swivel chairs until they were too dizzy to stand, then she'd let Charlie try on wigs and play with makeup while Bea painted her toes a reddish-brown to match the color of her hair. Charlie's broad smile was enough to make Bea burst with joy. But the joy was always tempered by the sense of the ticking clock. Bea wasn't able to learn much about their lives, but she did know one thing. Though April may have appeared quiet and serious when under the watchful eyes of her husband, inside her stony demeanor was a woman who loved her little girl with all her heart.

"Sometimes people do what they have to do," Bea now said to the girl, cringing at the utter uselessness of her words.

"What does that even mean? She said she'd come. She said she'd follow me. So what happened?"

Bea heard the catch in her voice, and reached out to fold her granddaughter's hand into her own. "Your mother loves you, Charlie. Don't ever question that. She had to have had her reasons."

"You've said that before."

"And I'll say it again. All I know is that your mother needs us right now."

"Us?" Charlie laughed. "Really? I don't see *you* packing any bags, getting any needles jabbed into *your* bony arms."

Bea's right hand instinctively went to the sore spot on her opposite arm.

Charlie stopped dead in her tracks, the duffel cradled in her arms. "What? You're not . . ."

"Well, just in case. I thought maybe you might want—"

"Seriously, Bibi? Are you kidding me?"

"I know, I know. What use would I be, an old fart who can barely see past her own crooked nose? It's just killing me, Charlie," she said with a sniffle. "How could I live with myself, knowing that something wasn't right and I didn't do a thing about it? I'm not about to go to my grave carrying that around my neck."

"Stop it, Bibi. You're not about to go to any grave." Charlie stood and grabbed a tissue from the nightstand.

"And I just worry about you, going all the way down there by yourself."

"You know you don't need to worry about me. I was just fine on my own for all those years, before I came back here to stay with you. Think of all the places I've been, and returned from in one piece to tell you all about." Charlie plopped back down on the bed and took her grandmother's hand in her own. They sat without speaking, the squeaky ceiling fan counting out the seconds like a metronome. Bea waited.

"I don't know, Bibi. All that travel? And the weather. You're not used to that kind of heat."

"I'm not going to melt."

"And I'll probably be doing a lot of running around."

"So go and run. I'm a grown-up. I can take care of myself."

"But you've never been anywhere."

"Well then, don't you think it's about time?" Bea waited for her granddaughter's response.

Finally Charlie let out a sigh. "Okay." Bea squeezed her hand, hard. "But here's the deal," she continued, shaking out her fingers. "I call the shots. All of them. No dreams. No premonitions. No 'I have a feeling, Charlie.' If you do, you keep it all to yourself. We're going on a fact-finding mission. Nothing more. We're just going to see if she's okay, make sure she's not in danger, and we're outta there. Understood?"

"Understood. I am completely at your command." Bea smiled and nodded, her middle finger crossing over her pointer as Charlie stood and headed to the door.

3

The thickset woman was perched on the edge of her seat, one hand anxiously gripping the handle of her suitcase, the other firmly atop a pile of belongings taking up the spot next to her. Charlie gestured toward the seat, the only one available on a busy morning at the airport, and the woman shifted her things to make room.

"I apologize," the woman said. "All this stuff I'm toting around. Hard to keep myself organized."

"Not a problem." Charlie guided Bea to sit, and thanked the woman with a slight nod, her gesture returned in a nervous smile.

"Y'all missionaries?" the woman asked, her voice telling of a Southern, or maybe Texas, background.

Bea's sharp laugh bounced across the waiting area like a billiard ball. Charlie shushed her grandmother with a nudge of her foot and replied. "No. Not missionaries."

"My mistake. I just assumed y'all were on a mission. I didn't think *anybody* who wasn't with the church went to Haiti. Well, at least not voluntarily."

"So you're a missionary?" Charlie asked, noting the gold cross hanging from a chain around the woman's neck.

"Oh, goodness, no." She shook her head. "Not me." The woman stuck out a hand. "My name's Lizbeth. Lizbeth Johnston."

"Charlie." As they shook, Charlie couldn't help but notice the perspiration coating Lizbeth's plump palm.

"Charlie," the woman said. "Isn't that an interesting name for a girl."

"My real name is Charity," she explained, sweeping her long curls over one shoulder. "Charlie for short. And this," she said as she placed a hand on her grandmother's shoulder, "is my grandmother, Bea."

Bea waved her hand in the general direction of the woman. "Hello."

"So I take it this is your first time going to Haiti?" Charlie asked.

Lizbeth looked at her as if she were mad. "My first time in *Florida*. I've never even been east of the Mississippi before."

"Well, I would hardly call this Florida." Charlie chuckled. "We could be in any airport, anywhere, right?"

Lizbeth shrugged. "I don't really know about that. I haven't traveled all that much, other than when we took our son to Disneyland, once, and a couple of cruises with my husband. We didn't get a start on cruising until after Darryl retired from his teaching job. He was always working before that, even in the summers. He's passed now." The woman's eyes seemed to lose their focus, as if she were thinking about times long past. "This is my first time traveling solo."

TMI, Charlie thought. The poor woman was obviously a nervous traveler. Charlie checked her phone for the time. She hated layovers. All those wasted hours. She always just wanted to get where she was going already. Especially on this trip. In and out. The sooner the better.

"And in all my fifty-eight years I've definitely never gone anywhere like *this*," Lizbeth added with a wrinkle of her nose.

Charlie cringed a little at Lizbeth's words. "Honestly, I'm not sure what you've heard about Haiti, but I doubt it's as bad as you think. Trust me, I've probably seen much worse."

"Oh, honey, don't get me wrong." Lizbeth placed a hand on Charlie's arm, her white-tipped acrylic nails putting Charlie's bitten-down nubs to shame. "I'm tore up over those poor people and all they've been through, what with the earthquake and all. My ladies' church group back home, we've done a bunch for the Haitian people—collecting clothes, shoes. We even made a hundred little dresses out of pretty flowered dishtowels, and sent them on down. I'm just not sure what to expect, going there by myself and all, it being so far, and so different."

"You're going down there to find someone?" Bea asked out of nowhere, turning in her seat to face Lizbeth. Charlie steeled herself in anticipation of the reaction that always came from those unfamiliar with her grandmother and her psychic abilities.

Lizbeth's eyes grew round behind the lenses of her wire-rimmed glasses, the kind that went from light to dark in the sun. "Why, yes, I *am* going down there hoping to find someone. How on earth did you . . .?"

Charlie jumped in before Bea could answer, going straight into full hairdresser mode—just as her grandmother had taught her—sitting down cross-legged on the floor and peppering the woman with questions. Soon Lizbeth was confiding in Charlie as if they'd known each other their entire lives.

Within three months, Lizbeth had lost both her husband and her son. Her husband to an aggressive form of cancer that took him before she barely knew what was happening. Her son's death came in the form of a speeding car that swerved across the dividing line, hitting him head-on. Luke had been temporarily living at home with her, having arrived shortly before his father's passing, planning on staying until he felt his mother would be able to cope on her own. If only he hadn't. If only she'd been stronger. He was a good boy, Lizbeth told Charlie, with tears in her eyes. Always trying to help others, watching out for those less fortunate than him, bless his heart. That was what had taken him down to Haiti in the first place. It was a job with a group that was teaching people to manage their water, you know, by building wells and capping springs? One of those NGOs, you know. Maybe Charlie had heard of them? Luke claimed to have loved it there, but Lizbeth always wondered if he just told her that to keep her from worrying too much. She felt badly that he had given up his engineering work to come help her, and the guilt of knowing that he would still be alive today if only he'd returned to Haiti after his father passed, instead of sticking around to babysit her.

Lizbeth stopped, blinking and fanning her eyes with her hands in an attempt to stave off the tears. It didn't take Bea's sixth sense for Charlie to see how broken the woman was by so much tragedy hitting in such a short time. Who wouldn't be broken? She watched as Lizbeth took a deep breath and continued with her story.

It wasn't until eight months after her son's passing that a letter found its way to her house. Lizbeth's hands shook as she took it from her purse to show Charlie. It was addressed to Luke, in what looked to be a schoolgirl's best writing, all loops and straight lines, the i's carefully dotted and the t's firmly crossed. Lizbeth hadn't had any idea what to expect when it first appeared in her mailbox, smudged and tattered like a weary traveler. Luke didn't talk about his private life much. He was a lot like his dad in that way. Sweet, but not a sharer. Maybe Charlie wanted to read it?

Dear Luke, the letter read. *Why have I not herd from you for so long? I have tried your email, but have had no answers. I have your family's house address from your job. I hope your mother is ok. I pray to the saints and the spirits and anybody who will listen for this.*

I mis you every day. I smell your skin in the pillows, I hear your voice in my ear when I sleep. I want the day to come fast when you are here with me again in Port-au-Prince. I am sad in the city without you.

When I see you, I hope you will be happy like me, because I have news. We will have a child. Soon I will be big like a truck. Already he is starting to move. I am sure it is a boy. I will name him Lukson. But if it is a girl, I will name her Lucille. Whichever it is, I know the baby will be beautiful like you. I hope you are home before the baby is here. Please be fast. Mwen renmen ou anpil. I love you.

Senzey

Lizbeth had looked for a return address, but, as you can see, she told Charlie, there was none. The folks Luke worked for were no help. They said they'd never heard of a Senzey. And, for the life of her, she could not find a way to get into his computer to look for her via email.

Who was this girl? Her friends told her she was crazier than a loon to even pay it any mind, that Senzey was probably just some girl looking to get her Green Card. That there probably wasn't ever any baby at all, and if there was, who's to say it was Luke's?

But Lizbeth could not stop thinking about it, going back and forth in her head for months, dreaming of her son who she'd never see again, haunted by the possibility of a grandbaby she'd never meet. And now, here she was. On her way, alone, to Haiti to find out the truth for herself.

"But really, how am I gonna navigate?" Lizbeth leaned forward toward Charlie's spot on the floor. "The only language I speak besides my own is Spanish, and I only had two semesters of that, a long, long time ago. And getting around? I don't have a clue. My husband always took care of that sort of thing, wherever we were." Charlie watched her twisting the wedding band around and around on her finger as she spoke. "And, not to mention, how am I gonna actually find this child—if there is a child. The only thing I have is the mother's first name. My friends are right. I have truly gone nuts." Lizbeth's head dropped into her hands, her fingers clutching at her yellow-blond hair that was so stiff with spray it looked as though it might crack.

Charlie felt a sudden surge of protectiveness for this woman. "You're doing the right thing," she said quietly.

"You'll be fine, dear," Bea piped in. "Sometimes things just fall into place when you least expect them to. By the way, what's your sign?"

"But Bibi," Charlie interrupted, "perhaps Lizbeth could use some of our help. You and I both have so much to offer, right?"

Bea narrowed her eyes at Charlie. "Me? I have your rules to follow, remember? And, unfortunately, I doubt you'll be able to find the time down there to truly help Lizbeth in the way that she needs. In and out, I think is what you said, isn't it?"

"Well, I'm sure I could make some time . . ."

"Don't forget your promise, Charity," Bea said, using the name that came out only when she was perturbed.

"I won't forget my promise."

Charlie turned back to Lizbeth, who seemed to be lost in her own thoughts. "I'm not sure exactly what we can do, but we can certainly try to help you."

Lizbeth placed a hand on Charlie's forearm. "I don't want to be a burden."

Charlie turned to her grandmother, then back to Lizbeth. "It's no bother."

"Bless you for offering. You don't even know me." Lizbeth seemed to choke a little on her words.

"You don't need to know somebody in order to offer them help. Think about your son, and all the people he helped."

"We'll do what we can, dear," Bea added with a sigh.

"But I—"

"Seriously," Charlie said. "Consider it an adventure. We'll be like the Three Musketeers!"

"More like the Marx Brothers," Bea said. And Lizbeth laughed for the first time since Charlie had set eyes on her.

"You'll be fine, Lizbeth." Charlie stood and shook out her long legs, the blood returning to her feet with the sting of a hundred needles, prodding her attention back to her own situation. "You'll be fine," she repeated, slower this time. "We'll all be fine."

4

Lizbeth felt like she'd suddenly been plopped smack-dab into somebody else's dream; the sights, the sounds, the whole atmosphere were so unfamiliar that they couldn't possibly be real. The plane ride had been one thing. As she'd passed by the other gates—all those lucky folks heading to Aruba, to Jamaica, to Barbados—the crowd had started to become decidedly darker. And by the time she and Charlie and Bea were settled into their seats on the plane, Lizbeth was well aware of the fact that hers was one of only six white faces onboard. She felt as if she were glowing like a neon sign on a rainy night. She was definitely out of her comfort zone.

The passengers around her were quiet and still, some seemingly in prayer as the plane lifted into the air. A woman wearing five fancy going-to-church hats on her head, each one stacked upon the other, stared silently out the window through the passing clouds at the ocean below. The man next to Lizbeth slept, his hands folded over a small blue paperback book on his lap. Something in French, it looked like. The flight attendant had asked if she were a doctor. A doctor, for heaven's sake! Imagine. Of course, Lizbeth told her no, she was not. But she could kind of understand the woman's assumption, that being *one* good reason for a person coming down here. Then they commiserated together over the plight of the Haitians. "Those poor people," the girl had whispered. "They just can't seem to catch a break. As soon as they get going another disaster strikes. In fact," she added, "we aren't even allowed to do layovers there, it's so dangerous."

Now here Lizbeth was, on the ground, bouncing around in the back seat of a four-wheel drive like a Mexican jumping bean, the words "so dangerous" still ringing in her ears. How could anybody call these *roads*? She prayed she was doing the right thing in agreeing to go with Charlie and Bea to their hotel. She'd been planning on staying at the Best Western, but when she told them she was going to take the courtesy shuttle, Charlie had laughed. Now Lizbeth understood why. The minute they got off that plane, everything turned into sheer chaos. People running around like chickens with their heads cut off, no signs to tell you where to go—or where not to go. And not a help desk in sight. Charlie had Bea on one arm. She had looped Lizbeth in with her other, literally guiding her through the maze of immigration, to the luggage carts, and to the carousel where their bags came tumbling down the chute like boulders in a landslide.

Outside was even worse, the heat and the swarm of strangers pressing together under the shade of a corrugated tin roof practically making her faint. And everyone, simply everyone, wanting to help. Carry your bags? Find you a hotel? Sell you some beads? Get you a taxi? Lizbeth, clutching her slash-proof zipper-locking travel purse close to her chest, didn't know which way to turn. She marveled at Charlie, the way she just kept marching straight ahead in her flip flops and ripped jeans, tossing out a million smiles and what sounded like a "no, messy" to anyone and everyone.

On the other side of the tinted car window, life was exploding onto the streets. Everything was in motion. Little buses and covered pick-up trucks painted from head to toe with slogans— *"The Best"*, *"Nice Girl"*, *"Merci Jesus"*, *"Thank You Lord"*—and plastered with images of queens or superheroes or people she did not recognize. Bigger trucks roared on by, weighed down with water or gravel, their wobbly wheels looking as though they were about to fly right off and follow their own route through the city. An endless swarm of motorbikes flitted in and out of the heavy traffic carrying three, sometimes four people, some of them just babies barely big enough to hold on, and not one of them wearing a helmet!

Then there was the parade of pedestrians, spilling out from the sidewalks and onto the streets, merging into any space left open for a body to pass, like a steady stream finding its way along the bottom of a rocky canyon. Everyone seemed to have somewhere to go. Was it rush hour? she wondered. Or was there always this much activity on the streets?

And the colors! It was as though someone had emptied a giant bucket of ice-cream sprinkles from the sky. Everything was screaming with color, from the walls of the shops to the merchants' umbrellas lining the curbs, the bananas and melons spilling from their baskets, the uniforms of the children on their way home from school, the T-shirts and dresses of the grown-ups out tending to their business under the blazing afternoon sun.

Thank you, sweet Jesus, for air-conditioning, she thought as she settled back into the seat behind Bea. What a funny old bird she was, all trussed up in her scarves and turban, those big round glasses giving her the look of an owl. And how brave she was to make this trip, what with her eyesight failing and all. What must this craziness look like to her? Lizbeth squinted her own eyes and watched as the bustle on the other side of the glass melted into a rippling rainbow swirl.

She tried to picture her son among these people. With his shaggy blond hair and his big blue eyes, he must have stood out like a sore thumb. His father never did understand why Luke would choose such a job. She could still hear their last argument in her head. "All that money we spent on your education, and *this* is what you decide to do with it? If you want to help people," her husband had hollered, "why does it have to be *them*? There are plenty of deserving folks around here who could use your help." Lizbeth remembered being taken aback by her husband's anger. She didn't always agree with his way of looking at things, and often wished he'd keep his opinions to himself, especially when it came to his son. But she imagined he had to have been pretty upset at the thought of their boy going to live so far away. She knew she was.

Luke had wanted them to come visit and had invited them down to Haiti plenty of times. But her husband had stubbornly refused, insisting if he were going to spend his hard-earned money on a trip, there were hundreds of other places he'd rather go. Now she wished she'd fought back. At least she would have maybe got a better sense of what Luke's life was like, who he'd been seeing. Being as good-looking as he was, Luke never did have a problem with the girls. And he was so darn trusting. It would have been no surprise to her, she thought as she watched the circus outside, if he'd fallen prey to a local girl more attracted to his wallet than to his face. How easy it must have been for a woman to wrap that sweet boy around her finger.

The car made a left turn up a slight incline, onto a road even more pitted than the last. Lizbeth felt as though her kidneys were being pounded flat with every bounce. Pretty soon they'd be like two little bean-shaped pancakes.

"This must be it," Charlie said as the car slowed to a stop at a solid steel gate, one side open to the road. The driver waved to a guard slumped in a chair on the edge of the property, a shotgun resting across his lap. Lizbeth, her eyes darting around the teeming streets surrounding them, wondered if he'd ever had reason to use it.

When the guard bolted upright and waved them through, they were transported to another world entirely. Gone in a flash was the frantic hubbub of the city. Here, hidden behind thick walls of solid concrete, was a tropical Garden of Eden, as green and lush as she imagined a jungle would be. There were leaves as big as elephants' ears, and skinny palms stretching up to the sky. She saw the most beautiful purple bougainvillea, and clusters of flowers in a shade of orange she'd never before witnessed in nature. She half expected to see a monkey swinging from branch to branch. Now out of harm's way, she lowered the window beside her.

And then she saw the statues. At first, from a distance, she'd thought they were some sort of scarecrow, that maybe that was how they did them down here, out of metal and twigs and chunks of wood. But on closer inspection, there was something strangely mocking and lewd about the figures, whose eyes seemed to follow her as the car rolled up the driveway. There must have been at least two dozen of them—skeletons and stick figures, skulls in top hats and crowns and pith helmets, some wearing sunglasses, some draped in fabric, and others naked as jaybirds with their big old red-tipped private parts hanging out for all the world to see. It was like a graveyard of crazy walking dead people.

Lizbeth shuddered as the car lurched to a stop, the rickety white hotel looming above them like a wedding cake made out of matchsticks. One little fire, or teensy earthquake, and the place would be history.

Dear God, she thought, shrinking back in her seat. What have I done?

5

Charlie peered up through the windshield at the grand old hotel, which seemed to be welcoming her like a quirky great-aunt, draped in filigree and lace, her face plastered in layers of white as if she were trying desperately to hold on to the illusion of a more youthful and innocent past. Charlie hopped out of the car and flung her arms wide to embrace the glorious air—thick and wet, like you could stick out your tongue and take a lick. What a relief to be out of chilly Carmel-by-the-Sea, where summer and winter were indistinguishable. She'd always loved the tropical heat. It was something she was used to, something that made her feel like herself in a visceral way that was hard to explain. Some people might call it being comfortable in your own skin. To Charlie, it was as though she were home—as surprising as it might be, even to her, that she'd come to think of the Amazon as home. Of course, it was not nearly as hot and humid here as it had been in the rainforest, especially at night when the generators went off, when her long braid would become so damp with sweat she'd have to practically wring it out with her hands. Now Charlie twisted up her curls and held them in place with an elastic band, pushed up the sleeves of her linen shirt, and turned to help the driver unload their bags from the back of the SUV.

What the hell had her grandmother packed, she wondered as she struggled with the old red Samsonite, and exactly how long was the woman planning on staying? Charlie had to laugh. She probably shouldn't worry about Bea. Charlie knew how adaptable she was. Her determination to retain as much independence as she could as her eyesight slowly disappeared was testament to that. The woman never complained, at least not about her own situation. And she was curious. Once something or someone caught Bea's attention there was no letting go. Which is what made her apparent disinterest in Lizbeth seem out of character. She was probably just tired. Once her grandmother was settled into her room at the hotel, Charlie thought, she'd be fine.

Lizbeth Johnston was another story. Judging by the look on her face during the ride from the airport you'd think she'd landed on Mars. Her fingers had turned stiff and white from their grip on the car's armrest, her blue eyes as round as coat buttons, her wrists pre-emptively protected by a trio of mosquito bracelets that looked like old coiled telephone cords and worked like a flea collar. Still, Charlie had to admire the woman, sucking it up to do the right thing. Please, she thought, whatever god or spirit or holy being is listening right now, let this poor woman find what she's looking for.

Charlie herself felt more alive than she had in years. During the drive through the city she'd noticed her heart quickening to keep pace with the pulse of the crowd, her eyes darting from person to person with envy at the sight of the beautiful faces and wide, easy smiles. And the way the Haitians walked! Especially the women. Even the youngest girls exuded a surety and pride in their straight-backed posture and long, even strides, as if sending a message to the world, loud and clear, that they were a force you couldn't mess with.

Charlie marveled at the cleanliness. Not in the streets, of course, where you couldn't ignore the Styrofoam and plastic and paper and who-knows-what-else pushed into piles in a lame attempt to keep the filth somewhat contained. What impressed her was the fact that, despite all the garbage and exhaust and rubble and dust and heat, the people of Port-au-Prince managed to keep their clothes looking crisp and spotless. Even the color-coded uniforms of the kids pouring out of schools seemed as though they'd just come out of the wash, the trousers and skirts neatly pleated, flouncy ribbons shiny and firmly planted in the hair of the girls. She could never manage to stay as neat as that as a child, not in the sweat of the jungle. She found herself smiling at the memory of her mother taking her down to the river for a bath, where she'd allow Charlie to jump right in with a bar of soap, clothes and all. Some evenings, they'd bring inner tubes to use as floats, and drift together under the full moon, making stories out of the formations of the stars that seemed to live so close to Earth.

Charlie listened to the cacophony of horns outside the hotel's wall and tried to imagine how her mother survived the free-for-all that was Port-au-Prince after being so isolated in the Amazon, where they were an hour and a half away by plane from the nearest town of any kind. She'd never forget the first time she, her mother, and Jim took off from the edge of civilization into the sky above pure rainforest, with nothing below them but trees and waterfalls and rivers, until they landed at the tiny mission base, with only one other mission family and a handful of tribespeople to greet them.

Their move to the jungle hadn't been terrible, at least not at first. Charlie was too young to look upon it as anything but an adventure. And what an adventure it was. Dropping from the trees with a splash into the mighty river, learning from the local boys how to fish and hunt—at first just for lizards and small birds, and later alligators, wild pigs, monkeys and capybaras, anything that could be considered dinner. It wasn't long before she became a true tomboy, an accepted member of the ragtag gang of kids who made the riverbanks their playground.

Back then she had been blissfully unaware of the dangers that came with the life they were leading. Of course, she learned early on to jump out of the water, fast, if she cut or scraped herself on a rock. The piranhas were quick to converge on the weak or injured, but they usually didn't bother with just anyone, unless blood was drawn. And most of the insects were simply an annoyance that they became used to, though everyone knew to avoid the bees, the scorpions, and the 24-hour ants, so-named for the full day of excruciating pain you'd suffer from one of their stings. The snakes were another story again.

But for Charlie, the real danger was within the walls of their jungle home. It was the growing sickness in her stepfather's mind—a toxic combination of ego and anger—that had shattered her family into a million pieces.

After depositing Bea's suitcase on the veranda of the hotel and making her way back down the long flight of wooden stairs to the taxi, she hoisted her own duffel onto her shoulder with a groan. The thought of Jim had suddenly turned the paradise she'd arrived in into a darker, more foreboding place. In and out. That's what she'd sworn to herself, what she'd maintained to her grandmother. In and out. She'd do just what she came to do, and before you knew it they'd be heading back to sleepy, foggy Carmel, to the little world of Bea's Hive.

6

The spongy wood of the worn stairs beneath her feet made Bea feel as though she were descending on marshmallows. She held tight to the dusty railing, the chipped paint rough and bumpy against her hand.

"Six more to go," her granddaughter said as the bannister made a tight U-turn on its path from the upstairs rooms down to the hotel's main floor.

"So is this place a dump, or what?" Bea called back over her shoulder.

Charlie laughed. "I wouldn't call it a dump. I'd call it—charming, interesting, a place with character."

"In other words, a dump."

"Give it a chance, Bibi. It really does feel like your kind of place." Charlie took her arm and led Bea out into the open air, some sort of veranda by the feel of the hard tile below and the anemic breeze from fans above. "TripAdvisor gives it three and a half stars," her granddaughter said. "The Abernathy is sort of famous, you know."

"And so was Jack the Ripper."

"What's the matter with you, Bibi?" Charlie helped her grandmother to a tall-backed wooden chair. "Are you feeling okay? Do you want to go back upstairs and rest a little more with Lizbeth?"

"I'm fine," Bea snapped back, wiping the sweat from her cheeks. The truth was that she was anxious, and a bit frustrated. She'd got this far in her plan to reunite Charlie with her mother, and now all the girl seemed to be interested in was babysitting some widow from Texas. She'd even promised to get a translator and a car for the next day, to drive the woman to her son's apartment. *First things first*, Bea had wanted to shout. But she didn't, and so here she was, facing a day of being left behind while her granddaughter got herself all messed up in somebody else's business.

It was obviously a stalling tactic. Bea understood that. She shared the girl's apprehension at the thought of seeing her mother and dealing with that despicable man again after all these years. The last thing she wanted was for her granddaughter to get hurt even more than she already was. Healing those wounds was the whole point of this adventure, after all; recovering that sense of wholeness and security that Charlie was so obviously lacking. At least she'd had the love of her mother to keep her grounded during all that time in the middle of nowhere. Being tossed out alone into the big wide world had turned the girl into a nomad. It was clear that she was struggling to settle in at the salon with Bea. What concerned Bea even more was the struggle Charlie might be facing long term, the struggle to find peace within herself while she remained crushed by the void created by her mother's absence.

As well as obvious, Charlie's latest attempt at avoidance was also brilliant, as Bea would have a hard time calling her on it. How could she question a show of empathy?

From the moment Charlie had started working in the salon a year ago, Bea had tried to instill in her granddaughter the code every good hairdresser knew to follow. No matter what, you needed to act as though you cared, as if all those sagas you listened to day in, day out were the most fascinating, most gut-wrenching, most tear-jerking stories ever. You had to keep track of the names of the cheating husbands, the dying dogs, the ungrateful friends. You had to ask about the illnesses and the aches and pains, about the troubled kids and the aged parents. It was all part of the job. And it was okay to really care, to a point. But that's it. Because if you let yourself get too sucked up into everyone else's problems you would drown in a sea of sorrow, not to mention the valuable time it would take away from your work. And though Charlie hadn't much patience for the gossip, when push came to shove, her empathy could be off the charts. Bea chalked it up to her strange childhood, growing up among people whose lives were so harsh, so raw. It seemed to have saddled Charlie with a worldview that made the pain of others very real, as opposed to some distant tale observed through a TV screen.

"This is a great spot for you, Bibi," Charlie said. "Really interesting. Lots of weird art around, kind of primitive looking. Plenty of room to sit. Looks like the perfect place for people to gather."

"It's dead as a doornail right now, though, isn't it?" Bea could detect the sounds of engines revving and horns honking, people yelling to one another out on the street. But there was neither a single human voice, nor the clink of a fork, nor the rattle of an ice cube, nor the scrape of a chair leg to be heard around her.

"Maybe it's too early for service. Let me see if I can find someone to get you a drink."

Bea swatted at a bug that was tickling her arm and settled back against the chair. She had to admit, at least to herself, that this ghost hotel actually gave off a surprisingly good vibe, or juju, or whatever they called it here. It was almost as though she could feel the presence of all the guests who had stepped across its creaky floorboards before her. These old walls must have seen quite a lot in their day, Bea thought, as she breathed in the heaviness that signaled the promise of rain.

"Gin and tonic." Her granddaughter delivered the drink with a small thud. "The quinine in the tonic is good for malaria. Which reminds me, don't forget to take your pill. I'm going to check on the arrangements for tomorrow, then head back upstairs to finish unpacking. You okay down here?"

Bea took a sip of the tall, icy cocktail, delightfully strong. She shrugged her shoulders, still not quite ready to concede her growing fondness of this place to Charlie.

"Okay then, Bibi. I'll be back down soon to join you for dinner."

Bea settled in with her drink, her eyes cast toward the mass of green beyond the boundaries of the veranda. *Haiti*. The very sound of it conjured up images of jungle drums and magic potions, like in those old zombie movies. And, of course, all those dictators and coups, all the corruption and greed. She could still picture the face of that crooked Papa Doc, with his little black glasses, and his chubby playboy son practically sitting on his knee like a ventriloquist's dummy. The nightly news had always portrayed the country as a pitiful cesspool, its people as victims of violence and crime, poverty and disease. And those commercials with the poor, wide-eyed, tiny orphan children who could be fed for just pennies a day. It got even worse after the earthquake—all those camera crews tripping over each other to capture lifeless limbs sticking out from beneath piles of rubble, the tattered tent cities clawing at the hills, and the people covered with dust wandering around the city like, well, like zombies.

She remembered the earthquake being the talk of the salon. It seemed like the whole town was scrambling to figure out how they could help: car washes, bake sales, food drives, all raising money for one organization or another. Everywhere you turned, there was someone with a hand out for the earthquake victims in Haiti. Bea didn't mind. It was good for the town to look somewhere beyond its own nose, for folks to have something to be up in arms about other than illegal bonfires on the beach or the "unsightly" moss sprouting from the roofs of the shops downtown.

However, it wasn't long after the disaster, maybe five years later, before the conversation took on a more reproachful tone. *All that money, where did it go? What good has it done?* It wasn't a bad question. Bea knew there'd been billions of dollars given for relief efforts. But the way people talked made it sound as though the Haitians had been blowing the cash betting on horses and bingeing on caviar. That, or burning it for fuel. Bea suspected the truth had more to do with the system, with the ones doling out the money rather than the ones who were supposed to be receiving it.

Bea's vision grew suddenly darker as a gust of wind barreled across the veranda. The rain started in a rush, as if someone had turned on a faucet full-force, muting the sounds of the city beyond, sending the temperature into a glorious nose-dive. The roof above offered shelter from the deluge—until it didn't. Bea scooted her chair over a bit to avoid the *drip-drip-drip* that was turning her silk turban into a soggy mop.

From behind her came the sound of leather soles on the tiles, one hitting hard, the other dragging behind. "Please, I will help you," she heard a man say, his soft, accented voice fighting with the racket of the rain. Bea felt two rough, dry palms against her skin, gently lifting her out of one chair and leading her to another, further back from the rain. Then the man left, only to return shortly after with a fresh drink and a towel.

"It will happen each night," he said. "It is the rainy season for Haiti."

Bea loved it. So much more dramatic than the fog back home, which crept in unannounced and lingered far too long, like an uninvited guest. This weather had a purpose, a job to do. She breathed in the sweet smell of wet soil.

"My name is Stanley."

Bea held out her hand. "Bea. Pleased to meet you. You work here?"

"I have worked at the hotel for twenty-five years."

"Tell me, Stanley, does it ever pick up around here?"

"Pick up?"

"I mean, do you get more business, more guests? It's so quiet."

"Well, that depends."

"Depends on what?"

"It depends on what is happening."

"What does that mean?"

"If there is a lot of unrest with the people, then the journalists come."

Bea nodded.

"If there is an election coming, then the politicians come."

"I see."

"When there was the earthquake, then everyone came."

"And now?" Bea had to practically shout to be heard over the strengthening storm.

"Nothing is happening now."

"What about tourists?" Bea tried. "Do you get them?"

"Not so many, anymore."

"Okay. So what about missionaries, those kinds of people?"

Stanley laughed. "A few. Most of them do not really like it here."

"Why not?"

"They think the hotel is full of Vodou."

"And is it?"

Whatever the man's answer was, Bea never heard it. It was lost beneath a boom of thunder accompanying a flash of lightning so bright that, for a minute, she thought she could see again.

7

Lizbeth was standing at the bottom of the stairs wearing a turquoise visor that plastered her hair flat onto her head, with her purse strapped snugly across her ample chest, when Charlie pulled up in a rented white Mitsubishi—a tank of a car that made her feel like a trucker behind the wheel. "Everything okay with my grandmother?" she asked out the lowered window.

"Bea's just fine," Lizbeth answered, pointing above her, toward the veranda. "I left her parked up there talking with some folks from England, with a big old cup of coffee and breakfast on the way. Have you tasted the coffee here? That coffee's so strong it'll walk right into your cup."

Charlie noticed Lizbeth's brows raise almost imperceptibly at the sight of the dark, handsome man in the passenger seat. She waited as the woman let herself into the back of the car and fastened her seat belt. "This is Mackenson," Charlie said. "He's going to be interpreting for us. Mackenson, this is Lizbeth."

Mackenson twisted around and offered Lizbeth his hand. "It is good to meet you."

"Pleased to be making your acquaintance as well," Lizbeth answered politely as they shook.

Charlie turned the car around and headed back down the driveway. In the rearview mirror she could see Lizbeth gaping at the field of sculptures standing at attention as they passed. "What do you think?" she asked her.

"I think they should put some fig leaves on those things!"

"They are the *loa*," Mackenson told her. "The spirits."

"Look like demons, if you ask me."

"See over there." He pointed to a sculpture in the far corner of the garden. "That is Èrzulie Dantòr. The Black Madonna."

Charlie glanced at the life-size figure draped in tulle, her skeletal face frozen in a grimace under a metal crown, a rotted rubber baby doll nestled in her arms.

"And do you see this one?" Mackenson pointed toward a squat carved figure on the lawn, basically two legs and a skull with a battered top hat almost as tall as the statue itself. "That is Baron Samedi. He is the *loa* of death and sexuality, and keeper of the cemeteries."

"Well, I don't give a lick if they're barons or goddesses, saints or sinners," Lizbeth said. "I still don't want to be looking at their hoo-has."

Charlie laughed as she waved to the guard and pulled the car out into the street. She was in awe of how alive the city was at this early hour, as if no one had slept at all. People were marching behind wheelbarrows stuffed with everything from mangoes to car batteries. A woman glided by with a bowl of bananas balanced perfectly on her head, followed by a man with dozens of brooms resting on his head, one arm holding them in place, the other swinging back and forth as if he were simply taking a leisurely stroll down a leafy boulevard. She braked for a young man draped in power cords and adaptors and boxes with dials, like a walking electrical store. Everybody everywhere seemed to have something to sell. Already the streets were lined with open umbrellas that were emblazoned with Digicel and Natcom logos, men and women settling in underneath them for the long day of commerce ahead.

"Can they make a living doing that?" Charlie wondered out loud.

"Yes, it is possible," Mackenson answered. "My mother was a seller. She had six children, and sent all of us to school, by herself. I have one sister, she is a nurse. Our brother, he is a priest, back in my countryside, where I grew up."

"Oh my goodness," Lizbeth said. "She raised y'all by herself? How on earth did she manage? When did your father pass?"

Mackenson didn't respond.

Charlie shivered, the relentless blast of air-conditioning sending goose bumps crawling up her pale arms. As they slowed to a stop in the morning traffic, she cracked open the window to allow some warmth to enter, and with it came the odor of diesel and smoke, as well as the sight of a street vendor balancing an impossibly huge wire basket on his head.

"Papitas?" He pointed to the plastic bags filled with thin, flat yellow strips, arranged in a way that made him look as though he were sprouting a giant marigold from his hair.

"It is chips *bannann*. Fried plantains," Mackenson explained.

Charlie dug deep into the pocket of her jeans. "Will he take dollars?"

"Dollars or *gourdes*. Whatever you wish. Money is money here. But do not expect him to have any change."

Charlie lowered the window further. She could see Lizbeth in the mirror, shifting in her seat. "Two please." She held out some bills in exchange for the bags. "*Mèsi*. Thank you." She handed a bag to Mackenson, and passed the other over her shoulder to Lizbeth.

Lizbeth wrinkled her nose and shook her head at Charlie's offer. "It's just fried bananas," Charlie explained. "With salt. Nothing too exotic." The woman still declined.

With the traffic still not moving, Charlie glanced over at Mackenson, sitting tall in his gray, long-sleeved Nike jersey and matching baseball cap. The guy could be a model. "So have you always been an interpreter?" she asked.

"No. I was a teacher of electrical engineering at the college. Before the earthquake. Now there is no college."

"What a crying shame," Lizbeth said. "You were a teacher and now you do this?"

Charlie thought she noticed Mackenson roll his eyes.

"Mostly I do jobs for people," he explained. "I fix electricity, things like that. I work as a guide sometimes when the hotel needs me."

"Seems like their electricity could use some of your fixing," Lizbeth said. "Went out yesterday afternoon just as I was trying to take a little catnap. Got hotter than a two-dollar pistol in that room."

Mackenson nodded. "The electricity from the city is only available for a few hours each day. Then they must use their own generators."

"Well then, somebody should tell them to turn those things on. A person is likely to explode in that kind of heat."

"It is very expensive to use power from a generator. Most people do not use them in their homes."

"How do they make their supper, then?" Lizbeth asked.

"They use charcoal for their cooking."

"What do you know? Just like our barbecues back home, right, Charlie?"

"Yep." Charlie nodded. She was by now well aware that Lizbeth was the kind of woman who talked when she was nervous. Here she was, about to come face to face with a part of her son's life she knew nothing about, and maybe—if they were lucky—find the woman and baby they were looking for. Yet all she could do was talk about barbecues. "You like to barbecue, Lizbeth?" she asked.

"I sure do." Lizbeth was quiet for a brief moment as Charlie continued to follow Mackenson's finger-pointed directions through the crowded streets. As they inched their way up a gentle hill behind a bus that had passengers piled on top of the roof and spilling out the back—"*Courage, Maman*" was the motto blazoned across its side—she began to notice the neighborhood changing slightly. Here the streets seemed to be a little cleaner, the stores a little more plentiful, the sidewalks a little less crowded. It was not pristine, by any sense of the word. It was just different. Still busy, but in a less chaotic way.

Shops vied for attention with competing neon colors splashed across their facades, the low, cinderblock buildings home to businesses offering car parts, groceries, dry cleaning, and a couple of restaurants. And everywhere, the ubiquitous lottery shacks, where all one could buy was a bit of hope for tomorrow.

But what Charlie took most notice of were the hair places. Barbershops, unisex salons, "studios de beauté", all easily identified by their handmade signs: men drawn with dark, razor-thin beards, women with long, straight hair or updos, all with very serious—she supposed it was meant to come off as alluring—looks on their painted faces, chipped and flaking from the year-round sun.

"I think we are close to the street where we are going," Mackenson said.

"*This* is where he lived?" Lizbeth asked.

"It's lively, right?" Charlie answered.

"That's one word for it."

Charlie braked hard as a stray dog darted in front of the car, chased by two small boys with sticks.

Lizbeth let out a muffled scream from the back seat. "Likely get ourselves killed in this damn place."

"We're fine, Lizbeth. Nothing happened."

"Yes," Mackenson added. "We are fine. But maybe just a little lost."

8

Mackenson lowered the window and shouted to a woman selling *aranso*, dried fish, from a crate on the side of the road. "Hey!"

Charlie pulled the car to a stop.

"Hey!" he repeated before the woman turned her attention his way, approaching the car at a lazy pace, one hand resting on her hip. "*Koman ou ye?*" How are you doing? he asked with a smile, holding out the address on the slip of paper in his hand. The woman peered through the open window at Charlie and Lizbeth, a gust from the air conditioner rustling the brim of her canvas hat. She wiped the sweat from her forehead and pointed ahead, and handed the paper back to Mackenson with narrowed eyes.

He closed the window and sat back, trying to shake off the sting of her look as they continued toward their destination. Mackenson was used to receiving looks like hers, from others who were jealous of this kind of job. One guy from his neighborhood, Cité Soleil, had even gone to a Vodou priest to ask for help from the *loa* to take Mackenson's job from him, he had heard. But why should he feel guilty? Sure, he was comfortable in this cool air, on these soft leather seats, but he had worked hard to teach himself English, had done plenty of work for the hotel before the owner started recommending him to the guests as a guide. No, he refused to feel bad about it.

It was true that jobs like this one weren't difficult to do, but they could test his patience. The two women with him now seemed nice enough, but it became tiresome trying to explain his country to people when he sometimes could not even explain it to himself. Especially hard for him was listening to those who came to Haiti thinking they were here to fix all the problems. Like the son of the older woman, the one called Lizbeth. Charlie had explained to Mackenson that Luke, she said his name was, had been working with an NGO. Mackenson had met many people like this Luke, living like kings from the money they made pretending to help. People who made promises to do certain jobs for the government, yet when you saw the NGOs' reports, you would find that three different organizations said they were spending money on the same project. There was never anybody watching, nobody telling them what should be done. They did not ask what the Haitian people needed. And some of the NGOs, the houses they had built, and continued to build? The rooms were too small, the materials too cheap. They only did what was easy. They didn't ask the Haitians how or where to build, what was best for this place. It was just a way for them to make more money.

Of course, not everyone who came to help was bad. But he had seen far too many people who came charging in to fix things, only to leave a mess behind. And what about those who thought that a week or two of work was enough to fix a country? Maybe being able to tell stories to their friends back home about what they did made them feel good, but it was like using a glass of water to put out a fire in the forest. Where did it leave the people they came to help? He had seen it a lot right after the earthquake. Back then Haiti was filled with *blans* rushing to help. Now they seemed to be almost invisible.

It was complicated. Even if things come from a good heart, they aren't always good for everyone.

This Charlie, she seemed to be different from the rest. The way she jumped into the driver's seat of the rental car while he was still standing there waiting for her to hand him the keys. He had not met many *blans*—and not one *blan* woman—who wanted to drive in Haiti. He had sat on the edge of the passenger seat, ready for her to turn to him for help, but when he saw how she fought through the traffic, how she made the big car move around the rubble and puddles, how she ignored the lane markers and stop signs just like any good Haitian driver would do, he relaxed. Now he was finding it funny to see people turning to look at her, people who didn't see many women at all behind the wheel in Port-au-Prince.

But the other woman, Lizbeth, looked as though she was just waiting for a pair of black hands to fling open the door and snatch her right from the car. And asking questions about his mother. Mackenson had no interest in sharing the story of his father leaving them for his other family. A *blan* would never understand this struggle, which was a way of life in so many Haitian homes. Of course, he thought, with a sudden feeling of shame, he should not be thinking this way about the poor woman. She had lost a son, and no woman should have to suffer the pain of a thing like that. Charlie had told him why Lizbeth was in Port-au-Prince. He felt sorry for her, chasing after some *souyon*, one of those girls who ran after *blans* just for their money, who treated guys like Mackenson as if they were no better than a piece of trash floating down the gutter in a storm, who would not recognize a good Haitian man if he were staring them in the face.

Stop, he told himself, as Charlie slowed the car to check the numbers on the houses. What was the matter with him today?

Charlie was slowing almost to a halt.

"It makes no sense," Lizbeth said. "The numbers are all mixed up. They were going higher, now they're lower."

They rounded a bend in the street before Charlie pulled the car up onto the sidewalk to park.

"Are you sure this is the right place?" Mackenson asked.

"It's the street number Luke's work gave me," Lizbeth answered, her wrinkled nose practically pressing against the glass of the car window. "Doesn't look like much, does it?"

Mackenson had to agree with her. He would never have guessed an NGO worker would live in a place like this. Usually they lived in big houses behind walls with locked gates, as if to keep the real world from invading their lives. This was a two-story cinderblock building, practically in the street, with a tailor shop and a snack bar below and a row of apartments above. It was fine, by Haitian standards. But he did not think that a *blan* would choose to live here.

"What did your son do for work in Haiti?" he asked, wanting to make sure he understood what Charlie had told him.

"He came down here to help with the water situation." Lizbeth's eyes remained fixed on the apartment windows above. "After the earthquake."

"And he stayed after that?"

"Yes."

"That is not the usual thing. Most people who came to help are gone now."

"Luke just loved his job, teaching people to help themselves. What's that thing they always say? Give a man a fish?"

The woman did not seem to want to leave the car. "I don't know what that is, about the fish," he answered.

"'Give a man a fish and you feed him for a day,'" Charlie said. "'Teach a man to fish and you feed him for a lifetime.'"

Mackenson nodded. "Your son was a smart man," he said into the rearview mirror.

"A do-gooder actually doing good, right?" Charlie said, as if she had been listening to his thoughts.

"Well, he certainly wasn't in it for the money, by the looks of things," Lizbeth said.

Mackenson reached for the door handle and felt Charlie's hand gently pulling him back. She shook her head a tiny bit, indicating with her eyes toward the back seat.

"Lizbeth?" she said. "You just tell us when you're ready. We've got all the time in the world."

9

Lizbeth could have sworn she was hearing the sound of her own heart pounding, until she noticed the rock in Mackenson's hand. The door was a rust-colored metal, battered and scratched from lord-knows-what. Above her, the green and white striped awning gave the building the appearance of a beach cabana, if beach cabanas came with security bars slapped across every window. Still, the place looked clean enough, at least from the street.

She waited on the cracked sidewalk as Mackenson continued to rap on the door while shouting for someone's attention. Perspiration rolled down her cheeks like the tears she'd only just managed to stop. She wasn't sure they'd find out much of anything here. But the address she'd got from Luke's work was all she had to go by. Even that had not been easy to get. Luke had neither sent nor received letters in Haiti, as the darn country had no mail system. Imagine. How could people live like that? The nice lady back in the States from the NGO had to dig through her paperwork to figure out where he was last living. Apparently the boy had moved homes quite a lot down here.

Finally she saw the door crack open. A muscular middle-aged man spoke with Mackenson. Lizbeth heard her son's name mentioned, and suddenly it seemed as though all eyes were on her. The older man opened the door wider and gestured for them to come inside. She went first, at his insistence, up an exterior staircase that led to another door.

Inside the building it wasn't much cooler than it was outside. At the end of a dark hallway the man reached around Lizbeth to open a door with a key from his pocket.

"He says this was where your son was living," Mackenson explained.

The one-room apartment was mostly empty, with just a few pieces of dark wooden furniture filling the space. The kitchen looked like one of those miniature play sets, a tiny two-burner hotplate and a fridge just big enough to hold a carton of milk and a jar of pickles. How a boy Luke's size could have fitted into a place this small was beyond her.

"This is Kervens," Mackenson added, by way of introduction. "He is the caretaker for this place."

"So you knew my boy? You knew Luke?" Lizbeth asked eagerly.

She watched Kervens' face as he spoke, his words sounding like popping corn to her, a mishmash of a language she couldn't even begin to understand. Kervens turned to brush the dust off a bed lodged against the wall, gesturing for Lizbeth and Charlie to sit, as Mackenson translated.

"He wants to know if you would like some water," Mackenson said, handing Kervens a wad of bills. Before they could answer, Kervens was out the door.

"You okay?" Charlie asked, her hand coming to rest on Lizbeth's knee.

"I think so." Lizbeth took out a tissue to wipe the back of her neck. It still seemed so unreal, being here in this foreign place with these folks she hardly knew. Even this room felt far from her comfort zone, though she knew in her head that part of her son's soul must be watching over her from somewhere in these walls.

Kervens bounded back through the door and delivered two sweating bottles of cold water to the women.

"I hope y'all didn't go to too much trouble." Lizbeth gratefully untwisted the plastic cap.

"They sell water on the street." Mackenson pointed through the room's one window.

Kervens leaned back against a table and said something to Mackenson.

"He says he knows your son. He is sorry to learn that Luke has died."

Lizbeth could see Kervens nodding in the background.

"He says your son was a good man. A good friend to have. Most of the *blans*, they live up in Pétion-Ville. Not here."

"*Blans*?" Charlie asked.

"White people. Foreigners," Mackenson explained.

Kervens continued to talk to Mackenson. Lizbeth could feel the tears about to start again. She dug inside her bag for more tissues.

"After his rent money was done, the landlord told Kervens to get rid of all the things belonging to your son, so that he can find another person to rent the apartment. But Kervens put all the things away for when your son came back."

Again Kervens left the apartment, this time returning with a large cardboard carton.

"Did he know the girl?" Lizbeth asked. "Ask him if he ever met a girl with Luke."

Mackenson seemed to frown a little as he interpreted her words for Kervens.

But Kervens broke into a smile. "Senzey?"

Lizbeth nodded. Kervens continued to speak to Mackenson.

"He says yes, he would see her sometimes."

"And the baby?"

Mackenson repeated her question in Creole. Lizbeth saw Kervens' forehead wrinkle with confusion before he spoke.

Mackenson folded his arms across his chest and nodded. "He says he did not see any baby."

"I knew it!" Lizbeth blurted out. "I should've listened to myself. Damn fool is what I am. Letting myself listen to some gold digger looking for a ride out of this godforsaken place."

"Hold on, hold on," Charlie said. "Let's just slow down for a minute and think about this." She turned to Mackenson. "Ask Kervens when was the last time he saw Senzey."

Kervens thought about the question before answering.

"He says maybe last spring, or summer, he cannot remember exactly. Senzey sometimes stayed here when Luke was traveling, and sometimes when he was not. After he was gone the last time, for so long, Kervens did not see her again."

"Aha! So she skipped out when the money dried up," Lizbeth said.

Mackenson again spoke with Kervens.

"The rent money was not gone. Luke gave the money for one year before he went to the States."

Lizbeth held the damp water bottle against her forehead. If only she weren't so damn hot, maybe things would all make more sense.

"He says maybe she went back to live at the hotel where she works," Mackenson continued. "And that maybe she could have been carrying a baby in her. He did not notice. She did not say anything to him."

Lizbeth felt something tugging inside, as if all her organs were contracting at once.

"Does he know which hotel?" Charlie asked.

"Hotel le Président," Kervens answered.

Lizbeth removed her glasses and peered into the cardboard box. She almost didn't want to touch it, remembering how painful it had been when she'd finally forced herself to go through Luke's things at home. He didn't have much of anything there, and he didn't seem to have much here, either. She wondered if the girl had taken anything for herself. She picked up a T-shirt, worn and faded, and held it to her chest.

"Do you want me to help?" Charlie asked gently.

"Please." Lizbeth watched as Charlie emptied the carton, one item at a time: two books, a pair of jeans, a knapsack she remembered from his college days, a crusty pair of sandals, and an old rain poncho. Luke never did believe in having more than you needed. *Leaving a small footprint*, is what he used to say.

Charlie stopped when she was near the bottom of the pile. In her hands was a small, carved photo frame, which she turned over and gently handed to Lizbeth. The sight of her son's face nearly knocked her over. But it was the face next to his that truly threw her for a loop. The girl was not at all what Lizbeth had expected. She was dressed nice and simple, in a sleeveless shift with a string of beads around her neck, her hair braided in neat rows. And she had a beautiful smile, Lizbeth had to admit. The two of them looked happy, seated against a picture-postcard background of a sea so blue it matched the sky. But the girl's deep, dark eyes were not on the view, they were fixed on Luke, fixed on him in a way that made Lizbeth wonder.

She slumped back onto the bare mattress, remembering the words from Senzey's letter: *I smell your skin in the pillows.* She knew that feeling. She'd caught herself doing it often, after Luke died, sitting in his room holding his sheets up to her nose until the day they'd lost his sweet scent, and the last shred of his being, forever.

"So what do you want to do with all this?" Charlie asked.

Lizbeth dismissed the box and its contents with a sudden wave of her hand. "You two take what you like," she said to Mackenson. "Maybe someone around these parts can use some of these things."

"There is a television, too," Mackenson said.

"Kervens can keep it, if he wants," Lizbeth answered.

"And he says he is taking good care of your son's cat."

"Oh, I don't know," she said, the photo and the T-shirt still clutched in her hands as the tears began to flow. "What will I do with a cat?"

Kervens hurriedly spoke to Mackenson.

"It is fine," he assured Lizbeth. "The cat is doing a fine job keeping the pests under control."

Mackenson handed her a clean handkerchief from his jeans pocket. His kindness made her cry even harder.

Kervens crossed the room and placed a warm hand on her shoulder. "*Kouraj, Maman. Kouraj.*"

10

Was it too early for a rum punch? Bea wondered as she awoke from a snooze on the veranda, easing her stiff legs off the wicker footrest, using her hands to shift the limbs, one by one, onto the floor below. It was no surprise she'd dozed off, right out here in the open, after having been woken so damn early by Charlie rustling around the room getting ready. The girl was literally up with the roosters, who were making so much racket themselves that it was a miracle Lizbeth had stayed asleep through it all.

Charlie had helped Bea out of bed and guided her through the huge room they'd upgraded to—one big enough to sleep the three of them surprisingly comfortably—and into the bathroom. Once Bea assured Charlie she'd be fine, the girl was off to find the car and translator she had organized through the hotel. Though the hot water was tepid at best, and the towels as thin as napkins, Bea had managed all right. Thank God for Lizbeth, who finally woke up and insisted on helping her down those rickety stairs that led to the veranda.

It must be near noon, she thought now, based on how hot and muggy it had become. She peeled her cotton tunic away from her sticky body, fanning it to let in some air. How long had Charlie and Lizbeth been gone, anyway?

"Pardon me," Bea asked over her shoulder, when she heard evidence of a human presence at the table behind her. "Could I trouble you to tell me what time it is?"

"No trouble at all," a man answered. "It is 11.07, on the dot."

"Thank you." She picked up her crocheting from the table and listened for Stanley's shuffle. "Must be a long trip here from France," she said to the man.

"Ah, my accent?" He laughed. "I try to hide it. I guess I'm not very good at it."

The man's voice was deep, and seasoned. She figured him to be somewhere in his sixties. "I'll bet you're here writing a book."

"Well done. You must be psychic," the man teased.

If only he knew how true his words were. She turned around to face him. "Lucky guess," she said with a laugh. "Actually, it's those little clicks that computers make when someone is typing. My hearing is superb. My eyes, not so much." She pushed the bridge of her glasses up to the top of her nose.

"I thought that maybe you were aware of the hotel motto," he said.

"And what would that be?"

"Check in, write a book."

"I hadn't heard that. Nobody has told me much of anything about this place. All I know is what I hear. And what I feel."

"And what is that?"

"Well, right now I hear the car horns and the motorcycles out there, of course. And the birds—maybe macaws, and grackles. I'm pretty good at birds. By my guess there are a few other folks here, either hotel guests or people here for lunch. Nobody's eating yet, I can tell that. Earlier I heard someone down at the pool, swimming laps, and I listened while a couple had an argument about whose fault it was that they got lost yesterday."

"And what do you feel?"

Bea sat for a minute, breathing in the air around her. "I feel," she finally said, "like there are a lot of ghosts in this place. Maybe not literally, but then again, who knows?"

The two of them remained silent until the man asked, "Do you mind if I join you?"

Introductions were made. Rum punches ordered. Robert was a professor of cultural anthropology from Lyon, here in Haiti researching a book on "loogarros", she thought he said.

"Lugar-whats?"

"The loup-garou. Werewolf, you would call it."

"Oh. They have those down here?" Bea was unable to control her smile.

"Well, according to most of the people who live here, yes."

"Really? Well now, that's interesting." She tried to picture the face that went with the man's wonderful voice.

"It is. Everyone is brought up on stories of the loup-garou. They say that the loup-garou is a person possessed by a spirit, who can turn into a dog or cat or snake, or any kind of beast, and who steals and eats young children."

"Yikes." Bea pulled a fan from her purse and unfolded it.

"I am specifically writing about the role of the loup-garou in post-earthquake Haitian culture," he continued, as if reading out the title of his thesis.

"You can write a whole book about that?" she asked as she batted at the thick air closing in on her face.

The man laughed. "Yes. Well, I hope so."

"So what do they have to do with the earthquake? Did the broken ground unearth a whole new batch of these creatures or something?"

"In a way," he explained. "You see, after the earthquake people were feeling very vulnerable, and very frightened, as you can imagine. They needed to give a name to their fears. There were many reports of loup-garous. And there were things that did happen—children *did* disappear. But, you see, it was more likely human monsters, rather than mythical beasts."

"Human monsters?" Bea, curious, leaned forward in her seat.

"Sadly, there were many instances of kidnapping and trafficking by local gangs after the earthquake, with so many children left homeless or orphaned."

"That's despicable."

"Yes, it is. And sometimes it was foreigners who were the culprits. For example, do you remember the story about those American aid workers who were accused of trying to smuggle homeless children across the border?"

"I do," Bea responded. "It was kind of a big deal at the time." She recalled reading newspaper accounts about the controversy, the members of a church group claiming they thought they had the proper permission for taking the children to an orphanage in the Dominican Republic. In the end, the woman leading the group served jail time for it.

"It *was* a big deal. Do you know that more than half of those thirty-three children still had parents?"

"Disgusting! The poor babies."

"So, you see, the loup-garou was a way to explain these kinds of atrocities that were too hard to process after living through such a disaster."

"I can imagine." Bea smiled at the man's enthusiasm for his research. He barely seemed to catch a breath between sentences. She again wondered what he looked like, what he was wearing. She pictured him thin, but not too thin. Tanned, with deep crinkles sprouting from the corners of his eyes, which were maybe blue. His shirt would be white, or perhaps khaki-colored, and crisp, with a collar.

"But that is enough about the loup-garou," Robert said. "What brings a lovely woman like you to Haiti?"

Spoken like a true Frenchman, Bea thought, smoothing back some stray tendrils of gray hair, tucking them under her turban. "It's my granddaughter," she explained. "Well, actually, it's my daughter."

"You have family here?"

"We think she's here."

"You do not know?"

"It's complicated."

"Ah. I understand."

"Well, I'm not so sure *I* do. All I know is that I've got to get my granddaughter—Charlie's her name—to gather up her courage to go see her mother. That's the only way the girl's ever going to find any peace in her life." Bea went on to explain April's situation, about how Charlie hadn't heard from her mother in ten years. How Bea had tried, over and over, to contact her daughter, only to have her letters returned, unopened. How Charlie had seen through Bea's lame attempts at sending birthday cards and Christmas gifts to Charlie, forging April's name surrounded by x's and o's. How Charlie was now avoiding a reunion with her mother—the fear of rejection holding her back like a magnetic force.

"It sounds like your granddaughter needs to have more faith in the situation, and in herself."

"You've got that right."

"Well then, you must teach Charlie this Haitian saying: '*M ap degaje mwen kon Mèt Jean-Jacques.*'"

"And what does that mean?"

"It means 'I will handle myself like Mr. Jean-Jacques.' Jean-Jacques Dessalines was one of the founding fathers of Haiti, the man who led the Haitian people to victory in the first successful slave revolt in the world."

"So Charlie is supposed to start a revolution?" Bea raised one eyebrow.

Robert laughed. "No, no. All it means is I will do my best to handle a situation. I will find a way, no matter what."

He paused, and Bea heard him take a sip of his drink. She wondered if he had that head of thick, gray, pushed-back hair so many elegant older French guys had. She wondered if he still had any hair.

"It is quite an astounding story, Dessalines and the slaves defeating Napoleon's army to start a new country."

"That *is* impressive," Bea agreed, her voice oozing with flattery intended for him as much as for the Haitian revolutionaries. "So what happened? It sounds like this place got off to such a good start, and all I ever hear about now is how it's the poorest country in the western hemisphere."

"Well, that truly is a complicated story, one that is tangled by a series of unfortunate events. Unfortunate for the Haitians, that is, though not always for others. But I'm sure you do not want to hear all of this."

"But I do!" she answered, urging him on. She could listen to this man talk forever. Bea heard Robert's chair scrape across the tile as he pulled it in closer to the table between them. I'll bet he's a Taurus, she thought. Strong, creative, dependable . . . sensual.

"So," he began, "as you can imagine, the white slave owners deliberately left their Haitian slaves uneducated. As brave as the revolutionaries were, what did they know about politics and government? All they were familiar with was how things worked on the plantation or in the tribe. So they rebelled against slavery and replaced it with nothing."

As he spoke, Bea could just imagine him pacing back and forth at the front of a lecture hall, with thick, solid arms that waved around to help make some point or another. Those French co-eds must be lining up to get into his courses.

"But some people say the problem after the revolution was that people didn't want to continue working the plantations," he continued, "so the money from export crops declined, and the government went broke. Whether that is true or not, what also happened was that the rest of the world—your country and mine in particular—feared that the revolution would threaten the future of slavery elsewhere. So they refused to recognize the new country, in effect cutting Haiti off."

"Shameful," she responded absently, and she did think it was terrible, even if she was somewhat distracted by the purr of Robert's voice.

"Yes, it was. And if you take that, and add in invasions, political corruption, outside interference, profiteering, disease, earthquakes, drought, famine, hurricanes, and overpopulation, that is the short version of how we got to where we are today, why people look at this country with only pity, and look at its people only as victims."

"I think I need another rum punch," Bea said when he finally stopped.

"I understand. It can be overwhelming. Even all these other things I've mentioned are complicated. I have probably told you more than you wanted to know."

Bea dabbed at the beads of sweat that had cropped up on her forehead. "Not at all. I've thoroughly enjoyed listening to you. But it is a lot to digest in one sitting."

"Well then, perhaps we can continue another day, if you'd like."

"I'd like that very much. But before you go, Robert, would you mind writing down that thing about being like Mr. Jacques? I want to give it to my Charlie. It'll be our new battle cry."

"Of course."

Bea waited while he found a pen.

"It has been a pleasure meeting you," he said as he placed a slip of paper in her hand. "There is another saying they have here in Haiti: '*Fanm se akajou: plis li vye, plis li bon.*'"

"And what does that one mean, may I ask?"

"A woman is like mahogany: the older, the better."

11

Charlie couldn't remember the last time she'd been in a proper church. Thanks to her stepfather, religion had become such a source of confusion for her that it seemed easiest to avoid it altogether. It wasn't that she didn't believe in anything. On the contrary, sometimes she felt as though there were too many options when it came to explaining the universe. She just didn't feel it necessary to pigeonhole herself into a single doctrine. And she definitely didn't feel it necessary to proselytize anything to anyone else.

Outside the car window, the low stone building beckoned like an ogre in a fairy tale. *Come, little girl, take a look inside. Have no fear, no harm will come to you.* She half wished she had agreed to Lizbeth's offer of accompanying her to the church. But the woman had been through enough for one day. Instead, Charlie had driven her back to the hotel, asking her to please check in on Bea. She'd said goodbye to Mackenson for the day as well, confident that someone at the church would be able to speak English.

She ran her fingers through her tangled curls and stepped out of the car. Ahead, a row of classroom doors adjacent to the church were open to any promise of a breeze. Charlie smiled at the sweet sound of a children's choir, and proceeded toward the church entrance, only to come to a halt before the solid double doors, her ripped jeans and flip flops giving her pause.

"*Bonjou*," came a voice from behind her.

She turned to see a serious-looking man, probably around her own age, with a clipboard under one arm. "*Bonjou*," she answered back. "English?"

The man nodded.

"Are you the pastor?"

Now he shook his head. "No. I am the head of discipline for the school. Do you need to see Pastè Samuel?"

Charlie felt his disapproving eyes upon her apparel. "Yes, if it's possible."

The man opened the door to the church and gestured for her to enter. "Then I will go find him for you."

Inside the church it was slightly cooler, and dark—the only light came from behind orange curtains covering the windows that flanked two sides of the room. Charlie could imagine the churchwomen busy at their sewing machines, whipping up the fringed valances that made the place look more like an Old West saloon than a house of worship. The ceiling was high, making the room almost as tall as it was wide, its beams supporting huge sheets of corrugated tin.

But it was the flowers that truly got her attention. Huge bunches of faded silk flowers—in bundles that were wired to the walls between each window, spilling out of boxes lining the raised stage at the front of the church, in vases atop the two pedestals flanking the pulpit, a centerpiece atop the piano—a massive quantity of synthetic bouquets that someone had obviously arranged with great pride. Charlie had just bent down to blow some dust off a tired-looking peony when the pastor entered.

"Good afternoon," he said, holding out a hand that was cool and dry in hers. "I am Pastor Samuel. How can I help you today?"

Charlie looked at the man before her, in his crisp, dark slacks and boxy short-sleeved shirt buttoned up to the neck. His eyes seemed to sparkle behind a pair of dark-framed glasses. The man exuded a serenity she could only wish to attain. She couldn't remember possessing that type of calm since she was a sleepy child resting at her mother's side, counting the stars in the black jungle sky.

"My name is Charlie. Charlie Clark," she added, using the name she'd been given before changing it back to Barnaby, the one she shared with Bea. "April Clark's daughter."

Pastor Samuel seemed to stiffen a little, his gentle smile freezing in place. "Pastor Jim is your father?"

"My *step*father."

"I see." The pastor took her arm, his hand on her elbow. "Please, have a seat." He led her to the last in a row of white-washed pews, taking a seat beside her. "And how is Pastor Jim?"

"I have no idea. I haven't seen him or spoken to him in nearly ten years."

The pastor nodded slowly. "And your dear mother? How is she getting along?"

"I'm not sure."

Now his eyes widened.

"Actually," Charlie continued, "that's what I was hoping you could help me with. I'm trying to find her, my mother. I need the location of my stepfather's mission."

Pastor Samuel cocked his head. "His mission? He has no mission. Your stepfather is no longer with our church."

Charlie's first reaction was a stab of satisfaction. She knew Jim's arrogance and intimidation would catch up with him sooner or later, that he'd get himself booted from the one job that made him feel like a king. But then, at the thought of her mother cut adrift from the church community, a panic set in, and with it the fear of never being able to find her again.

"What do you mean 'no longer with the church'?"

"Your father—I mean, your stepfather—has chosen other ventures to devote himself to."

"Like what?" Charlie couldn't imagine the man without a Bible as his shield.

Pastor Samuel didn't answer. Instead he lowered his eyes to the red and white checkered floor and left them there, as if he were contemplating a chess move.

"When did this happen?"

"It seems that he started, after the earthquake, to make the acquaintance of some . . ." He hesitated. "He was involved with some people who had access to the money that was coming into our country."

"And?"

"And their activities were not exactly the kind of things the church supports."

"So he got kicked out?"

"No. That is not what happened. The church urged him to go back to the States for a sabbatical, to take some time to refresh after so many years in the field. But he refused."

"And then they kicked him out?"

The pastor shook his head. "We all agreed that him leaving would be best."

"But are they even still here, in Haiti?" Charlie could hear her voice cracking, the way it did when things seemed to be falling apart.

The pastor nodded. "Yes, as far as I know they are still here."

"Can you tell me where?"

"The last I heard, they were living at a place I think he is calling the Freedom Farm. Wait, no. Farming for Freedom. That is it. Up north. I can give you directions to get you close to there."

Charlie was surprised at the relief that flooded through her. "That would be great," she said. "Thank you."

"Just a minute." The pastor left through the double door, the harsh afternoon light flashing across the room as it swung open and shut.

Charlie slumped forward on the hard wooden bench, her head coming to rest in her hands. The brief moment in which she thought she might not ever see her mother again had brought out something deep inside her that she'd thought was long gone, something she'd fought back so many times that she'd assumed it had been vanquished for good. It was as though a hole in her heart had opened and shut just like those heavy church doors, her love for her mother flashing in and then out again, like a ray of light from the searing Haitian sun.

She shifted positions to ease the pressure on her tailbone. How could anybody last through a sermon on these things? she wondered. Was being uncomfortable a requisite for piety?

So she'd check out this Farming for Freedom thing, whatever that was. She'd determine that her mother was okay, as she was sure she was, and she'd go back to Carmel with Bea, and life would go on as it had before. She'd survived ten years without her mother just fine, and she'd survive dozens more, God willing.

She turned her eyes to the huge wooden cross at the front of the church and chuckled a little at her uncharacteristic use of the phrase. *God willing.* It was as if religion was seeping right back in through her skin by her mere presence here.

The pastor returned with a map he'd drawn on the back of a used school worksheet. "Here is where you should go," he said. "When you get to here," he pointed to a spot on the map, "turn left. Then stay on the road for an hour. Then you will get to a place with lots of trees, a tire-fixing place, a lotto place, and a solar phone-charging place. At this market town is where you turn for the property where your stepfather is."

Later that evening, after Bea and Lizbeth had settled in for the night, Charlie returned to the empty veranda with her laptop, switching from table to table along the length of the porch until she found a spot with decent internet reception. Only Stanley remained, working the late shift, perched on his tall chair against the wall like a sleepy sentry guarding a castle. He roused himself to bring her a small glass of rum, then nestled back onto his roost.

Bea had been in rare form during dinner. Charlie hadn't seen her that animated in a long time. Sure, she was always funny, but not *that* funny. And Charlie was pretty certain it wasn't the gin and tonic talking. She seemed to know everybody, greeting the entire staff and each of the handful of guests by name, introducing Charlie as "my wonderful granddaughter" and Lizbeth as "my dear friend". Bea just somehow seemed more alive, as if the place had erased years from her life. Not a bad trick for someone who'd spent the entire day sitting in a chair.

Dinner—*cabrit en sauce* for both Charlie and Bea, with Lizbeth playing it safe and choosing pasta for the second night in a row—had been accompanied by a spectacular thunderstorm. As they waited for the cooked-to-order meal, munching on *akra*—fritters made with malanga, a starchy root vegetable—Charlie filled in Bea and Lizbeth on her visit to the church. If her grandmother had the same first reaction as Charlie to the news of Jim leaving the church, she hid it well. There was no satisfaction at his downfall. Instead she focused on encouraging Charlie, and on the tender chunks of goat swimming in citrus on her plate. Bea downed the meal with gusto before calling it a night.

Now Charlie sat alone under a full moon that had appeared from behind the retreating clouds, her laptop open and waiting. *Farming for Freedom.* She recalled the way Pastor Samuel had said the name. He might as well have used air quotes. What the hell was her stepfather up to, anyway? She carefully typed in the letters, taking a sip of rum as the browser struggled to connect.

The name was condescending, or ironic at best, considering how the Haitians had already fought hard for, and won, their own freedom way back when, without the help of anyone. They'd talked about that over dinner, after Bea had told them about the Frenchman she'd met that day, and about the Haitian saying he'd shared with her. How did it go? *I will be like Mr. Jean-Jacques*, or something like that. Anyway, it was clear to her, even after only a couple of days in Haiti, that this was a proud country, not one whose people needed to turn to someone like Jim for liberation. And from what, exactly, was he promising freedom? she had to wonder.

As the website resolved onto her screen, Charlie scrolled past the huge red "giving" button and went straight to the photos. There was an empty classroom, with neat rows of desks facing a shiny blackboard. And a field, where a handful of teenage boys were crowded around a man in khakis and cowboy boots crouching down, pointing to the soil, a man she recognized as Jim. *Here at Farming for Freedom*, the text read, *our goal is to provide the keys to a better future for those lacking resources, by providing meaningful skills through a comprehensive education in sustainable agriculture.*

Not terrible, thought Charlie as she scrolled down further. There were more pictures with captions: a composting project, a solar-powered pump designed to bring water to the fields. She scrolled past bundles of sugarcane, and a pile of smooth red peanuts newly harvested from the earth.

Then she reached the bottom of the page, and came face to face with her mother, her smile as wide as those of the students surrounding her. Charlie's fingers remained frozen on the keyboard, her eyes locked on the image before her. She leaned in closer to the screen, searching for clues. Her mother looked just fine, standing tall and still thin, her strawberry-blond hair streaked with a little gray, the crows' feet springing from the corners of her eyes a little deeper, the freckles a little darker, but there seemed to be absolutely nothing wrong with her, as far as Charlie could tell.

I should have just googled Jim's name before I came down here, Charlie thought. It had never occurred to her that he'd even have an online presence, always having lived off the grid in the past. She could have simply shown all this to her grandmother back in Carmel, and they would have left it at that. Maybe, she thought, she might still be able to do that—she could convince Bea that everything was fine, and she could return home without her ever having to see that man again, without having to face the woman who had erased Charlie from her life.

A warm wind kicked up from the garden below as Charlie closed her laptop. She took another sip of rum and sat back in her chair to watch as a gecko scurried down a post, in search of a mosquito or two for a midnight snack. Then she closed her eyes and listened to the rustling palms speaking of yet another storm to come.

12

Charlie stabbed her fork into the shiny brown mound on a plate in the middle of the table. *Pain patate*, Mackenson had called it. Haitian sweet potato pudding. He'd been excited to see it on the menu here at the Hotel le Président. "Yum," she said, her mouth still half full. "You gotta try this."

Lizbeth nodded absentmindedly while Mackenson wiped off his knife with a clean napkin and carefully sliced the dessert into thirds. Charlie scooted herself further under the umbrella to avoid the sun's midday wrath. Beside them, the glassy blue surface of the hotel pool beckoned convincingly. It was nice to take a meal somewhere other than at their own hotel, Charlie thought. She hadn't realized that practically nobody went out at night in Port-au-Prince, which was certainly going to put a damper on their culinary adventures. Mackenson seemed to be enjoying himself as well. His plate was as clean as one straight off the kitchen shelf. And he'd been absolutely right about the passion fruit juice. Amazing.

But Lizbeth had been quiet throughout the entire meal, picking at her food, understandably disappointed by the news at the front desk that Senzey no longer worked at Hotel le Président. The desk clerk knew nothing about her whereabouts. However, she told them, there was another worker who had been close to Senzey. Perhaps she knew something? She'd be done with her shift in about an hour. They were welcome to wait.

When they saw a girl descending the stairs to the patio, none of them took much notice. She looked so young that Charlie assumed she was a teenager out to lunch with her parents. But then she approached their table, addressing Mackenson.

Lizbeth perked up at hearing the name "Senzey" coming from the girl's mouth. "*This* is her friend?" she asked out loud. "Is this girl even old enough to work?"

Mackenson pulled up a chair for the girl, who he introduced as Guerline, and ordered her a Coca-Cola. Charlie and Lizbeth waited as they chatted for a while in Creole. Charlie noticed the girl smirk a little when Mackenson asked her a question, gesturing toward them as he did.

"Guerline says she has been working all her life," Mackenson explained. "She came to this hotel after escaping the home of her cousins, where she was working as a *restavek*."

"A rest-a-what?" Lizbeth cocked her head, as if she hadn't heard right.

"A *restavek*. In English it means something like 'stay with'."

"And what does a 'stay with' do?"

"Actually, it is very sad. Many poor parents, especially in the countryside, send their children to live with family, or sometimes strangers, to do work for them. They are sometimes only five or six years old. They cook, they clean. For no money. They are just allowed to sleep and eat in the home, even if the bed is only rags on a floor and the food is scraps from the family's meal."

"Do they go to school?"

Mackenson shook his head. "No, not usually."

"How in heaven's name could a parent do that to their child?" Lizbeth's eyes were glued to the girl.

Charlie noticed Mackenson stiffen in his chair. "Many parents cannot afford to educate all their children," he answered, with an odd snippiness in his tone. "But these types of parents," he added more gently, "they also cannot even feed them. And they do not always know if their children face abuse or mistreatment once they are in their new homes."

"Poor darlings!" Lizbeth clucked. "I've a right mind to take this one home with me right now."

The girl was listening eagerly to Mackenson's telling of her story. "Guerline says she stays here now, in a small room, and works at the hotel. She takes classes in the mornings, with the money she earns. The people here are okay. She says Senzey was watching out for her, before she left. She showed her how to draw, and was teaching her some English. Guerline says Senzey knew what it was like to be a girl alone."

"Doesn't Senzey have any family? Where are her people?" It was no wonder she glommed onto Luke, Lizbeth thought.

Mackenson relayed Guerline's answer to Lizbeth. "She has only one sister. Darline."

"And where is Darline now?"

Mackenson asked. "She says she is here, in Port-au-Prince. Down in Cité Soleil. Senzey and her sister do not get along, they are not the same."

Guerline tapped Mackenson on the arm, with something to add.

"Sometimes, she says, Senzey would go to stay with her sister, but most of the time she stayed here, at work, closer to the place where she was taking classes. Then she started staying with your son."

"Did Guerline know Luke? Ask her if she knew my son," Lizbeth pleaded.

The girl smiled at the mention of Luke's name. He used to come to the hotel to eat, she said. That's how he and Senzey met. After a while, she seemed to always be with Luke. That is, until she came back.

"Did she say why she was back?" Charlie asked.

The girl shook her head. Apparently Senzey came back angry—and very sad. And she was no longer talking about Luke, would not even allow anyone to ask about him. Did they want to see where she and Senzey had lived together?

Mackenson tucked the box of Lizbeth's leftovers under his arm, and the three of them left the shade of the patio to follow the girl upstairs to the hotel. The place was really quite lovely, Charlie thought, beautifully landscaped. Tree branches heavy with breadfruit and mangoes, bougainvillea spilling over the terraces, palms casting shadows across the broad driveway. As the girl led them through the kitchen, Charlie nodded and smiled, saying "*bonjou*" to the workers scrubbing the last of the lunch dishes, their sweat mixing with the suds in the deep sinks. Behind the kitchen was a tiny, windowless room, barely big enough to hold the three single beds lined up one against the other. Lizbeth stood in the narrow doorway, speechless.

"Poor girl," Charlie said, wiping her brow. "It's like living in an oven."

"I'm sure it is better than where she was living before," Mackenson said. "And here, there is nobody to bother her. She is safe."

Charlie could only imagine what went on in those homes. It was outright child slavery. And in a country where so many had proudly fought for, and won, freedom from slavery. It made absolutely no sense to her.

Guerline eased her way around the beds and pointed to a row of small paintings tacked to the wall. "Senzey," she said, gesturing for the women to come closer.

Charlie was blown away by what she saw—tiny, intricate brown figures, dozens of men and women set against the backdrop of a two-dimensional city teeming with life. You had to practically squint to see the detail. There were five paintings in all, each one an urban explosion of vibrant reds and cobalt blues, lush greens and sunshine yellows.

"Senzey did these?" she asked, running a finger lightly over the rough surface of a lively market scene.

The girl nodded. Mackenson stepped in for a closer look.

"Wow. These are incredible, aren't they, Lizbeth?"

Lizbeth nodded, her curious eyes moving from one canvas to another.

"So why did Senzey leave here?" Charlie asked.

The girl shrugged, as if the answer were an obvious one. They weren't going to let her stay here, she told them. But she wasn't sure where Senzey went. Charlie couldn't take her eyes off the paintings. They were so joyful, so romantic, as if they were telling the story of a city seen through rose-colored glasses.

If they did find Senzey, the girl continued, please tell her hello. The last time Guerline had seen her, Senzey was not looking so good.

13

Mackenson picked up his pace as he weaved through the labyrinth of narrow roads, his feet kicking up dust and pebbles with every step. The sun was nearly set, and he was anxious not to be out here after dark, when the sounds of gunshots and shouting between gangs kept many, like him, behind closed doors. Charlie and Lizbeth had wanted to come with him down to Cité Soleil to look for Senzey's sister, but he had insisted that he do it by himself. There were too many places a car could not pass, and even in the streets where driving was possible, a strange, new car with *blans* inside would draw attention he did not want. *It is my neighborhood*, he told them. *I know it well. It is better I do this alone.*

He had thought he would go in the morning to look for Darline, but one look at Lizbeth's face told him he could not wait. She seemed to be in so much pain over this search for the girl. The sooner the woman understood the truth and accepted what Senzey was, the better, in his opinion. But then a vision of the paintings they'd seen in the little room behind the kitchen at the Hotel le Président came to his mind. Who was this girl who could create something like that? And, of course, he thought, there was also the baby. No matter what type of girl the mother turned out to be, the baby would be Lizbeth's own flesh and blood. And that was something he knew a person could not turn their back on.

He had spent two hours so far asking around, urging his friends to ask their friends if they had ever heard of Darline. He was tempted to quit and head back to his home on the edge of the neighborhood, where things felt a tiny bit calmer, a tiny bit safer. Looking at the rubble around him, the crumbling shacks that people called homes, he felt lucky. He was proud of the small house he had managed to rent for his family, a house that was now filled to the roof with the addition of the two children of his cousin, who had been left with Mackenson and Fabiola to raise as their own. He had worked hard to get the money to put down for the rent, and even harder to fix up the place. He had recently added a square concrete patio in the front, where Fabiola could sit in the sun and wash the clothes, and the children could lay it all on the trees and bushes to dry. Someday, he hoped, he would have enough money to buy the house, and make it theirs forever.

He was headed toward what would be his last stop, no matter what. If he did not get any answers at the place his friend Wilner had suggested, he would go home. Fast. Behind him, he could hear the sound of footsteps growing louder. Mackenson lowered the brim of his cap and shoved his hands in his pockets, spreading his shoulders to make himself appear bigger. He held his breath as a group of young men passed and then turned toward the same spot he was headed to.

The nightclub stood out like a fish in the desert. Even so, it was just a small concrete box of a place, no bigger than a single-car garage of one of the fancy homes up in Pétion-Ville, its painted front chipped and scarred with graffiti. He was grateful for the crowd outside, as there appeared to be only one small window looking in, and he was wary of what he might find should he need to actually enter.

He had been told of a man named Evens, who was the boyfriend of Senzey's sister Darline. It did not take long to find him in the group that was socializing under the sky. Evens stood from a crouch near the nightclub's front door. He was a tall, skinny guy wearing a sleeveless basketball jersey with *Lakers 23* across his chest, as if he were about to be called into the game. Seeing Mackenson following pointed fingers toward him, he stood eye to eye with Mackenson and asked, "*Kisa ou vle nan men mwne?*" What do you want from me?

"*Bonswa.* Good evening. I am here only to ask about Darline."

Evens narrowed his eyes. "What about Darline?" His friends drew nearer, as if lining up to welcome the entertainment a fight might bring.

"I would like to talk with her."

"And what do you want to talk to her about?"

"Is she here?"

The man shrugged his shoulders.

"Do you know where I can find her?"

Evens looked away.

Mackenson reached into his pocket for a few *gourdes*, hoping that the offer of enough to buy a drink of *kleren* inside would help to loosen the man's lips.

Instead, Evens grabbed the bills, shot Mackenson a smirk, and went straight inside.

His friends laughed. "I will tell you where Darline is," one of them said, sidling up to Mackenson. "She is with her 'papa'. Her sugar daddy. That brother," he gestured toward where Evens had disappeared through the door, "he has no job, no money. But the old man, he gives her whatever she wants." Then the man started to dance, all elbows and knees, humming the song that had become so popular the year before. "*Madan Papa*", Daddy's Girl. Mackenson had heard it blaring from every moto-taxi and tap tap, its words telling of the girls who become "sugar babies" to older, richer men. Though it was a song everyone liked to dance to, Fabiola had told Mackenson that she found it sad, thinking about all the girls who were called on to support their entire family, or who wanted an education, and had no better option than to turn to an arrangement like this, girls whose parents looked the other way when their daughters traded their bodies to rich men in exchange for security. He thought she was probably right.

"So do you know Darline's sister as well? Do you know Senzey?"

Mackenson turned to see that Evens had returned from inside the nightclub, this time looking much happier.

"Senzey?" Evens seemed surprised by the question. "Sure. I know Senzey. But I do not know what happened to her. I have not seen her since she got big as a house." He bent his knees and thrust out his middle, patting his stomach.

"Would Darline know where she is?"

Evens shook his head, continuing his little dance.

"Do you know who the father of the baby is?" Mackenson asked, ignoring the guy's mocking gestures.

"How the fuck would I know, man? You know how those *souyon* can be."

14

"Aren't you concerned about your granddaughter going up into the mountains alone?"

Bea's laugh echoed across the veranda of the Abernathy. "You don't know Charlie," she told her new friend Robert—or, rather, "Row-bear", as he pronounced it. As soon as he'd joined her at the table after her breakfast, she began to fill him in on the note she and Lizbeth had found earlier that morning. Lizbeth had read it aloud as Bea brushed her teeth with water from a bottle. Charlie had gone to look for her mother.

"My granddaughter," she assured Robert, "is a very independent young woman. And tough. That girl could wrestle a tiger and have it purring like a kitten before you'd even see it coming."

"She must take after her grandmother."

Again Bea could feel herself blushing. What was it about this Frenchman that made her feel so giddy? She pressed a glass of cold water against her cheek and tilted her face toward the ceiling to catch the breeze off the whirring fan above. "Well," she said, "Charlie *is* stubborn like me, that I'll admit to. But she is a lot more, shall I say, *worldly* than I am. She can handle herself just about anywhere."

"That surprises me, Madame Bea. You have the air of a woman who has seen quite a lot in her day."

Bea laughed again. "Oh, I've seen a lot, all right. I just don't need to leave my chair to do it."

"I understand. Sometimes I feel as though my life is spent always between the covers of a book."

Bea didn't bother to explain that that was not exactly what she had meant. She didn't want to scare the poor man off by talking about her "gift", after all. Behind her, she heard the shuffle of Stanley's feet approaching the table.

"Good morning, Professor," he said. "Is there something I can get for you?"

"Good morning, Stanley. A cup of your magnificent coffee would be very good, if there is still some to be had."

"Of course." Stanley limped away toward the kitchen.

"And what are your plans for the day, Madame Bea?" Robert asked.

"Me? I'm finally breaking out of this place." She waved an arm across the empty veranda. "After Lizbeth finishes putting herself together, we're being taken to a late lunch by the interpreter my granddaughter has hired. Mackenson. Do you know him?"

"Yes, of course. Everyone knows Mackenson around here. A very nice young man. You will be in good hands."

Stanley returned with the coffee and Robert invited him to sit. As the two men began speaking in French, Bea's mind started to wander. Despite what she'd told Robert, she *was* worried about Charlie. Not about her physical safety; no, it was her emotional well-being that Bea was concerned for. She imagined the girl could stand up to Jim, if need be. Anger could be a powerful weapon. But what shook Bea to the core was the thought of her granddaughter having to do battle with the feelings of rejection she'd tried so hard to bury for so many years. Bea had to believe that April must still hold love for her child, but she also understood the power of a man like Jim, and knew all too well what a blinding influence a husband like that can become. It had nearly happened to her, when she was young.

April's father had turned out to be one of those controlling types who, not long after their baby was born, had become consumed with jealousy at the drop of a hat. Bea couldn't even say hello to the mailman without her husband flying into a rage. She tried to reason with him, over and over. But things just seemed to get worse. There was no way in hell Bea was going to live her life that way. And there was no way a man like that was going to make an even halfway decent father for April. After the divorce, he disappeared from their lives. She never did tell April the full truth of the matter, choosing instead to explain his absence with a story about a helicopter crash during the evacuation of refugees from Vietnam. Maybe she'd taken it a little too far with that tale, but she'd wanted to protect her daughter, just like she now wanted to protect Charlie. Bea could only hope that her instincts about April were right.

The two men continued to talk. About what, Bea had absolutely no idea, but that didn't bother her. She was thoroughly content to simply close her eyes behind the huge lenses of her sunglasses and be calmed by the lullaby of a foreign language drifting lazily through the steamy morning air. Just as she was beginning to melt into her chair, she felt a sudden chill pass over her, as if a gust of ice-cold air had blown in her direction. As quickly as it had appeared, it was gone.

"What the heck was that?" she asked the two men.

"What was what?" Robert said.

"That cold breeze. Didn't you feel it?"

Both said they had not.

"But I swear, it just blew right over me."

"There is no breeze at all," Stanley said. "The air is very calm right now."

"Well, I felt something." Bea paused for a moment. "Or someone. Did anyone pass by just now?"

"Only Mambo Michèle," Stanley said.

"Mambo Michèle?"

"She's a Vodou priestess. She lives near the hotel."

"Seriously?"

"Yes. She is probably here to see a guest."

"Mambo Michèle is a healer," Robert said. "One of the best, from what I have been told. I have heard she has quite a talent. There is probably someone who has come to the hotel to seek her help. Someone with a problem."

"I'd sure like to be a fly on that wall," Bea said.

"A fly?" Robert asked, apparently unfamiliar with the expression. Bea explained it to him. "Ah," he said. "In French we have a similar phrase about a little mouse."

"Do you believe in Vodou?" Bea asked him.

"It is not my religion, but I respect the power that it holds."

So much for scaring him away, Bea thought. Maybe she'd offer to do a reading for him later. "What about you?" She turned to Stanley.

Stanley hesitated with his reply.

"It is a complicated thing, here in Haiti," Robert interjected, looking at both of them. "Vodou is misunderstood, and frowned upon by many outsiders, and also by some Haitians—though those Haitians doing the frowning are probably turning to

Vodou themselves, at times. You know," he added, "here there is a saying: Haiti is seventy percent Catholic, thirty percent Protestant, and one hundred percent Vodou."

Stanley let out a knowing chuckle.

"I see. So what exactly is it about Vodou that gets people so worked up?" Bea asked.

Again, Robert answered. "Well, in the old days, Vodou was seen as a threat. There is a story about how the slaves had help from the *loa*, the spirits, in overthrowing the French."

"There was a woman possessed one night by Èrzulie Dantòr, the Black Madonna," Stanley added, his eyes wide. "She slit the throat of a black Creole pig and gave its blood to the revolutionaries, who drank it and promised to kill the *blancs*."

"The white settlers," Robert clarified.

"Oh my." Bea removed her glasses and placed them on the table. "That's quite an image."

"It is," he agreed. "But, you know, perhaps the threat was less magical than it sounds. You see, the revolutionaries used Vodou ceremonies as a cover for their meetings. The slave owners did not have a clue."

"You make it all sound so interesting," said Bea.

"I think it *is* very interesting. So, of course," Robert continued, "whether it was magic or not, other colonists and slaveholding nations, including yours and mine, feared the same thing could happen in their own territories, with their own slaves. So they did all they could to demonize the religion, and erase it altogether."

"You seem to know an awful lot about Vodou," Bea said.

"He wrote a book about it," Stanley said.

"Of course he did." She dabbed with a scarf at the perspiration forming on her brow. "Can I ask, Robert, have you ever seen it yourself?"

"Seen it? That is a difficult question, as Vodou is something that is all around us here in Haiti. But I have met many people who have told me stories."

Bea sat up straighter in her chair, her attention piqued. "Like what?"

Robert laughed at her eagerness. "Well," he began, "for instance, there was a woman, an American, a guest at this hotel. She asked to talk to Mambo Michèle because her husband had left her, after thirty years of marriage. He swore to her that there was no other woman, but she did not know whether to believe him or not. Just in case, she wanted to make sure he could not . . ." Robert hesitated. ". . . would not be able to, you see, *perform* with anyone, if you understand what I mean."

Bea found his sudden shyness adorable. "I understand perfectly," she laughed. "Go on."

"So, she asked Mambo Michèle what to do. Mambo Michèle told her to pick a saint. Any female saint will help with an unfaithful husband, she said. Pick one, and find out her favorite color and food and drink, and make an offering."

"And?"

"She did just that. She decided on Èrzulie Fréda, the *loa* who rules over the heart. In her garden, she placed a strawberry cake under a tulip tree, and poured some pink champagne into the ground. Then she asked for what she wanted."

"That's a lovely image, but how would she ever know if the spell worked or not? It's not like he'd come running back to her, complaining about not being able to get it up."

Robert made a sound as though he were choking on his coffee, and Stanley excused himself from the table to go and get him some water. "Well, Madame Bea, all I can say is that just doing the ceremony made her feel better. So, in a way, it worked."

"Don't you have anything juicier?" Bea asked Robert.

He laughed, in that way that made Bea feel as though she were the wittiest person on Earth. "Oh, there are plenty of those stories. But most of Vodou is not what people think."

"I don't get it. What is it, then?"

"You ask some very difficult questions, Madame Bea. You are not wrong to expect stories of poison and zombies and sorcery. There *are* practices intended to do evil, and there *are* spells cast in order to seek revenge and satisfy jealousy. But it is much more than that. Vodou is a way of life, a system of beliefs that lives in the music, the art, the stories, the medicine, even in the justice system of this country. It is something to which every man or woman can turn to make order out of chaos, to give them something divine in a world that has presented them with such harshness. Some say it is the very soul of the Haitian people."

Bea nodded her head slowly. It was all so complex. And it was all so wonderful.

"Perhaps you would like to meet Mambo Michèle?" Robert asked.

"You bet I would," she said, practically stepping on his words before they were out of his mouth. "I'd love to compare notes with her."

"Compare notes?" Robert asked, confused.

"I mean," she quickly added, "I'm thinking why wouldn't I want to meet Mambo Michèle, after all you've had to say about her? She sounds like such an interesting woman." Bea adjusted her scarf and smoothed out her long skirt. "Besides, there's absolutely nothing wrong with letting a little magic into our lives. Am I right, Monsieur?"

15

Why a person who was blind would want to go look at a bunch of art made out of garbage was beyond Lizbeth. Personally, she would have preferred returning to the hotel after lunch, where at least she could lie down under a fan to wait out the afternoon heat. That is, if the electricity was on. But Bea, she was something else. That woman was so full of energy she was jumping around like hot water on a skillet.

Lizbeth was exhausted. She was looking forward to heading back home to Texas the next day. Hearing what Mackenson had to say when they'd met up that morning had been enough to make her go straight to that nice woman at the hotel's front desk to arrange for a seat on the first plane out. He'd hit a dead end. If her own sister didn't know where she was, how were they ever gonna find that girl? And what kind of a girl doesn't let her own family in on her whereabouts? Why, Mackenson had almost said so himself—Senzey was a fraud, looking to point the finger at her son for putting her in the unfortunate condition in which she found herself.

So here she was, waiting out the time until she could leave by babysitting Bea while Charlie was off on her own fool's mission. What was that girl thinking, driving around here all by herself? Why, anything could be happening, and they wouldn't even know. She could get robbed or carjacked or kidnapped—Lizbeth had heard that those things happened around here. She could likely have an accident, with the horrible roads and crazy drivers, and animals walking right in front of a car as if they owned the place. She'd seen pigs and dogs and goats wandering around clueless right in the middle of the city. And what about getting lost? Charlie could find herself out in the middle of nowhere, where nobody spoke a word of English. Not to mention the weather. They'd seen rain coming down in buckets practically out of the blue. Those roads were bound to turn into rivers right in front of her eyes.

Lizbeth mopped her forehead with a balled-up tissue. Even out of the sun, it was hotter than blazes. Mackenson had borrowed a car from the hotel for a couple of hours, and had escorted them to a small restaurant nearby, run by Haitian women. They were seated on the patio under the shade of a mango tree, Lizbeth on high alert the entire time, fearful of a falling piece of heavy fruit. That's all she needed, to get a concussion while she was here. Bea had ordered goat in some kind of sauce, while Lizbeth asked for the pizza. There was no sauce on Earth that would convince her to eat a goat.

Again she noticed Mackenson's impeccable manners, and his attention to cleanliness. She'd tried not to laugh the day before when he discreetly sliced up their shared dessert, leaving the portion Charlie had already attacked with her fork facing in her direction. He even used a napkin to pick up a piece of bread from the basket. She supposed his habits must've had something to do with living in a country with so many diseases. Lord knows she'd had to endure a boatload of vaccinations before heading on down here, though her doctor had claimed she was more likely to die from a car crash while she was here than from a mosquito bite or some tainted water.

And his fingernails! She'd never seen such a perfect set of nails on any man; smooth and buffed and not a speck of dirt. How he did that in this dustbowl of a city was a mystery. Folks back home could also learn a thing or two about courtesy from him, the way he excused himself from the table every time his mobile phone rang, bless his heart.

And now, here he was, smiling and nodding at Bea's request to drive them downtown to some place where they make art out of rubbish. Wasn't there enough trash for her right out there on the streets? Lizbeth had half a mind to fake a headache, just to get out of the heat and grime of the city. But the handsome Frenchman at the hotel had told Bea she would enjoy the place with the garbage art, so it was off to the garbage art they went.

"Found objects," Bea corrected her, when they were in the car. "They are called the Atis Rezistans, Artists of the Resistance—the sculptors of the Grand Rue."

Lizbeth didn't answer. She was too busy hanging on for dear life as the car bounced across a pitted intersection, toward a traffic jam worthy of the parking lot at Costco just before a Fourth of July weekend. Only this was far worse. It wasn't just cars, it was also a jumble of trucks and motorcycles and those painted tap tap things, people selling plastic bags of water and soda bottles carried in gigantic bundles on their heads, and pedestrians going every which way. There were men hanging over the open hood of a car, deep in discussion, and others unloading piles of lumber so raw the boards still held the outline of a tree. Any open space that might've been left was taken up by the umbrella-shaded "shops" that seemed to grow like weeds from the sidewalks. And no traffic cops, not a one, anywhere. It was a miracle anyone got from place to place in one piece.

But somehow Mackenson managed, finally squeezing the car into a tiny parking space just off the main street. "Be careful," he said as he opened the door and took Lizbeth's hand. "There is mud."

She stepped down gingerly in her open-toed sandals to avoid the puddle, her foot landing smack-dab on a pile of trash instead. Mackenson led the two women across the busy thoroughfare, dodging the traffic amid a sea of honking horns. Lizbeth felt like she was inside one of the old video games her son used to play, where the frog had to make it across the street without getting himself squished to death. Once safely on the other side, she thanked the Lord and turned her attention to her surroundings. They call this "downtown"? The buildings were low, some of them crumbling, almost as if the earthquake had happened eight days instead of nine years ago. The street was wide, covered by a canopy of powerlines strung willy-nilly across the sky. Mackenson had said they were on boulevard something-or-other, but it looked more like a junkyard to her. Old tires and auto parts in piles everywhere, and not a tree in sight.

They turned right, Mackenson's hand resting on Bea's arm as he gently led her through a maze of abandoned cars and rusted motorbikes, lazing cats and pecking roosters, Lizbeth following closely behind.

"We are here," he said. Lizbeth's gaze was drawn upward, where, from atop a wrought iron arch, a human skull was staring down at them, with Christmas-light eyes hanging from its sockets. She thought she'd arrived at the gates of hell.

She quickened her pace to catch up with the other two as they continued down a narrow alley bordered by a row of dilapidated wooden shanties, which looked like they might topple right over with one sneeze. Could anyone even live in those things? Lizbeth had to wonder. "Are you sure there's an art gallery back here?" she asked.

At the end of the path was a courtyard, an open-air space jam-packed with the kind of sculptures she'd seen outside the hotel. Only this was different. There were tons of them; huge statues towering overhead, knee-high figurines crowding shelves along the cinderblock walls, life-size likenesses that met her face to face, and each one of them spookier than the next.

At first glance, they reminded her of those popsicle stick figures Luke used to bring home from kindergarten, with yarn hair and little googly eyes from the craft store, only bigger, and made from trash, and way scarier. But some of them were actually quite complicated, when you really looked at them. It was pretty clever, the way they used marbles for eyes, hubcaps as hats, springs for necks, vacuum cleaner hoses as arms, tire rubber for clothes. Some of them were almost beautiful, decorated in lacy golden fabric and shiny mirrors. But mostly they were creepy, the bones and skulls and dismembered baby-doll parts sending chills down her spine.

They followed Mackenson into the cool shade of a three-walled room as big as a garage, Lizbeth hanging on for dear life to Bea, fearing the woman might trip up on something, what with everything so cluttered and all. She felt herself being pulled forward as Bea stepped in close to a tall wooden figure, pausing to remove her thick, round glasses to wipe them with a scarf. "What's this one?" she asked Lizbeth.

"Well," Lizbeth replied, moving in for a better look, "it's kind of hard to describe. I think it's supposed to be an angel, or maybe a queen. I can't tell if that's a crown or a halo on her head." She watched as Bea carefully ran her hands down the front of the statue.

"That is the pussy," came a deep voice from behind.

Lizbeth turned to see a dark man in baggy shorts and cropped, bleached white hair emerging from the shadows. "Pardon me?" She could feel the blood rushing to her cheeks.

"Ha! So these are the pubic hairs?" Bea's fingers rested on a cluster of rusted nails that had been hammered halfway into the rough wood. "That's fabulous!"

Lizbeth lowered her eyes and backed away from the piece, only to find herself poked from behind by a large, red penis hanging from a totem-like creature with a bucket on its head. She barely managed to stifle a scream.

"Are you the artist?" Bea asked the man.

"We are a group of artists here. But this is my space," he answered, his English near perfect. "Would you like me to show you around?"

Lizbeth was already inching her way back out, toward the courtyard. "That's so kind of you, but we really must—"

"We'd be delighted," Bea insisted.

Lizbeth was wilting in the afternoon heat, her capri pants practically glued to her thighs, the money belt she wore hidden under her blouse damp with sweat. She reluctantly followed Bea, Mackenson and the artist through the ground-floor rooms, her eyes wide with wonder at the pieces the artist claimed had been on display in art shows all over the world. Paris, Venice,

New York. Why anyone with half a mind would voluntarily go see these naked, nasty things was a mystery to her. She stuck close to the group as they climbed a crumbling stone staircase, not wanting to be left alone.

"You don't mind if I touch them, do you?" Bea asked.

"Please," the man said. "Go ahead."

Bea, now latched onto Mackenson, made her way very slowly through the mess, exploring every sculpture up close as her hands ran over each and every crack and crevice.

"Shouldn't we be getting back to the hotel?" Lizbeth asked. "Maybe Charlie's come back."

Bea ignored the question. "You know, you should really try this, Lizbeth. With your eyes closed. Sometimes people find they can see better with their hands than with their eyes."

Lizbeth did not have the slightest desire to see things any clearer than she already had.

"Where do you find your materials?" Bea asked, rubbing her fingers across a pair of nipples made from metal bottle caps.

"There is an endless supply of trash here in Port-au-Prince, as I am sure you have seen. There is no system for proper disposal. So it is not hard to find things for us."

"Recycling! I love it," said Bea. "And the bones? The skulls?"

"Those were taken from the cemetery by people, after the ground was broken up by the earthquake."

Lizbeth gasped a little. Bea simply continued to ply the man with questions about his so-called art. Apparently she was looking to buy a souvenir for her salon back home. Lizbeth began to grow impatient. That woman could talk the legs off a chair.

Her thoughts wandered as the group drifted through a seemingly endless maze of rooms. Outside a window she could see the crumbling rooftops of the shacks surrounding downtown, roosters and stray cats perched atop homes that looked more suited to accommodate them than humans. She couldn't get her mind off of Senzey. Surely she would have tried harder to find Luke, or his family, if the baby was actually his. That baby wasn't her son's. No sirree. That girl had no doubt gone and got herself in trouble, and then looked to sweet Luke as her ticket out of it. What had she been thinking, chasing down a girl like that in a place like this? It was downright crazy, just like everyone had said. Everyone, that is, except for Charlie, who seemed certain that something would turn up. To Lizbeth, it seemed that the only thing likely to turn up around here was trouble.

She ground to a halt when, behind her, she heard Bea ask, "Why so many penises?"

"These are the *Guédé*," Mackenson explained, without missing a beat. "The family of spirits that embody the powers of death and fertility. Baron Samedi is their leader, the head of the cemetery, which he rules with his wife, Maman Brigitte." He smiled at Lizbeth.

"Yes," she said, trying to cover her embarrassment. "I do believe we already met him, back at the hotel."

"The *Guédé* are very mischievous, very sexual *loa*," the artist said, beaming with pride.

"I see."

"They make fun of people, swear a lot. Every year, in November, there is a big celebration. That day there are thousands of people in the streets who become possessed by the *Guédé*. It is very fun. Very wild."

Lizbeth clucked her tongue. "It sounds like an excuse for bad behavior, to me."

"How do they know they're possessed?" Bea asked.

"Their voice, the way they act. When it happens, it is the *loa* doing the talking for them. And then, to prove that it is true that they have been possessed, they use the *piman*."

"*Piman*," Mackenson interjected, "is *kleren*, raw rum, with peppers soaked in it."

"Here. I will show you," the artist said, then left the room for a second. He returned with a bottle filled with a nasty-looking, cloudy liquid.

"And they drink that?" Bea asked, incredulous.

The artist nodded. "Some do. But mostly they rub it on themselves, on their face, or like this." And then the man actually began to rub his own private parts, right there, right in front of them, with a grin the size of the Grand Canyon on his face.

Lizbeth felt herself once again blushing, and turned away. "They're probably so drunk they don't even feel it," she muttered.

"Exactly," Mackenson said.

Bea was laughing. "One can only hope!"

They weaved their way back through the warren of shacks, a rusted aluminum goddess type of thing almost as tall as Mackenson slung over his shoulder like a victim rescued from disaster. How on earth did Bea plan on getting that monstrosity onto an airplane, for Pete's sake? Why, she'd practically have to buy it its own seat to get them to allow that. Lizbeth shook her head and continued leading the old woman toward the street until, suddenly, she came upon a sight that stopped her in her tracks.

"Ouch!" Bea said as she plowed into Lizbeth's back. "Whadya stop for?"

Lizbeth remained silent and still. She was looking at a darkened doorway to her right, where a woman stood, stooped and gray-haired. In her arms was a child, naked save for the thin diaper covering its tiny behind. The woman's broad hand cupped the back of the baby's head as she gently swayed to and fro, dancing to a tune only the two of them could hear. But it was the woman's eyes that Lizbeth would never forget. Two round buttons, like the ones on some of those statues they just saw. Two dark round buttons that bore right through her soul and into her heart. Lizbeth felt as though she'd been peeled open like a grapefruit.

They did not return to the hotel until close to dinnertime, hungry, tired, and soaked from the short walk from the car to the hotel. The rain was coming down in buckets, turning the staircase from the veranda down to the parking lot into a waterfall. Lizbeth unlocked the door to their room to find it empty and dark, with no sign of Charlie anywhere in sight.

16

At first Charlie wasn't sure if she was in the right place. The sign was almost invisible, half hidden behind a thicket of orange bougainvillea. But there it was: *Farming for Freedom*. And next to it, a larger sign, reading *Prive*. Private.

She stopped at the gate and turned off the ignition, road-weary and dying of thirst. The drive had taken far longer than she'd expected. For the first forty-five minutes or so, she'd inched her way through city traffic, already so dense so early in the morning that she had to wonder whether people had simply stayed out all night. Then, driving through the outskirts of Port-au-Prince, she got stuck behind a fat truck belching black smoke straight back into her windshield, the roads too narrow and windy to offer the slightest chance to pass. After that, when she finally began to climb higher into a less populated area, it was the crumbling asphalt, overloaded tap taps, and careening motorbikes that had forced her to keep her speed well under the limit.

As she left behind the hillsides stacked with little houses climbing halfway to the sky, she found herself surrounded by green. But even this far from the city center, life was led on the streets—vendors chatting as they crouched near their wares, children skipping and running and just plain goofing around, and always plenty of people walking to and fro. She was tempted to ditch the car and join them for a while, just to feel a part of things. Ever since she'd stepped off the plane in Haiti she'd felt as though she were living in a bubble, tucked away like a precious china doll, behind a dusty windshield or the walls of the hotel. For days she'd traveled by foot only as far as the distance between the car door and the front door, and it was beginning to make her stir-crazy.

Charlie turned off the air-conditioning and lowered the window all the way down. She could feel the temperature outside dropping as the car continued its ascent. She passed a schoolyard full of kids playing, a sea of navy blue uniforms in perpetual motion, the sounds of recess the same as anywhere in the world. By now she'd climbed so high that the mountains across the way looked like patchwork quilts, their fields in varying stages of harvest. Plumes of white vapor seemed to levitate from the ridges, whether smoke or fog Charlie could not tell. In the distance, she spied a farmer crouching in an impossibly steep plot; a tiny dot of red among the green of the crops and the brown of the earth.

And now here she was. The pastor's directions had been good, though there were so many spots along the way with lottery shacks and solar-charging stations and those ubiquitous piles of tires for sale—which made sense, considering how damn hostile the roads were—that she wasn't sure which was the landmark she was supposed to be looking for. And it seemed to be market day everywhere, a jumble of umbrellas and baskets and produce spilling out into the streets at just about every turn. She did get a bit lost a couple of times. Finally, she took a wild guess at the intersection of a pebbly, red-dirt road bordered with pines, and luckily had been right.

She exited the car, gulping down the last of the water in her bottle, staring out at the distant mountains across a deep valley frothy with fog. It felt unreal, being here, so close to her mother, to Jim. It was hard to imagine his ugly presence in a place as beautiful as this. But of course, he'd blighted the Amazonian jungle with his sanctimonious bile as well, sticking out like a sore thumb among people so genuine and true.

Charlie took in a deep breath of the mountain air, feeling the anxiety she'd managed to keep in check during the drive here starting to surface. As she bent to stretch her legs she heard a voice coming from behind the closed gate.

"Yes? Can I help you?"

She stood and found herself face to face through the bars with a broad-shouldered young Haitian man cradling a rifle in his arms. Charlie's forced smile bounced back at her off the dark lenses of his Ray-Bans. "*Bonjou!*" she chirped. "How are you doing today?"

The guard returned neither the greeting nor the smile. "What are you looking for?"

"I am in the right place, aren't I?" She gestured toward to the sign. "Farming for Freedom?"

The guard nodded.

"Well, that's a relief," she said, shaking out her curls. "Would have been a shame to come all this way and be in the wrong place. Is Pastor Jim here?" Her heart was pounding as she peered through the bars of the gate and up the long driveway, toward some structures in the distance.

The man shook his head. "The pastor is out doing business."

"Well, that's too bad," she said, breathing a sigh of relief.

"Who are you?" He pointed with his chin as if challenging her to come up with a good answer.

"Me?" Charlie stuffed her damp hands into the pockets of her jeans. "I'm from one of his backer organizations."

His brow furrowed in confusion.

"We're a group who gives him money. From Virginia. He didn't mention to you that I was coming?"

"No, he did not." The guard dropped the rifle to let it rest against his side.

"Darn. I was hoping for a tour of the place. You know, to let our folks hear firsthand about all the good things their money is doing." She tugged at the T-shirt that was beginning to cling to her torso. "And your name?"

"Eddy. My name is Eddy."

Charlie nodded. "Tell me, Eddy, is the pastor's wife around?"

Again the guard shook his head. "No. Madame April had to do some errands in the city. She will be back later also."

Charlie looked down at her watch. "Well, you see, here's the thing. I'm supposed to be back in Port-au-Prince for a meeting with my bosses in a couple of hours, so I really can't wait around."

"You should come back tomorrow."

"I'd love to, but that's just not gonna work. I'll be flying out first thing. So this here is my only chance."

Eddy thought about it for a few seconds. "I do not think it is possible. We do not usually see visitors here. The pastor, or his wife, will maybe be back soon. You can wait."

Charlie frowned. "You know, Eddy, as much as I'd like to see them, I just can't take the chance of missing out on my meeting. It's really important. In fact, we're going to be talking about this very place, about how much we can afford to give to Pastor Jim next year. I'm sure he'd be extremely disappointed to hear he'd missed an opportunity to show off his wonderful project to a donor."

Charlie felt bad for lying to Eddy. The last thing she wanted was to get anybody in trouble. But now that she was here, all she wanted to do was take a quick survey of the place, find some evidence of her mother's well-being, and report back to Bea without ever having to face Jim or her mother.

The guard removed his baseball cap and wiped his brow with his forearm. Charlie followed his glance down the road, praying not to see an approaching car.

"Let me try to call him," he said, beginning to punch in the number.

"No, no." Charlie waved a halting hand in his direction. "No need to bother him. I'm sure the pastor's a very busy man. Honestly, I promise this won't take long. I just need a quick peek." Again Charlie flashed her famous smile.

"Pastor Jim does not answer." Eddy shoved the phone back into his pocket.

"You know what he'd say," Charlie urged. "You know how important this place is to him, how much he relies on his donors to help this dream come to life." She swept her arm majestically across the horizon, as if there were a grand palace before her eyes instead of a dusty driveway leading to who-knows-what.

Again the guard hesitated. "I don't know—"

"I'm *sure* it's fine," she insisted. "In fact, Eddy, I will be sure to mention you in my report, to let the pastor know just how helpful you've been."

Charlie's pulse quickened as she saw the guard's eyes soften slightly. "Okay," he said finally, as he pushed a button that caused the gate to slowly swing open with an electric hum. "I will give you a tour. But we will make it quick."

"Thanks." Charlie began to follow him up the long, pebbled driveway as the gate closed itself behind them. "I'm sure your boss, and my boss, will both appreciate it very much."

The first thing Charlie noticed was the smell—a mix of barnyard and sewer that hit her like a punch in the face. She held a hand over her nose as they neared the closest structures to be seen on the compound, a cluster of shacks with rusting tin roofs.

"What are those?" she asked.

"That is where our people live."

"The dormitories?"

The guard didn't answer. As they approached the buildings Charlie began to see just how dilapidated they were. Many appeared as though they'd collapse with one swift breeze. Some lacked roofs altogether, instead relying on tarps to provide shelter from the sun and rain. There were no real doors, just bent pieces of corrugated metal, or hanging blankets, or nothing at all. And everywhere, goats and chickens picked through piles of trash, and pigs wallowed in mud puddles the size of small lakes.

"Is there running water? Electricity?"

"There is a pump. I will show you."

She followed him down a rutted path that led away from the shacks, stopping in front of a roofless concrete enclosure divided in two by a crumbling wall.

"This is our bathing facility," he explained. "One side for the men, the other for the women."

"You have women here, too?"

"Yes, of course."

"And children, too?"

Eddy shook his head. "The pastor, he says this is not a place for children."

She followed him around a bend in the path, where two shirtless men were taking turns swinging their blades at the twisted trunk of a leafy green tree, its gnarly roots seeming to be clinging to the ground for dear life. Behind the men was a graveyard of stumps beneath a tangle of dismembered branches.

"That tree's so beautiful. Why are they cutting it down?" she asked.

Eddy didn't answer.

"Is it sick or something?"

The guard was already ten paces ahead of her as the tree fell, its leaves shivering as it hit the dirt with a crack. Charlie scrambled to keep up.

"Where is everybody?" she asked as they continued down the path.

He pointed to a distant field, half green, half bare, where Charlie could barely make out the dozens of tiny figures, bent with their backs to the midday sun.

"Those are the students?"

"Those are our farmers, not students. Their job is to cut the sugarcane and strip the leaves. Then it will be chopped and put into piles," he explained. "It will be sold to make rum."

"So you call them farmers?"

"Yes, of course. They work the fields."

"But they also attend the school, right?"

The guard looked confused.

She gestured to a low, rectangular building that seemed somewhat sturdier than the rest. "What's that?"

"That is the church. Where Pastor Jim gives his sermons," Eddy said with some pride.

"So the classes are held there as well? Or are there separate classrooms?"

"Classes?" Eddy stiffened. "I think it is time for you to go, to get to your meetings, am I right?"

"Are they being paid for their work?" Charlie persisted.

"Everyone receives a bed to sleep in, and plenty of food to eat," he said as he started back toward the gate, his manner now abrupt.

Charlie was disgusted, though not surprised. The place looked nothing like what she had seen on the Farming for Freedom website. The place was a scam, her stepfather a fraud, no better than a slaveholder disguised as a man of the cloth. But almost worse was the fact that her mother was obviously complicit in such shameless deceit.

"But wait!" Charlie called after the guard. "I haven't seen the pastor's house. I'm sure our people back home would be curious to see how he lives. And I'm sure he'd want to show it off to them as well."

Charlie's heart was pounding against her ribs. She had to get out of this place. She had come with no plan, had never really expected to get this far. If she could just get a quick look at the house, maybe take a photo, perhaps give Bea some sense of her mother's well-being, that would be enough. She wouldn't even have to leave a note. Her mother would never have to know she'd been there.

The guard sighed and turned, and motioned for her to follow him down a hill, away from the squalor and stench of the sorry living quarters. Here the vegetation turned lush, with palms and pines and banana plants living side by side, blending together to shelter the path as they descended further and further away.

"There is the house."

Eddy pointed ahead, where, sitting smack in the middle of a pristine, freshly mowed lawn, behind a white picket fence, was a tidy stone house with lace curtains in the windows and a chimney up one side. Without the tropical heat to remind her, she might have thought she was back home in Carmel.

She approached the cottage with trepidation, as if Jim and her mother might suddenly appear in the doorway. But the place was still. Then she noticed the garden—a meticulously manicured patch of color, bursting with what looked like irises, birds of paradise, hibiscus, oleander, and other even more exotic plants whose names she did not know. It was stunning. The hand of her mother was unmistakably present. She remembered how, in the jungle, her mother—frustrated by the insects and ants chewing up her garden and carrying it off leaf by leaf—learned to grow orchids in the trees. She'd mount the flowers onto the trunks by attaching them with cotton string, which would eventually disintegrate, leaving the blooms clinging safely to their hosts, far above the clutches of nibbling predators.

"The pastor's wife," she asked the guard, "is this her work?"

"Yes." Charlie noticed a smile creep onto his face. "Madame April is a good gardener. I see her here sometimes, digging in the dirt, pulling the weeds and cutting the bushes."

"And how is she?"

"How is she?" He raised his eyebrows beneath the brim of his cap, obviously perplexed by the question. "Madame April, she is a fine woman, very kind."

Charlie felt a twinge in her chest. But, of course he would only say something like that. Who was paying the guy's wages, after all? She took out her phone and snapped a couple of photos before hurriedly following him back up the hill. Passing once again by the tumbledown shacks, she snapped a few more.

"No pictures!" Eddy barked. He hustled her back down the driveway to the gate, arriving just as a canary-yellow 4x4—with tinted windows, a snorkel running up its side, and a Farming for Freedom logo plastered on its door—came roaring to a halt.

Charlie froze as heavy cowboy boots hit the gravel, one by one.

17

"I tell you, the guy was downright obsessed with genitalia," Bea said, laughing, as she filled Robert in on her afternoon visiting the Atis Rezistans with Lizbeth. The three of them were sipping rum punch, snacking on fried *akra* and spicy *pikliz* while waiting for Charlie to arrive back at the hotel for dinner. Bea used a napkin to dab her bare arms, slick with the smelly insect repellant she'd learned, the hard way, to apply before each foray onto the veranda. The rain had stopped, but the sky remained ominously dark. She pulled her thin scarf tight around her neck in anticipation of the next downpour.

Lizbeth seemed jumpy, as if the air were filled with tiny electric charges that only she could feel.

"Who will join me in another rum punch?" Bea offered, listening for Stanley's shuffle.

"Perhaps we should order our meal," Robert suggested.

Bea agreed. She appreciated how long it took the kitchen staff to prepare an order. Everything made from scratch. Not a thing going to waste. And besides, there was absolutely nothing wrong with a good, long cocktail hour, in her opinion.

"What about Charlie?" Lizbeth asked. "Shouldn't we wait?"

"She'll catch up with us. It'll be fine," Bea insisted.

"Your granddaughter is not back yet?" she heard Stanley ask. "There is a big storm coming, and sometimes the roads get flooded."

"She'll get here. I know my Charlie. A little water won't stop her."

"How can you be so sure, Bea? Why, if it were my grand-child—" Lizbeth stopped mid-sentence, as if the word had frozen her tongue.

"I am somewhat concerned too, Madame Bea," Robert added. "I know how these roads can be. And if there is any problem, her phone will have no service out there. Perhaps I should find somebody here with a car and go look for her."

"We should have never come here anyway," Lizbeth added. "Not a one of us. Not you, not me, not your granddaughter. Y'all should do like me and just pack up and head home first thing tomorrow morning."

"Would everybody please relax?" The vibe at the table that night was making Bea crazy. Both Robert and Lizbeth seemed particularly on edge. "If something happened to Charlie," she said, "I would know."

"How can you say that, Bea? How would you know?" Lizbeth swatted at a mosquito buzzing around her head.

"I know things."

"Well, I know things too. But that doesn't make me a psychic."

Bea laughed. "You never know, Lizbeth. Maybe you simply haven't tapped into your powers. They say we all have the ability. It's just that some of us choose to develop our skills, and others don't."

"What, Madame Bea?" Robert said. "Are you telling us that you are a seer?"

"These days they call us sensitives. Me, I like to think of myself as a plain old-fashioned psychic."

"Oh, good Lord," Bea heard Lizbeth say, not quite under her breath.

"That is very interesting," Robert said. "And what is it that you are so sensitive about?"

Bea pushed her round glasses up the bridge of her nose. "Well," she began, wondering how far she should take this. "I can read people's energy. And, sometimes, I have dreams."

"Ha! I can do that, too," Lizbeth said. "It's called intuition and imagination, where I come from."

Bea shook her head. "This is different. Trust me. A whole other ball game."

"So where's your crystal ball?" Lizbeth teased.

Bea ignored the crack. "My real specialty is as a medium."

"You're trying to tell us you're one of those folks who talks to dead people?"

"I *communicate* with people who have crossed over, and relay their messages to those who are still living."

"Madame Bea, you are even more fascinating than I first thought."

Bea lowered her eyes and pulled at one of her dangly earrings. "I don't know about that, Robert. It's just what I do. Something I was born with."

"I've seen those psychics on TV," Lizbeth said. "The way they get people to talk, the way they spit back whatever they've heard? And who's gonna tell me they weren't just told everything there was to know before those cameras started rolling?"

Bea shrugged her shoulders. "Nobody says you have to believe it." She removed her glasses, and turned to Robert. "To be quite honest with you, Robert, I've been picking up on something all evening. In fact, I'm sensing someone standing beside you right now."

"Remarkable," he replied, almost in a whisper.

"Oh, please," Lizbeth muttered.

"Is it all right with you if I pass on a message?"

"Go right ahead," he answered.

Bea closed her eyes. The hum of the city beyond the wall filled the air as they waited.

"Someone with an M in their name is coming through. A soft-spoken woman. She says to tell you the pain is gone. A Marilyn? Marcie? A woman with long brown hair, hair that she wears piled up on top of her head. A very elegant woman, with beautiful hands."

Robert was silent for a minute. "Marie-France. My wife," he said softly. "She passed away three years ago."

Bea should have known. The woman was as stunning as Robert was charming. What a couple they must have made. "She needs you to know she's okay."

"That's incredible, Madame Bea."

"She's been with you, on your travels. She says to keep up the good work."

Robert was silent for a moment. "Is that all?" he finally asked.

"A question for you, Robert. Is there something you keep finding in your luggage when you travel? Like a pebble or something?"

"A seashell," he answered excitedly. "A small conch. I always wonder how it gets there."

"Marie-France puts it in your suitcase, to remind you of the vacations you took together, at the beach."

"*Mon dieu.*"

"And she's asked me to tell you to please stop forgetting to water her plants."

Now Robert laughed. "Astounding. Simply astounding."

Bea took a deep breath, placed her glasses back on her face, and returned to her drink. After a few moments she turned to Lizbeth. "Now let me ask you something. Have you ever sensed Luke's energy about you since he passed?"

"Oh, quit it, Bea. This is nonsense."

"So there's nothing strange you've ever noticed around the house, like objects moving, not being where you left them?"

"Of course I misplace things. I'm getting older."

"That's not what I mean. Think, Lizbeth. Think hard."

"Well," the woman finally said. "There *is* this candle, right in front of Luke's picture on the mantel. Keeps going out. Must be a draft coming from someplace, but Lord help me, I haven't been able to locate it."

"That's your son. Luke's trying to communicate with you."

"Now, come on, Bea."

"I'll stop if you'd like, but I'm feeling right now like he really wants you to acknowledge his presence. Shall I go on?"

When Lizbeth didn't answer, Bea took it as a yes. "And he's not alone, he's coming through with someone else. He's making me feel a 'D'. A very strong 'D' is coming through. Who's Darryl? He says to tell you thanks for sending him off with his nine iron."

"My husband. Luke's father. I told you his name was Darryl. We buried him with his favorite golf club. I probably already told you about that, too."

"But he says he wishes you'd picked the sand wedge instead." Bea couldn't tell if the sound coming from Lizbeth was a laugh or a cry. "They want you to know that they're together, and that they're getting along fine." She paused for a minute. "But it's really Luke that's coming through strong. He's the one who wants to be heard."

"Oh, sweet Jesus," Lizbeth said.

"He needs you to know that he felt nothing. That his passing was fast, and painless."

"How could you possibly know that?" Lizbeth asked.

"I'm supposed to tell you that he knows you often wish it were you instead of him who had the accident," Bea said. "He wants you to stop that. And he knows how hard you've been trying to cope. He sees you sitting in his room, on his bed, at night. He hates how difficult it's been for you. He wants you to focus on the happy times you two had together."

"You could say that to anyone, Bea."

"But he's aware of what you're doing now," she added, "and he wants you to know that he's incredibly proud of you."

"It's him I was supposed to be proud of, not the other way around," Lizbeth said quietly.

"Lizbeth, Luke needs you to tell Senzey that he did not abandon her, that he loves her."

Lizbeth was silent.

"And he apologizes for not talking to you about her before he passed. He was waiting for the right time, but he waited too long." Again Bea paused. "And then there's the baby."

"You're trying to tell me Luke knows about the baby?"

"Senzey and the boy, they need to be together. Those are Luke's words."

"A *boy*?" she asked excitedly, before quickly composing herself.

"Luke says he's with you, and not to be afraid."

And then he was gone.

"You are most amazing, Madame Bea," Robert said, his voice far quieter than usual.

Bea dabbed at her forehead with the edges of her scarf and slumped back in her chair.

"She has quite a gift, it seems, hasn't she?" he asked Lizbeth.

"I don't know what to think. But if she's so gifted, then why didn't she say all this to me before?"

"You didn't ask," Bea piped in.

"I think I need that second drink," Lizbeth said.

"If only you could use your powers to find Charlie," Robert said, as the sky broke open and lightning flashed behind the palms.

"Now, *that* would be worthwhile," Lizbeth agreed.

Bea again shook her head. "Actually, it doesn't work that way. Usually a person needs to have passed on for me to hear from them. Sometimes I get feelings, but it's just too difficult to get anything from a person you're close to. And there's nobody on this Earth closer to me than Charlie."

"So, is that why you couldn't simply use your senses to check on your daughter here in Haiti, instead of coming all this way yourself?" Robert asked.

Bea let out a mischievous giggle. "Well . . . maybe."

"Maybe what?"

"Maybe yes and maybe no."

"And what is the 'no' part?"

"I actually told Charlie I had a dream. But truth be told, I needed Charlie to come here. *Charlie* needed to come here. The girl needs her mother in her life. Not to be living with memories and nightmares that are eating up her insides like worms.

I've waited way too long for those two to come back together, and I wasn't about to wait any longer. How much time can an old woman like me have, anyway?"

"Please, Madame Bea. You radiate youth."

Bea laughed. "That's very kind, Robert. I think. But we all know how short our time on this earth truly is. And what's the point of wasting that time holding negative feelings toward those who are closest to us?"

"That is true," he answered.

"Family belongs together. That's all there is to it. Am I right, Lizbeth?"

Perhaps Lizbeth's answer was drowned out by the sea of rainwater spilling down the eaves, cascading onto the pavement below and rushing down the long driveway into the streets of Port-au-Prince, or perhaps she hadn't answered at all. The only thing Bea knew was that, for all of them, their adventures in this crazy country were far from over. She pulled her scarf even tighter, sat back, and waited for Charlie's return.

18

Her stepfather's face turned the color of raw beef when he recognized her standing there at the gate of his compound. "Well, well, well," he said through clenched teeth. "Lookie who's here. If it isn't the prodigal daughter, come home to roost. What happened, Charity? You get yourself in trouble or something?" His gaze came to rest on her belly.

"Hello, Jim," she said coolly, determined not to let loose the fury boiling just under her skin. "Don't worry—I'm not planning on staying."

Her stepfather slowly nodded, his beady eyes looking up the driveway. He punched a code into the keypad. "So, what can I do for you?" he asked as the gate swung open.

Charlie moved into the road. "Not a thing, Jim. I came to see my mom."

He took a step toward her, running one hand through what was left of his greasy head of hair. "She's not here."

"I heard."

Jim's eyes flashed briefly at Eddy. "So?"

Charlie shifted her feet, her sandals filling with pebbles as she struggled to come up with what to do next. "Where is she?" she asked.

"Church errands."

"Really," she replied, remembering what the pastor in Port-au-Prince had told her about Jim and her mother's break with the church. "Will she be back soon?"

Her stepfather shrugged his shoulders. "Can't honestly say."

"Will you give me her phone number?" She already knew the answer.

Jim shook his head.

"Well, then can you give her a message from me?"

Again Jim shook his head. "I don't think I can do that, Charity. It wouldn't be wise."

"Why the hell not?"

"Because she doesn't want to hear from you."

Charlie couldn't escape the sting of his words.

Jim took another step closer. "She has no interest in you. You can't just waltz out of someone's life and expect them to welcome you back with open arms, can you? You're the one who chose to leave. Don't forget that."

"I *chose*? Are you serious? I don't believe you gave me that choice. And she knew I had to leave, wanted me to go. She saw what I was living with. She was living with it, too."

"Your mother knows who you are, Charity. She knows exactly who you are."

Charlie stood with her hands planted firmly on her hips. "Who am I, Jim? You tell me. Because I'd really like to know."

"A smart girl like you should know the difference between right and wrong—between being a good, obedient daughter and one who turns her back on the family who sacrificed so much to raise her."

"Turned *my* back? And sacrifice? That's a laugh."

"How dare you!" he roared, his anger suddenly igniting.

"How dare *I*?" she yelled back.

"Think about it, Charity. Why would your mother want an *ungrateful daughter* such as yourself, one who runs off and gallivants all over the world like some sort of *tramp*. One who turns her back on the Lord and everything he stands for?"

"How do you know what I've been doing? And how dare you, of all people, accuse me of turning my back on the Lord? I've seen what's going on up there, at your 'mission'."

Her stepfather narrowed his eyes at the guard, who'd been standing stock still with his rifle resting against the fence. His anger seemed to have cooled as quickly as it had flared. "The fact is, Charity, your mother never wants to see you again. Why do you think she hasn't written, or called?"

Charlie bit the inside of her lip, desperate to keep her tears at bay.

"Your mother sees the truth for what it is," he continued calmly.

"You are a disgusting, horrible man!"

"And you," he countered, "are a heathen. Just like your Satan-loving grandmother. Now get the hell off my property."

Jim took another step toward her, his chest puffed out like a rooster. Charlie walked backward to the door of the SUV, not taking her eyes off of him. She jumped into the driver's seat and threw the car into reverse, spitting gravel into the air as she peeled away from the compound in a race to put as much distance as possible between herself and the man and everything he stood for.

She flew down the mountain, the four-wheel drive bouncing over rocks and rattling across potholes. The sky was darkening, the clouds gathering into one thick mass that hung over the valley. But it wasn't the threat of bad weather that was driving her to speed so recklessly. It was anger—a rage so overwhelming that it was filling her brain to the point where it felt ready to explode.

She'd barely made it back to the turn at the little market town when the skies opened, turning the road into a muddy waterfall and leaving the last of the street vendors scrambling for cover. Charlie continued ahead, grateful for the four-wheel drive and a half-decent wiper blade, which provided a slender crescent of clarity that came and went with every swipe. Her stepfather's accusations echoed in her head. What kind of a mind did it take to twist the facts into a painful web of lies? Did Jim actually believe his own stories? The man was deranged, pure and simple.

In retrospect, Charlie could recognize the signs. She and her mother had adapted quickly to life in the jungle, learning the language and making friends. They were easily embraced by the community. Jim, not so much. Any psychology student could have read what was going on in his head. He thought he'd be marching right in as the Great White Savior, a god to these people. Yet nobody was really all that interested in a word he had to say. Not that he let that stop him. In fact, all it did was stir up his resentment until he began to exert his ugly power over anybody and everybody, including his wife and family, projecting his own demons onto them in a perpetual tirade of suspicion and abuse. Charlie would never forgive his behavior. Nor could she forgive her mother for staying behind and pandering to his madness.

The day Charlie left the mission had started just like any other. She'd woken to the smell of smoke from the morning fires and the sounds of the village coming alive—the echoes of voices, children laughing and babies crying to be fed. She finished her breakfast quickly, mopping up the remains of the runny eggs from the plate with a hunk of her mother's bread. She was anxious to get her schoolwork done early, to escape her stepfather's disapproving eyes and short-fused temper. She hated being back at the compound, missed boarding school, which had felt like a vacation after life under Jim's roof. But he'd ruined that, just as he ruined anything good in her life, with his ugly suspicions about what went on there, his certainty that she was a girl who could not be trusted to keep her pants on.

Until she hit puberty, Jim had left her pretty much alone. Her mother had told her the facts about what to expect from her impending womanhood. Charlie already knew all about the tribe's traditions around a girl's first period, which seemed sort of mysterious and romantic to her. First the girl would be put into a tiny shelter made of leaves, allowed only to drink water from a gourd that must not touch her teeth. When she emerged, after the bleeding stopped, she had to speak in a whisper for weeks. Then, when the women in her family decided it had been long enough, they'd tickle her until she burst out laughing, then would take her to the water for a ritual bath, rubbing her in "young woman leaves" and encouraging all the littler girls to swim downriver in the runoff, so that they, too, would soon become young women. Finally, her body would be painted and decorated in feathers, she'd be clothed in new skirts, and escorted like a queen back to her village.

Charlie's experience was nothing like that. By Jim's reaction, it was as if the blood coming from her body was a sign of evil, a declaration to the world that she was shameful.

At first she'd done everything she could to try to be a good girl, not even understanding what she'd done wrong. Her mother helped as best she could, cautioning Charlie to stay out of Jim's way. But that was difficult. He seemed to be everywhere.

When she turned fourteen, her mother finally, somehow, convinced Jim that sending Charlie to the boarding school for missionary kids two hundred miles away would be best for everyone. And though she'd missed her mother terribly, Charlie loved being away at school. Now she was condemned to long mornings at the kitchen table, buried in textbooks she'd struggle to get through between the constant interruptions from the tribespeople, who always seemed to need something from her mother.

But the worst part about having to live back at the compound, besides her stepfather, was that there was no one, beyond her mother, to hang out with. Here, all the girls had been living the lives of grown women since they were five—tending to gardens, carrying firewood, and hauling around newborn siblings practically as big as they were strapped to their sides. At her age, they'd already been married for years. And the boys, they all spent their days hunting and fishing for real now, with families to feed. There was no room for a daydreaming seventeen-year-old girl among their ranks.

Thank goodness for Cole. He'd arrived in the jungle full of hope, to join his parents on their mission after completing Bible college in the States. He was quiet and serious, yet to Charlie he offered a welcome relief from loneliness. They'd spent much of the month he'd been there sitting and talking in the afternoons, under the shade of the palm grove by the river, away from the commotion of the compound. Cole would tell her about what it had been like going back to Michigan to live, after a child-hood of hopscotching across the world with his parents as they worked. She laughed at the image of him arriving in his plaid pants and crew cut, in a place where nobody would be caught dead without their skinny jeans or their messy bedhead. He told her of his confusion over putting gas in a car, let alone learning to drive one. Always, he said, there was that feeling of not quite "getting it", a fear of messing up by saying or doing the wrong thing. Charlie had heard these stories before, from other kids who had left the mission field for extended periods of time. And as much as she dreamed about getting out, the thought of going "home" to the States also terrified her. But a hard slap across her face, one that sent her reeling backward in the dirt, was enough to make her conquer that fear.

She'd just put away her math book and stepped outside when Jim arrived home from his morning rounds of the village.

"Where do you think you're going?" he said, blocking her way, his cowboy boots planted firmly in the dirt.

"Out," she answered, her eyes darting around for her mother.

"You've no business parading around like that, showing your skin like a tramp," he hissed. "If you can't show respect for who you are, then at least show some for who your family is."

Charlie tugged at her cutoff jeans, the sweat already pouring down her limbs. "It's hot. I'm just going down to the river to cool off."

"Don't make your excuses to me, Charity," he said, the volume rising. "And quit your lying."

"I'm not lying." Charlie forced herself to look him straight in the eye, anger beginning to simmer inside her.

"I know where you're going."

Charlie stood facing him, her hands on her hips in a silent challenge.

"I've seen the look in your eyes. Don't think I haven't. And I know that look—it's the look of the devil."

"Oh, please." Charlie tried to step around him, but immediately found her arm pinned in his grip.

"Don't you 'oh please' me," he seethed. "Ever since that boy showed up you've been prancing all over the place, waving your lust around like a flag on a ten-foot pole. How do you think that looks to people? How do you think it makes me look?"

Charlie should have seen this coming. There was no hiding here, in the middle of the jungle. She'd tried to be discreet, for her own sake, about her afternoons hanging around with Cole. And that's all they were doing, anyway. Just hanging around. She couldn't deny that she'd had thoughts about maybe, someday, doing more than that. But Cole was so damn serious. And so much older, almost twenty-two! Besides, she barely knew the guy.

"I know what you two have been doing, down by the river. I have eyes everywhere, young lady. Don't you forget that. And I'm going to tell the church exactly what those eyes have seen. That boy will wish he never set foot down here, in my house of the Lord."

"But we haven't done anything!" Charlie shouted back. "And even if we had, so what? You know why? Because it's normal!"

That's when he struck.

"You whore!" he spat, standing over her with his hand open and ready to hit her again.

Facing the man, Charlie felt any lingering traces of fear from a lifetime under his rule escape her body, leaving her emboldened by anger. She remembered seeing her mother running toward them through the compound as she and Jim went at it, April's feet flying across the dust. She pushed her way in between Charlie and Jim, with her back to her daughter, her words to her husband measured and controlled.

She said it was time for Charlie to go. "We can't handle her anymore," she told her husband. "Think about it. What good can come of having a girl like that interfering with the work you're trying to do down here? You've put too much into it to have everything ruined by her shamelessness."

Charlie had been stunned. She'd never heard her mother say anything like this before. This was not her mother speaking. Had Jim hypnotized her or something? She numbly packed a bag of belongings, her mother watching with her lips pressed tightly together. The weekly boat heading upriver would be leaving soon.

Charlie had wanted to shake her, to grab her by the arm and force her to come along, to run as fast and far away as she could from the ugly, pitiful excuse for a man who was poisoning her with his hatefulness. Instead, all Charlie was left with was a fistful of dollars sneaked into her pocket and a hushed promise, whispered into her ear as the two of them embraced on the riverbank. "I'll come," she had sworn she heard her mother say.

Yet, ten years later, here her mother was, still following that fucking man to the ends of the Earth. There was not an excuse in the world for allowing herself to be pulled even deeper into his clutches, Charlie thought as she raced down the mountainside, rain pelting the windshield. Not loyalty, not God, nothing.

She struggled to suppress the echoes of Jim's mocking tone, to erase the image of his thin, mean lips and the skin that stretched across his sharp features like crinkly leather on a couch.

Just being in his presence made her feel slimy, as if his treachery were contagious.

"*I hate you!*" she shouted out loud, speeding through the rain, anxious to put this day behind her as fast as she could. "*I hate you both!*"

The words were barely out of her mouth when she found herself skidding around a hairpin turn and straight toward a line of boulders spread across the road.

Charlie slammed on her brakes, praying that nobody was following behind her. The car came to a halt and slid into the roadside barrier with a thud. She sat for a minute, her heart thumping. It was nearly nightfall, the rain was slowing, and there was not a soul in sight. Charlie unbuckled her seat belt and stepped down from the car to check for damage.

The thick black bumper had done its job. She returned to the driver's seat and backed the car up, but it was clear that there was not enough room to pass between the evenly spaced rocks. Suddenly she found the car surrounded by a handful of teenage boys, their arms crossed rigidly in front of their chests.

"Need some help, *blan*?" one of them asked.

"I'm good," Charlie said out her window. "Just need to get around these rocks. Why are they even here?"

"So that we can help you," answered another of the boys, a cigarette hanging from his lips. Next to him was a smaller boy, in a backward baseball cap and a Michael Jordan T-shirt. Charlie watched as he tapped his mouth twice with two fingers, touched his stomach, and then held out his open palm toward her.

"You're hungry?" she asked, knowing full well he was looking for money.

Nobody moved. Charlie reached across the front seat for her bag and pulled out a power bar. She tossed it out the window to the boy, who unwrapped it, took a bite, and chucked the empty wrapper down to the road without ever taking his eyes off of her.

"So?" Charlie pointed to the roadblock ahead.

"So what?" one of the boys answered. The boys' laughter rang out across the misty valley.

"What are you going to do about those rocks?" she asked.

They stood their ground, all eyes locked on Charlie.

She gave them a minute, then flung open her door and once again stepped out of the car. The rain had stopped, leaving the pitted asphalt a maze of puddles.

"Now," she said, placing her hands on her hips, "are we going to just stand here? Or are we going to keep playing this little game until the sun comes up?"

The boys looked confused by this skinny white woman who charged toward the nearest rock, dug in her heels, and began to push. The tallest one was the first to make a move, joining in to help. The others followed.

"*Mèsi*," she said as she returned to the car and slammed the door. "And stay out of trouble," she added as she shifted the car into gear and rolled forward, cramming a fistful of *gourdes* into the hand of the nearest boy as she passed.

The sky had turned from dark to pink as the sun sank below the clouds toward the horizon. A rainbow sprouted out of nowhere, arcing toward the heavens like a beautiful arrow shot from a bow. Charlie smiled, then remembered the warning she'd learned from her friends in the jungle: Beware of the rainbow. It is a mystical path where the demon watches human beings to capture their souls. And, they told her, there is nothing beautiful in that.

19

Charlie was flinging her belongings into the suitcase with a vengeance. Despite Bea's protests, it was clear the girl had her mind set on going home as soon as possible. She'd come back late the previous night, after Lizbeth was already mostly packed herself and in bed with her eyes closed. Lizbeth had listened while Charlie ranted and raved to Bea about some scam, about her stepfather being a tyrant and a bully—the man did sound like a real creep. All hat and no cattle. Lizbeth didn't say a word, just lay there listening to Charlie go on and on until she was all talked out. Lizbeth didn't mind. It wasn't as though she was going to get a lick of sleep anyhow, not after all that hooey with Bea.

By the light of day, Lizbeth was thinking she might've had too much of that rum the night before, sitting there on the veranda all that time with Bea and Robert. After Bea was done talking about Luke and all, she'd just kept going, pouring herself nips straight from the bottle. Now her mind felt as fuzzy as an old shag carpet.

Charlie woke up still madder than a wet hen. Lizbeth felt sorry for the girl. If Charlie were *her* granddaughter, she'd charge right on up that mountain and give that man a piece of her mind, and then some. At least she'd like to think she would. Bea wasn't talking about any of that. She was too busy trying to change Charlie's mind, to get her to stay a little longer, try a little harder. The woman was scrambling to unpack the bags almost as fast as Charlie was filling them.

But it seemed as though no matter what Bea said or did, it wasn't making a lick of difference. Lizbeth's heart ached for the girl.

She decided to give it a go herself. "Are you sure he's not just playing games with you, honey? That he's not lying through his teeth about your mom?"

"All I know is that if my mother truly cared about me, she would have found some way in all these years to show it."

"Well, seems to me just about everything else that comes out of his mouth is a darn lie. That man is slicker than a boiled onion. Are you sure your mother is all right?"

"That guard barely batted an eye when I asked about her. And her garden looks as though she's been up to a lot of hard work lately. Signs point to her being pretty all right, don't you think?" She crouched to check under the bed for anything left behind.

"Honey, I know it's none of my business, but I think you oughta go back on up there to that place."

"Not on your life," Charlie answered from the floor. "You couldn't pay me enough to look at that pig face again."

"Now, you can't let an ugly mug keep you from doing what's right. Why, if I had to place a bet on it, my money would be on you in a match with that man. You're a tough cookie, Charlie. The toughest in the batch."

Charlie straightened, her hands coming to her hips. "Well, this cookie has no interest in begging. If she wanted to see me, she would have done it by now. God, I wish we'd never even come down here."

Lizbeth heard her own words echoing in Charlie's. "You don't know what goes on behind somebody else's curtains, Charlie. That man could be threatening her, or keeping her hostage somehow. Why, anything could be happening up there."

"She was out, doing errands. Nobody is keeping her prisoner."

"All I'm saying is that you oughtn't give up so easily. You and your grandma came all the way down here with a purpose, and I think you should at least see things through."

"You came down here with a purpose too, Lizbeth. And you tried. And now you're leaving. And so are we." She handed Bea a comb. "Come on, Bibi. We'd better hurry. The plane leaves in just a few hours."

Lizbeth was tempted to share the truth of what she'd been toying with all night, tossing and turning in the hotbox of a hotel room. She had to admit to herself that, even though it might just have been the rum talking, she was a wee bit haunted by Bea's words, or Luke's words, or whoever's words they were supposed to be. She had half a mind to change her plans. But now how was that gonna work? They'd hit a dead end. And besides, she'd never be able to see this through without Charlie and Bea along to help.

Lizbeth was doing one final sweep of the bathroom for anything left behind when the knock came to the door.

"You came to say goodbye?" she heard Charlie ask.

Mackenson stood silhouetted in the open doorway, his cap in his hands. His eyes darted to the suitcases by the door. "You are leaving? I did not know."

"We are," Charlie confirmed. "So long, Mackenson." She shook his hand. "And thank you for everything." She reached into her pocket for some cash.

"But I did not come to say goodbye," he said, stopping her with the palm of his hand. "I came," he said, turning to Lizbeth, "because I have something to tell you."

20

"Well, lookie there. What's that on his head? Are those *pills?*" Lizbeth said, as they crawled past an intersection where a man was balancing a bucketful of medications for sale, the foil packets arranged in a circular tower reaching to the sky. "Don't they have pharmacies in this godforsaken place?"

Mackenson shifted in the seat beside her, biting his tongue to keep from responding. He tried to keep in mind how anxious this woman must be. She was probably just talking to keep herself calm, not really thinking about how her words might sound.

He thought of the look on her face that morning, when he told her that Guerline had called him the night before to say she had been thinking about Senzey after the day they had visited her at the Hotel le Président. The girl was sure that if Senzey were still in Port-au-Prince, she would have heard from her. And that had made her think about where Senzey might go. Her friend, Guerline said, sometimes talked about the city of Jacmel, how she dreamed of going there someday. She had heard it was a place full of artists, of people making beautiful things, and she thought she might learn to be a real painter there. Guerline thought it was just a crazy dream. She had doubts that a girl, alone, with a baby, could survive doing that, in a place without any family to help. But it was all she could think of, and she wanted to let Mackenson know.

Lizbeth's eyes had turned big and bright with the news. The old woman, Bea, was certain that they must go investigate. Charlie had taken one look at Lizbeth's face, which was full of hope, and agreed. So now they were on their way to Jacmel, with Mackenson coming along to help. Although he did not know how he would be of any help if this Senzey turned out to be the kind of girl he feared she might be.

Mackenson wondered if Lizbeth was planning on talking for the entire three-hour trip south. Now she was commenting on the tap tap in front of them, bursting with passengers, with a goat balancing like a surfer on its roof. But it wasn't the goat she was concerned with. It was the two little boys riding on the back bumper, smiling and laughing as they bounced up the hill.

"Lordy, that looks dangerous. Who allows their children to do a thing like that? Why aren't those boys in school?"

Mackenson shrugged. "They cannot afford to pay. They are probably street boys." He helped himself to a bottle of water from the bag at his feet, and handed one to Lizbeth.

"Street boys? You mean like homeless?"

"No. Maybe. I do not know. There are many kids whose parents cannot afford to send them to school, and who cannot be home to watch over them."

"So what happens to them?"

Mackenson sighed. It was sometimes hard to make people understand, to make some sense of the struggles of his people, his country. "Some of these children grow up on the streets. Sometimes they stay out two or three days, and their parents do not know where they are. Some do not go home at all." Mackenson thought about how lucky he was, in a way, to have Fabiola at home with their daughter, and the other two children who were now in their care.

"What kind of a life is that for a child?" Lizbeth continued, leaning toward the front seat, peering through the windshield to get a better look.

"You are right," he had to agree. "A lot of these kids, they get used by others, who teach them to steal and rob. You have seen the boys washing car windows? They are doing that for a gang person. The gangs make a lot of money from the small boys with cute faces."

"Can't something be done to help them?" Charlie asked from behind the wheel.

"It is a very difficult problem to fix. Even if you took them and gave them money to go to school right now, they would have to start at the beginning. Great big boys in a kindergarten class. Imagine. That is very tough."

Charlie put her foot on the brake, lengthening the distance between their Mitsubishi and the tap tap.

"So their parents have no control?" Lizbeth asked.

"The boys like to have money."

They watched as the two kids hopped off at a stop sign, disappearing into the maze of traffic.

Again Mackenson was thinking about his own household. It sometimes angered him, and even made him feel ashamed, that he did not seem to be able to do for his family what his mother, on her own, had managed to do for him and his brothers and sisters. Perhaps if the earthquake had not happened, they would not be in this situation. He would still be a teacher, and Fabiola might be still working as a cook. Even so, it was not as easy living in Port-au-Prince as it was living in the countryside, where he grew up. The cost for school—the entrance fees, ID badges, uniforms, shoes, books—was not as much there, and back when he was younger, there was enough work for the older children to help pay for the younger ones coming up behind them.

"What are those things, pigs?"

Now Mackenson turned to see Lizbeth wrinkling her nose. They were heading out of the city, passing over a canal buried so deep in garbage and plastic bottles you could not even tell if there was any water running through the channel or not. The black creatures had made it their home, rooting around through the trash as if it were an Independence Day feast.

"So much garbage!" she said, shaking her head. "It's no wonder y'all got the cholera down here."

Once more, he summoned the patience to explain. "Actually," he said, "it was the UN that brought the disease to Haiti. Everyone thinks it is because the Haitians are not clean people, that we do not know how to be sanitary. That we are poor. But poverty doesn't cause cholera. Bacteria does. And we do know about sanitation, although it is a difficult thing here, especially after the earthquake."

He thought back on the marches and protests that happened after it was discovered that some peacekeepers from Nepal had built a bad sewerage system at their camp, one that sent waste into a river that people used to drink, to cook, to wash, to bathe. There had not been cholera in Haiti for one hundred years, and now thousands were dead from it.

"Oh," Lizbeth said, "I didn't mean that as an insult. I just can't help but feel sorry for y'all. Everything just seems so darn difficult down here."

Mackenson smiled a small, sad smile. Although he was used to it, the misunderstandings, the insults and the judging never got any easier.

"It is the same with the AIDS," he said aloud, unable to stop himself from defending his country. "It is your country that blamed us for bringing the disease to them, when in fact some people say it came to Haiti with American sailors."

"I remember reading about that," Charlie said, her eyes looking back on them from the rearview mirror. "In a class. Back then they were saying that there were four groups who carried the disease: homosexuals, hemophiliacs, heroin addicts, and Haitians. The 'Four H Club' is what they called it."

Mackenson groaned quietly.

"Well, I'll be—Isn't that just awful? Shame on those people. It seems like it's just one thing after another you've had to deal with."

"Exactly. Because that is when the tourism we had was ruined."

"You had tourists?" Lizbeth asked.

"Of course. There were some very famous people who came to Haiti."

"Like who?"

Mackenson counted them off on his fingers. "We had Mick Jagger, Jacqueline Kennedy, the Clintons, people like that. And many famous writers, too."

"What do you know?" Lizbeth laughed. "I can just see Jackie teetering around those downtown streets in her white gloves and high heels and that little pillbox hat of hers."

Lizbeth turned to look out the window beside her. The road had begun to climb, winding through a handful of villages busy with market activities, and was lined with bundles of sugarcane and mangoes, and sacks of USA Rice for sale. Dogs with swaying teats wandered the street, looking for scraps. Through an open church door, a pastor waved his arms in the air, his yelling and shouting silent, replaced by the whir of the car's air conditioner and the calm of Bea's soft snoring from the front seat.

Mackenson savored the silence. He was tired of trying to explain, of trying to make people see the good he saw in his country and his people. He could not wait for the day when telling the story of his life did not bring pity from outsiders. He was proud of being a hard worker, even though he did not have much to show for it. It felt like he was always scrambling for money, that there was never enough to provide for the needs of his family, especially now that it had unexpectedly grown. He remembered the Vodou practitioner who once told him that he sometimes did numbers for people to win in the lottery. He would do it for Mackenson, too, he said. Mackenson was polite, and accepted the numbers the man chose for him. But he did not play them. Mackenson did not believe in that kind of magic. What he believed in was hard work. But what do you do when there is not much work to be had?

"Good God almighty! Poor thing." Lizbeth was wincing at the sight of a cow tethered to a tree. "Why, he's so skinny, there's nothing between his nose and his hooves but hide."

"How much longer?" Bea asked, straightening in her seat.

"She lives!" Charlie said, laughing.

"I think we will be there in about two hours," Mackenson told her.

"Too much rum with your boyfriend last night?" Charlie teased.

"Robert is not my boyfriend. That man must be young enough to be my son. That is, if I had been a child bride or something."

"Nothing wrong with being a cougar, Bibi."

"Stop your nonsense, Charlie. I simply find the man to be interesting, in an intellectual sort of way." Bea tucked her hair back under her scarf.

"He's quite a charmer, don't you think, Bea?" Lizbeth asked.

"Please. Any Frenchman is charming. Charm is their default mode."

"A bird in the hand, Bibi," Charlie said.

"Mind your own business."

The countryside had turned green, with banana trees and palm trees and open fields stretching right out to the horizon. But the going was slow, the road twisting and turning like a snake, cars and motorbikes flying toward them, horns blaring.

"You should honk on your own horn too, Charlie," Lizbeth urged, her fingers gripping the seat.

As they climbed, the acres of green became patched with brown, naked hillsides.

"What happened over there?" Lizbeth pointed out the window. "A fire or something?"

"The trees have been cut down," Mackenson explained.

"*All* of them? How come they haven't planted anything else?"

"It is complicated. It is something that has been happening for many years." Mackenson passed a bottle of water to Bea in the front seat. "The mahogany was cut for furniture, and later for fuel. It is a big problem now. There has been flooding and drought, and with erosion it is difficult to plant new crops."

They climbed further, to where the fields turned vertical, striped from side to side with rows of crops. If you squinted,

143

you could make out the farmers, like tiny ants crawling among the plants.

"And then, there were the Mapou trees." Mackenson pointed to a broad, green canopy off the side of the road in front of them, supported by a brawny trunk that seemed to rest on long, twisted fingers that clawed at the dirt. As a child, he had been taught by his grandmother about the mighty trees, how one must respect and worship the Mapou as a symbol of the power and strength of the Haitian people.

"Oh, I've seen one like that!" Charlie said.

"The Mapou trees were cut down by the church people."

"Why?" Lizbeth asked.

"It was during *rejete*, the campaign against superstition," Mackenson said. "The Mapou is the sacred tree of Vodou, the link between the spirit world and earth. It is a meeting place for the living and the dead, and sometimes ceremonies are held right around the tree."

"Magnificent," said Bea.

"He was having one chopped down. Up on the mountain." Charlie slowed the car to a crawl to get a better look.

"Jim?" Bea asked. "Figures. It's just like him to force folks to go against their own beliefs. The power in the tree probably scared the bejesus out of him."

"Your stepfather?" Lizbeth asked. "What did a little old tree ever do to him?"

"Nothing a sane person would take as a threat. I tell you, that man is pure evil, through and through."

"You do not need to worry." Mackenson reached his arm forward and patted Charlie's shoulder from the back seat. "This man's power is not that great. The Mapou trees are strong. They will never go away."

21

Bea wished that she could still see. It was the first time she'd truly felt that way since her eyesight started to fade years ago. At home, in Carmel, she could picture exactly what everything, and everyone, looked like, down to the last detail. After all, she'd lived there practically all her life. What was left to wonder about? But here in Jacmel, from the way Charlie and Lizbeth were describing it, there was plenty she'd have loved to be able to experience with her own eyes.

"It's kind of like New Orleans," Charlie told her as they parked and exited the car. "Wrought iron balconies, crazy-tall arched doorways, and pillars. Lots of brickwork. Old mansions, but kind of crumbly."

"Those are the houses where the coffee merchants lived, and stored their coffee," Mackenson explained. "And it is 'crumbly' because it has not yet all been fixed from the earthquake."

"And look!" Lizbeth said. "Bea, there's a woman holding a live chicken upside down, by its feet. Swinging it back and forth just like a handbag. And she's got pineapples on her head."

Charlie took Bea's arm and led her across a bumpy street. Cobblestone, by the feel of it under her feet.

"You okay, Bibi? Should we go check in to the hotel and save all this for tomorrow?"

"Don't worry about me. I'm on my second wind after that lunch." They'd stopped outside of town, at a fancy hotel with an outdoor restaurant hanging over the Caribbean. Bea could have stayed there all day bathing in the sea breeze. The only bad part was that now she couldn't get the stupid song that had been playing over the PA system out of her head. *We are the world*, she heard herself humming as Charlie helped her up the curb.

"So many shops!" Lizbeth said. "Why, there's one little crafts store after another. Just look at all these pretty things!"

"Jacmel is a city of artists. The cultural capital of Haiti. There is also a music and film school here," Mackenson said with pride.

"It sounds amazing." Charlie steered Bea to a shady spot away from the street.

"You want come inside?" came an accented male voice from inside a doorway.

"No, thank you." Lizbeth paused. "I mean, yes," she corrected herself. Bea heard her rustling through her bag. "We're here looking for someone. A girl with a child."

Mackenson repeated her words in Creole.

"He says he does not know her," he told Lizbeth.

And so it went as they canvassed one long street, shop by shop, showing Senzey's photo, looking for someone who might have seen her, someone who might know if she were here.

Everyone asked if they wanted help, disappointed when the help they needed did not involve learning the price of a painting or having a fragile purchase wrapped up for travel. Lizbeth was disappointed as well. Nobody seemed to know who Senzey was. Bea knew the others had to be as hot and sweaty as she was, and frustrated as hell. But, when they were nearly at the end of the street, one of the artisans gave them a tip. *Go ask Martine*, he told them. *She knows everyone. All the girls.*

He pointed them toward her place, around the corner and two streets away. Bea picked up her pace to match that of the others, her arm entwined in Charlie's. But when they reached the spot they were looking for, the group came to a dead halt. The gallery was closed, the door locked.

"There is a phone number painted on the door. I will call," Mackenson said.

They stood under the relentless afternoon sun as he dialed. Bea could feel her energy flagging, but there was no way in hell she was going to be the cause of them giving up now. She leaned against the concrete wall, its surface rough and cool through her thin cotton tunic.

"We will come back tomorrow," Mackenson said after a brief exchange on the phone. "She will be in her gallery then."

Bea heard Lizbeth sigh.

"Come," Mackenson said. "Let us walk back this way, by the water. It will be cooler."

Bea could feel the air turning sticky as they neared the sea, the sound of waves lapping at the shore a soft caress to her ears.

"Oh my god, it's beautiful!" Charlie cried out.

"What? The water?" Bea asked.

"No. Well, yes. But also the mural. Bibi, it's fantastic. A long wall that runs all along the boardwalk, covered with mosaic."

Bea squinted behind her thick glasses, but all she could make out from where they stood were some blotchy patches of color.

"Let's go look," urged Charlie.

Up close the splotches just looked bigger. But Charlie was in heaven. "This is amazing!" She described tiled flowers and birds and beach scenes and ocean life. "There's a huge Mapou tree, and a mermaid, blowing a golden trumpet. What's up with that, Mackenson? I see mermaids everywhere around here."

"That is La Sirène—the mermaid goddess of the sea. There are many stories about mermaids in Haiti, but the one I was told was that when the slaves were brought over from Africa, they were kept in the bottom of the ships, where it was wet and damp. It was dark, and they did not know where they were going. They believed they came here under the sea, and that it would be the mermaids who would guide them back home, to the promised land of Africa, when they died."

Bea ran her palm along the wall, trying to see if she might be able to make out the shapes by touch. Some tiles were square, some pointy, some nearly round, but there was no way she could see the full picture with her hands.

They walked, slowly, back to where they'd parked. Bea, hot and tired, was ready to leave. But apparently there was a problem, in the form of a little dog that had sought refuge from the heat in the shade underneath their car.

Charlie was reluctant to shoo him away. "Poor thing. It's too hot for him out there in the sun." Bea could hear her granddaughter clicking her tongue at the animal from the sidewalk below.

"*Ale!*" Mackenson urged the dog in a gentle voice. "Go!"

They drove to the hotel they had booked, along the coast toward the outskirts of Jacmel, in silence.

There they were greeted by the clamor of more dogs—definitely large, Bea thought, from the sound of Lizbeth shouting over the racket of their barking. "What the heck are those things up on the roof? Looks like a couple of wild hyenas, fixing to eat us for lunch."

"I think they're Dobermans," Charlie said.

"Well, whatever they are," Lizbeth said, "I'm not getting out of this car until they're leashed and penned up and given something to chew on besides my leg."

"Hello!" came a greeting from the direction of the barking. "Welcome. I will be right down to check you in."

Mackenson began to unload their bags as Charlie helped Bea out of the back seat.

"Do not mind my four-legged friends," the man said, in a vaguely European accent, as he approached the car. "They are very friendly. Unless you are an intruder, of course," he laughed, sounding to Bea like one of those villains in an old cartoon.

"How do they know the difference?" asked a shaky-voiced Lizbeth.

The man didn't answer. Bea flinched as a tuft of whiskers tickled her hand. "It's all vibes, Lizbeth. Dogs know things," she said as she held out her palm for a lick.

Perhaps it was the salty air, or the beckoning sea breeze, but all Bea knew was that she yearned for the touch of the Caribbean on her toes. After a quick stop at their hotel room, Charlie slapped a straw hat onto Bea's head and walked with her across the road to do just that.

"Careful," her granddaughter warned as they picked their way over detritus strewn across the sand—palm fronds and coconut shells, mixed with plastic bottles and other trash, all making the journey seem more like an obstacle course than a walk on the beach. But closer to the shoreline, Bea could feel the sand turn smooth and damp, left clear by the sweeping of the tide. Here, it felt as pristine as any beach in Carmel. But the water, she thought as it finally came to greet her feet, was much more welcoming, like a warm bath with Epsom salt after a day of hard work.

"Stay put," Charlie told her. "I see a couple of chairs."

Bea remained blissfully at the shore, her feet resting in two little pools churning with the mellow tide.

"Bracelets? You want bracelets? Look and see."

The surround-sound echo of a gaggle of young boys startled Bea. "No thank you," she said. "I have plenty." She shook her wrists toward them, her own bracelets clattering like shutters in the wind.

"*Blan* needs bracelets."

"No money." She gestured toward her pockets with open palms.

"Only three dollar," one said. "Very cheap."

"I'm sure they're lovely," she answered. "But no."

"We have more. Look."

"I said no thank you."

"Lady, you need bracelet. Very nice. Look."

"Please!" Bea said. "No money. No dollars. No *gourdes*. Nada. Understand?"

"Two dollar."

"Not going to happen. Now go."

"Two dollar. Very cheap."

"Give us some money."

Bea forced her lips into a scowl and pointed a bony finger toward the loudest in the group, shaking it like a stick. "*Wap konn Jòj!*" she shouted. "*Wap konn Jòj!*"

Charlie arrived by her side, and the boys turned their attention to her. Before she knew it, Bea felt her granddaughter's hand slipping band upon band onto her already crowded wrist.

"*Mèsi*. Very nice. Have a good evening!" Charlie said as the boys scattered. "What was that about? What were you yelling?"

"*Wap konn Jòj*. You will know George."

"Who the hell is George?"

"Hurricane. A bad one. It means 'don't mess with me'."

"Where did you learn to say that?"

"Stanley. He told me it works wonders."

"A bit harsh, don't you think? Poor kids were just trying to earn a bit of money."

Bea shrugged her shoulders. "It worked, didn't it? No harm done. I just wanted some peace and quiet, that's all."

Charlie positioned two plastic chairs at the shoreline, putting Bea directly above the tide, her feet sinking into the wet slush below.

"You know, you're going to have to go back up there," she said, her eyes closed, her face tilted up into the sun.

"Where, Bea?" her granddaughter asked with a sigh.

"You know what I'm saying."

"Do we have to, Bibi? I thought you wanted peace and quiet."

"I'll get enough of that when I'm dead." Bea straightened in her chair. "I'm serious, Charlie. Something's going on up there, and I don't like it one bit."

"Of course something's going on up there. People living in filth, working literally like slaves, while she sits like a queen behind her white picket fence."

"You know that's not who your mother is, Charlie. Not deep down."

"How can you say that? She's bought into that asshole's bullshit hook, line, and sinker."

"Well, she's obviously susceptible to the man, or you'd have never ended up in the jungle in the first place."

"Exactly!"

"But that doesn't mean she doesn't love you."

"Who said anything about that?"

"I did."

"So what, she's been brainwashed or something? That's what kept her from leaving—what let her go on with her life as if she didn't have a daughter at all?"

"I'm just saying I think there's more to this than we know."

Bea saw Charlie's shadow shift as she stood.

"Why do you defend her, Bibi? You don't think I saw those letters come back to you, all sealed up? You don't think I noticed the look on your face every time someone asked about her? I hate her for that."

Bea turned toward her granddaughter, her hands gripping the cracked plastic arms of the chair. "This isn't about me, Charlie. It's about you. You can't live the rest of your life carrying around all that hurt you have inside. A woman needs her mother."

"Tell that to your daughter."

"I tell you Charlie, something is *wrong*. I'm worried."

"Cut it out, Bea. Don't try to use your worry to save me. I don't need saving."

Bea heard the sound of a small stone bouncing across the water.

"Honestly, Bea? Sometimes I think it would be easier if she were just dead."

"Charlie! How can you say that?"

"All I mean is that, instead of all this shit we've been going through, we would instead have been sad, grieved, and it would be over with. One, two, three."

"It doesn't work that way, Charlie."

"I know."

Bea listened to the water lapping at the shore. She felt her granddaughter's arms embrace her from behind.

"I know," Charlie repeated. I'm sorry, Bibi. I think I'm going to take a walk. You okay here?"

Bea nodded. "I'm fine."

With the gentle waves tickling her ankles like a soft massage, Bea felt herself drifting off under the evening sun. She had no idea how long she'd been out when, suddenly, she was startled awake by someone removing her hat.

"Charlie?" she asked, her hand flying to her head.

"They're doing braids, Bibi. I just had mine done. See?" She took one of Bea's hands and ran it across her scalp. "Now it's your turn."

"Oh no, not me." Bea reached to retrieve her hat.

"Come on, Bibi. They're such cute little girls. And it's cheap. Only five dollars. Imagine what you'd pay for that at home."

"I wouldn't pay for it at home. And I'm not going to pay for it here. Braids? Me? Ridiculous."

"It's my treat. Seriously, what's the harm? I can always take it out later."

"Why don't you just give the girls the money, and skip the braids?"

"They're trying to earn their money, Bea. What kind of a lesson would that be? Just do it. It'll be fun."

Bea sighed as four small hands began to play with her short locks. She could feel the girls fumbling, and heard them giggling. It wasn't long before Charlie was laughing as well.

"What? What's so funny?" she asked.

"They're just having a bit of trouble."

"Well, they can stop, you know, if it's too much of a challenge for them."

"No, no. It's all good," Charlie assured her between chortles.

Now Bea started to giggle too, imagining herself looking like an old, wrinkled, white version of that rapper, Snoopy Dog or whatever his name was. She couldn't help herself. It was a funny image. This made the girls laugh even harder as they tugged gently at her hair. Which made Bea laugh even harder as well.

The girls suddenly stopped, and started talking. They seemed to be having a consultation on the sand.

"You should help them, Charlie," Bea laughed.

"Me? What do I know about braiding?"

"*Bèl . . . granmè . . . blan . . . kaka . . . chevè*" were the only words Bea could make out from the girls' conversation.

"What are they saying, Charlie?" she asked, wiping the tears of laughter from her eyes.

"I don't know. Something about the pretty grandma and her white shit hair, I think."

And there they sat, four hairdressers, sharing a moment that, in truth, needed no translation. Just another day behind the chair, Bea thought, as she listened to the welcome sound of her granddaughter's laughter rolling across the sea.

22

Charlie was happy to be alone. She sat on the patio outside the sliding glass doors of the hotel room, basking in the night air with an unopened book by her side, savoring the solitude.

At dinner, Bea and Lizbeth had both been particularly energized, Lizbeth howling at Bea's account of the girls and the attempted braids, Bea getting Lizbeth all pumped up about the possibility of finding her grandchild the next day. When Franz, the hotel owner, showed up with a trio of giant, twitching langoustines dangling from his fingers, the two of them practically squealed.

The meat was delicious, Charlie had to agree. They dined under the stars, cracking and picking and sucking every last bit from the shells, their chins dripping with butter, until their plates resembled little crustacean boneyards. Even the two Dobermans—who had been lurking behind a hedge, panting, all throughout the meal—had given up hope of snagging a taste.

Charlie had seen them trotting off together into the shadows, like a pair of sleek wolves on a hunt.

Now Bea and Lizbeth had gone to bed. Mackenson had taken the car, off to visit a cousin who lived in Jacmel, promising to pick them up in the morning to return to town and resume their hunt for the mother and baby.

Charlie was beginning to think that, in believing she was doing the right thing for the woman, she may have made a mistake in leading Lizbeth on with all this. Mackenson, in private, had shared his suspicions about Senzey with her. He sounded like Lizbeth had sounded at times, questioning the relationship between Senzey and Luke, questioning the baby's paternity. In the meantime, Lizbeth seemed to be getting more committed by the hour to tracking down the child. And exactly what, Charlie had to wonder, was she planning on doing if and when she found the baby? And Bea—had it been a mistake to lead her on as well, getting her hopes up about reuniting their broken little family? Maybe they should head back to Port-au-Prince first thing in the morning, before any more disappointments came their way. Besides, she'd already been away longer than she'd intended. She shuddered to think about the mess of appointments that would be waiting for her when she returned to Carmel.

Charlie closed her eyes and tried to enjoy the symphony of crickets and tree frogs blasting from the greenery around her. It reminded her of the jungle, which, of course, made her think of her mom. Sometimes, late at night, Charlie would find memories clawing to the edges of her consciousness, fighting to be recognized. She'd see her mother clear as day, her long hair loosely knotted on the top of her head to alleviate the heat, a ready kiss on her lips to chase away the scrapes and bruises that were the jungle's revenge on a curious Charlie. She remembered her mother's humor, like the time when, faced with an invasion of army ants that came marching across their dining room table one day during lunch, she turned the whole thing into a game. Charlie had panicked, knowing how hard the ants could pinch, knowing they could hold on so tight that when you flicked them away only their bodies would fly off, leaving the heads and pincers to fester under your skin. But her mother had cheered the army on, humming the "Battle Hymn of the Republic" as they made their way in formation over the plates of chicken and rice. Later she'd explained to Charlie that the army ants were her heroes, as they obliterated every tarantula, cockroach, grasshopper, and daddy longlegs in their wake.

One recurring image was the time she surprised Charlie with a gift for no reason whatsoever. It wasn't Christmas, or her birthday. So when her mother revealed the Polly Pocket toy she had hidden behind her back, Charlie had almost cried. She could still remember the feel of the smooth plastic case that opened to reveal the country cottage the tiny doll lived in with her dog. It was pink, and shaped like a heart. Her mother had to have planned this months, perhaps years, in advance, in order to include the doll in the barrels of supplies that were shipped down during each furlough, tucked away among the clothes, the underwear, the generators and chainsaws they could only get from the States. There was an empty slot in the heart-shaped case where Polly's cat was supposed to sit, telling Charlie that the toy was a used one, no doubt donated by some church member. But Charlie didn't mind. She spent countless hours playing with Polly, escaping into a fantasy world far away from the one she lived in, stopping only when she'd hear her stepfather nearby.

Then she'd slip the doll into her actual pocket to protect her from Jim's judging eyes.

That was all long before Jim's poison had seeped so deeply into her mother's soul. And allowing those memories to surface only made everything hurt more.

Now she thought about what she'd said to her grandmother earlier, on the beach, about wanting to grieve. A good, old-fashioned jungle funeral would do just fine. There, in the Amazon, the women really let it all out—wailing, mixing their tears with dirt and rubbing the mixture onto their cheeks to turn the grief into a thick, dark badge they'd literally wear on their faces. And then it would be over.

Charlie applied a fresh layer of insect repellant over the one that had already left her limbs sticky and smelling like a chemically reproduced eucalyptus grove, and slipped a couple of Lizbeth's plastic mosquito bracelets onto her ankles. Across the water, a trio of white lights winked back at her. Fishing boats, Charlie imagined. How serene it all seemed, at least from an inky distance.

A rustle in the bushes suddenly brought her attention closer to home, to where two pairs of eyes were glowing in the dark, looming larger as they approached her chair, accompanied by the pungent smell of cigar smoke.

"Bella! Hans!" a man shouted. "Leave it! Calm!"

All four eyes disappeared for a moment, only to reappear two by two on either side of Franz, who had taken hold of the collars of the Dobermans. "Sit!" he commanded them, waiting for an invitation from Charlie for him to do the same.

"A lovely evening, is it not?" he asked, running a hand through his snowy white hair.

"It is," Charlie agreed.

"Did you enjoy your dinner?" He helped himself to the chair next to her.

"Delicious. Thank you." Charlie had hoped the man would offer a polite goodnight and continue on his way, but for now it seemed as though her book would have to wait. "You have a lovely hotel."

"Thank you. It is mostly my wife's doing."

"Well, bravo to you both. How long have you lived here, in Jacmel?"

"It has been thirty-eight years since I came from Austria."

"Wow. I'll bet you've seen a lot of change since then," she said, at the risk of opening the door to an answer longer than she needed, or wanted.

Franz shrugged his shoulders. "Not really. Maybe some facades have been fixed up, and fake cobblestones put on the streets, but the mentality hasn't changed."

There was something about this man that made Charlie wary. Perhaps it was his military-straight posture, or that big cigar he carried around like a nightstick. Or perhaps it was those two dogs, which followed him around like a couple of bloodthirsty bodyguards. Still, she was curious. She turned her eyes to the night sky as she spoke to him. "So you think things are hopeless down here?"

"Haiti hasn't changed in my time here, and it never will."

Charlie turned toward him and raised her eyebrows.

"In my opinion," Franz continued, "it all comes down to the Vodou. It is a country running on fear. It is fear that keeps the Haitians from success. And those outsiders who tried— who still try—to abolish Vodou, they've made it even worse. Because if you are fighting against the devil, then you only make the devil more real."

"Okay," Charlie said, drawing out the word as he paused to puff on his cigar. "So you don't think there's anything anyone can do to help?"

"There is a welcome dependency." He blew a thick cloud of smoke into the air. "Foreign aid is respected. But it is resented at the same time. The people are used to it, and the government welcomes the money it brings in. It is a vicious cycle. And in the end, it is like putting a band-aid on a cancer."

Charlie found herself wincing at his attitude. "So if you find things so dismal here, why do you stay?"

"I will never leave. What can I say? We took a paradise and we turned it into a latrine. But it is our latrine." The two dogs suddenly leaped up and began to bark wildly, tearing toward the thick wall separating the hotel from the street. "And you"—he smiled, as if he hadn't even noticed the dogs' activity—"how are you finding Jacmel?"

"Well, from what I've seen, I like it very much. So peaceful. It's nice to be able to stroll around so easily, especially after being in Port-au-Prince."

"You should see it at Carnival time." He cackled.

"Maybe someday I will," Charlie said, deliberately ignoring the derision in his voice, and knowing full well she'd never be able to bring herself to set foot in Haiti again as long as her mother and Jim were here.

"And have you had the chance yet to purchase any art?" Franz asked.

Charlie had been awed by the art they had seen even in their brief time in the city. Especially the papier-mâché roosters and horses, painted with a fine hand to make them appear as if they had been showered with flower petals, their lips a ruby red, their wide eyes lined with gold.

"We did see some, but we're not really here on vacation," she said.

The man raised his thick eyebrows. "Missionaries?" he asked.

Charlie laughed. "No, not us. We're here looking for someone. A girl. And a baby." The man was not giving any indication that he planned to get up and leave any time soon, so Charlie took a deep breath and gave him the short version of the story behind their hunt for Senzey.

"And have you met Martine?" he asked, once she was finished.

"We tried, but nobody was there. You're not the first person to suggest that, though. Why?"

"Everybody knows Martine. She is one of the best painters in Jacmel. In my opinion, one of the best in Haiti. If you come up to my house tomorrow, I will show you some of her work. Very original, yet with the traditions of Haitian art still visible. And I have bought too many pieces from her. I think they will become quite valuable, someday."

"But why is everyone telling us to go see her about Senzey?"

"Because she helps women. Martine is a kind of activist, even more an activist than an artist. She takes the girls who are in trouble—prostitutes, abused women, those running away from a father or a husband—and tries to teach them a way to earn money by making crafts, by doing art."

"Ah, I get it. If Senzey is here, Martine would know."

Franz shrugged. "Of course she would know. You go there tomorrow, you ask her about her art. You *buy* some of her art. Then you ask her about your girl. You will find her, I'm sure."

"Thanks," Charlie said, the word muffled by a yawn as it left her mouth.

"Hans! Bella! Come!" Franz stood, and extinguished the tiny butt of his cigar on the concrete ledge beside him. "Best of luck to you tomorrow." He waved as he retreated toward his house, the two dogs by his side. "I'm sure it will be a most interesting day."

23

Franz had been right. The next day was interesting. But not exactly in the way that Charlie had expected.

They arrived at the gallery at ten, as arranged. But the door remained boarded up, the gallery shut as tight as it had been the day before. The four of them waited in the car for a good forty-five minutes, with the air conditioner blasting. Bea suggested they go for coffee, but Lizbeth was too keyed up, and didn't want to miss Martine should she appear. Charlie was concerned about Bea. The day could turn out to be a long one, and the heat was worse than ever. But her grandmother had insisted on coming along. "What?" she'd said when Charlie had suggested she stay behind at the hotel. "And miss all the excitement?"

"Let's give her a call," Lizbeth urged. "See what's holding her up." Lizbeth was convinced that today was going to be the day. Charlie was more worried than ever that she was setting herself up for disappointment.

Mackenson dialed and the three women waited as he offered greetings in Creole, the kind of endless back and forth that Americans never seemed to have the patience for.

"Tell her we're looking to find someone," Lizbeth prompted from the back seat. "Ask her about Senzey."

Charlie waved her arms in Mackenson's face, shaking her head no. "Tell her we want to buy some of her paintings," she suggested, remembering Franz's words from last night.

"What the heck?" Lizbeth grumbled.

After more discussion, Mackenson put down his phone. "She says we should come to her atelier," he explained. "Her studio. She is sending a boy down to show us the way."

It was another three quarters of an hour before the kid, a skinny teenager with a warm smile, showed up and squeezed into the back seat with Bea and Lizbeth to point out the route. The car climbed through a maze of narrow, rocky streets. Charlie could hear grunts and groans from the others as they were bounced around in their seats like cowboys at a rodeo. It wasn't long before she noticed that theirs was the only car amid a sea of motorbikes, two wheels obviously being better than four to navigate the ruts and ditches that only deepened as they ascended. This was a completely residential area, save for the lottery stands that popped up around every corner. Laundry hung on lines, or was laid flat to dry on corrugated tin roofs. A man waved hello to his neighbors from a moto-taxi, two kids sandwiched between himself and the driver. There were plenty of homes, but many appeared half-built, with twisted rebar sprouting from graffitied concrete, and piles of cinderblock that sat baking under the midday sun. But despite all those signs of progress, there was not a hint of activity, not a soul in sight with a hammer or a ladder or a trowel or a saw.

"Are y'all sure we're headed in the right direction?" Lizbeth asked from the back seat. Charlie was beginning to wonder the same thing herself. It seemed to be an odd spot for a studio.

Finally the boy gestured for her to make a U-turn. She slowed to avoid three goats grazing on garbage in the gutter, then pulled the car up onto the side of the road. The boy hopped out and pointed toward a narrow dirt path zigzagging through a maze of worn-out shacks. Again Charlie worried about Bea, but it was way too hot to even think about leaving her in the car. So, with Mackenson's encouragement, the odd little group followed single file behind the boy, Charlie steadying her grandmother from the rear as Bea held fast to the back of Lizbeth's floral-print blouse.

The boy shouted out a greeting as they approached the end of the road, where a row of cinderblock homes stood, separated one from another by shared, crumbling concrete walls. From the darkness of an open doorway a woman emerged, dozens of long, skinny braids falling from her head, a strappy dress billowing around her thick torso like a parachute, and a display of bling—trailing from her spangled ears down to her sequined toenails—that rivaled Bea even at her most bejeweled.

"*Bonjou*," the woman said, holding out a hand dappled with paint, sparkling with stacks of silver rings piled up to the knuckles of each finger.

"Hello!" Lizbeth cried out from the front of their little conga line, her floppy straw visor and oversize sunglasses making her look like a lost tourist. She stopped at the bottom of the two cracked stairs leading up to the doorway and began to dig about in her bulletproof purse, as Charlie liked to call it, for the photo. Charlie scrambled around Bea to grab Lizbeth's arm.

It was then that she noticed the paintings. There were tons of them—some tacked on to the walls, some set out to dry under the sun, others hanging on clothespins from the branches of trees, and even more piled high in the corners by the doorway. One, half-finished, rested on a paint-splattered chair, sharing the wicker seat with a palette where pinks and greens and purples and shiny golds butted up against each other in blazing harmony. To Charlie, it looked like a plate of melted candies.

These weren't the usual harvest or market scenes, the same old cats and tigers in the wild she'd spotted everywhere in Jacmel. These were portraits, pictures of women, outlined in a somewhat primitive style, yet with their bodies, limbs, and digits intricately adorned, like Martine herself. Their necks shone with glassy beads, their hair sparkled with glitter, the plastic buttons on their dresses were as real as the ones down the front of Lizbeth's blouse. But it was their faces that spoke to Charlie, specifically the eyes. They were eyes that told a million stories.

Charlie turned to Mackenson. "Please tell her I think her work is amazing."

Mackenson interpreted, and Martine immediately began to pull paintings from the stacks, fanning them across the dirt in front of her stoop. Then she cleared off the chair that made her makeshift easel, handing the work in progress to Charlie. "*Chita, Mami.*" She helped Bea up the two stairs to sit.

"This one's beautiful," Charlie said. Even though only halfway completed, the piece in her hands was truly a unique work of art. It was a woman, like the rest, but this one held a small child high in the air, their faces tilted toward each other in pure joy.

Martine spoke in Creole. "She says she will finish it for you, if you like," Mackenson told Charlie.

"Pardon me," Lizbeth interrupted, "but do you think we could get down to doing our business?"

"In a minute, Lizbeth," Charlie said. "I'm just trying to be respectful here."

"She says she has more," Mackenson added.

In a blink Martine was in and out of the doorway, bearing an armful of canvases for Charlie's perusal. She paged through them with a thumb, pausing whenever she sensed Charlie's interest in a particular piece.

"Ask her, Charlie," Lizbeth pleaded.

"I will," Charlie promised. "Just give me a minute."

"What is it you want to ask me?"

Charlie looked up from the paintings. "You speak English?"

"Some." Martine shrugged. "Is it my prices you want to know?" Her eyebrows rose into two eager arches.

"No," Charlie said. "I mean yes! I am going to buy something. But what my friend here is talking about is a girl. We're looking for a girl."

Martine's face turned to stone. She busied herself restacking the canvases and shook her head. "I don't know about any girls."

Lizbeth pulled out the photo and held it in front of Martine's face. "It's one girl we're looking for. Her name is Senzey."

Again Martine shook her head.

Charlie watched as Lizbeth's body seemed to deflate like a popped balloon. "She's an artist," she tried.

"A young girl, with a baby," Bea added.

Martine did not respond.

Charlie continued. "We think maybe she came to Jacmel to look for you."

"Why would anyone look for me? I am a poor artist."

"We were told you help women."

"Nobody here is getting my help," Martine insisted. "I cannot even help myself." She pointed back toward her house. "You see how I live. You have been listening to the jealous gossip on the streets."

"You're *sure* you haven't seen her, dear?" Bea asked.

Charlie turned to Mackenson. He made his own attempt with Martine in Creole, but the results were apparently the same.

As prepared as she'd been for yet another dead end, something was telling Charlie she should not give up. The woman knew more than she was letting on. They'd been told she knew everyone. That she was big on helping others. And Senzey, they'd been told, had wanted to come to Jacmel to learn art. Martine was an artist. Teaching art. What was this game she seemed to be playing? "Well then," Charlie said, entering into a little game of her own. "I guess we'd better get going."

Lizbeth looked devastated, but Charlie kept at it, helping Bea from her chair. The old woman turned her face to the artist, lowering her glasses as if that might help her see. "It's been a pleasure," she said, her blind stare cutting right through the woman's facade. Clearly Bea had her doubts as well. Charlie smiled, and thanked Martine for her time.

"You are not going to buy?" the woman persisted.

Charlie shook her head. "No thanks. I think my grandma might be feeling ill." She gave Bea a tiny pinch on the arm.

"Maybe we'll come back another day," Bea added. "If we have the time."

"But—" Lizbeth objected.

"But we need to go," Charlie finished for her as she began to head down the path that led to the street.

"I'm not ready to leave. Just one more sec," Lizbeth pleaded, desperately grabbing a stack of canvases from Martine's hands.

Charlie turned back to urge the woman along. She pulled lightly at Lizbeth's elbow. And as she did, she saw, peeking out from among the portraits, one piece that did not look anything like the rest.

Charlie grasped the painting between her fingers and pulled it away from the pile. The bustling urban landscape was unmistakable. The intricate scenarios played out on the canvas, the delicate brushstrokes, could have only come from one person.

Lizbeth saw it too. "It's hers, y'all!"

"What's going on?" Bea asked.

"It's Senzey's painting!"

Martine tried to grab the painting back, but Charlie held tight. "You know her, don't you?" she asked.

"I know lots of girls."

"Why won't you tell us where she is?" Charlie demanded.

"Where is the child?" Lizbeth cried.

Martine stood firm, hands on her hips, sizing the three women up. "Okay, so I know a lot of girls," she finally said. "But that does not mean I need to tell people about them." Her voice turned sharp with bitterness. "There are girls, they come to me, they are running away from terrible things. From husbands who beat them, from men who put them into prostitution, from people, sometimes their own families, who treat them like slaves. You know of *restaveks*? I do not even ask the girls I see why they come to me. If they want to talk about it, they do. So, no. I do not know your Senzey, and if I did, why would I tell you where she was? I do not even know you." She gathered up the canvases and turned toward the house.

"But Lukson!" Lizbeth cried out. "What about Lukson?"

"What about my baby?" a voice rang out from inside the house.

The group fell silent. Charlie turned, and there, silhouetted in the dark doorway, stood Senzey. A little older looking than in her photo, a bit more worn, a sadness clouding her dark eyes, but definitely Senzey.

"Where is he?" Lizbeth asked.

"Why do you ask me that, when you are the ones who would know?"

Lizbeth took a step forward. "How on earth would we know?"

'What are you talking about, Senzey?" Charlie asked.

"What did the orphanage tell you?" the girl cried.

"You do not have to speak to them, Senzey." Martine reached out a protective arm.

"What orphanage? I don't understand," Charlie said.

"So the baby is not here?" Bea asked.

"Tell them my baby is not for sale."

"You should go now," Martine told them.

"Wait," Charlie said. "You gave the baby up?"

"Oh, dear God." Lizbeth slumped down into the vacant chair, her hat tumbling to the ground as her head sank into her hands. "What have I done? Forgive me, Luke, for failing you." She took off her sunglasses to wipe her eyes.

Charlie saw Senzey freeze, her eyes landing on Lizbeth's face. "You are not from the orphanage," she said, more a statement than a question.

Lizbeth shook her head.

"And you know of Luke."

Lizbeth nodded sadly. "My son."

"Of course," Senzey gasped, then stepped closer to the woman. "You have the same blue eyes, like him. And like his son." She took another step closer. "He has talked all about you."

Suddenly she stiffened. "So tell me, where is he?" She gave a defiant jerk of her chin. "Where did Luke disappear to? What was so important to him that he could not come back, could not even write to me? Was he too afraid to be a father? Was it a woman? You must tell me. I need to know." Her eyes darted from Lizbeth to Bea to Charlie.

Finally Lizbeth spoke. She stood and stepped forward, folding Senzey into her arms.

"Oh, you poor, dear girl," she said, with a sob. "Luke is dead."

24

Nobody was talking as they sat around the heavy wooden table at the coffeehouse in Jacmel. The man, Mackenson, had guided them here after Senzey agreed to come with Luke's mother and her friends, to sit and talk somewhere cooler than the steps of Martine's house. She felt numb. She could not even cry. And, to her tongue, the coffee tasted like bitter medicine.

Senzey had never been inside this restaurant. With its brick walls and high ceiling, it still looked like the warehouse it once was, a place where they stored the coffee from the ships instead of a place where the coffee was turned into fancy drinks that probably cost more than most Haitians earned in a day. At the other tables, people did not seem to be talking much either, their noses deep in their laptops and their ears tuned to music playing through the speakers, the jazz that Luke had liked so much. She imagined, for a second, being here with him. It was then that she felt the first tear rolling down her cheek.

"Now, now, it's all right. You just cry all the tears you've got inside you."

Senzey felt Lizbeth's hand, warm and plump, patting her bare knee. "I did not believe him," she sobbed. "My sister, everyone told me that he did not really love me, that they knew he would leave. And I believed them instead of him."

"You can't beat yourself up, child. Don't you think Luke knew how you felt about him? Why, if I had a penny for every time I blamed myself for saying or not saying the things I did before it was too late, I'd be living in a big old mansion by now."

"I am a terrible person."

"Hush. That's no way to talk. Maybe if you get it out, tell us what all went on, you might feel just a wee bit better."

"I do not even know how to start."

"Well, there's no better place than the beginning. How'd y'all meet?"

"Luke—" Senzey paused to wipe her eyes. "He ate at the hotel where I was working. He was there many times for dinner."

"That boy never was one to cook much for himself. Woulda eaten a pepperoni pizza every single night, given the chance."

"I saw him sometimes, eating alone or with a friend, and we talked together a little. Then one night, when I was helping to clear the dishes, I saw that Luke forgot his wallet on the table. His passport was inside."

Lizbeth shook her head. "His mind was always on something else. Luke woulda lost his own head if it weren't screwed on tight."

"He was not gone long, so I ran after him. After that, Luke started coming into the restaurant almost every night." Senzey noticed Mackenson looking at her, judging her with his eyes. She knew what he was thinking. *Just another Haitian girl out to find her* blan.

"It was Luke who came to me," she said, setting her own eyes squarely on Mackenson's. "He wanted me to do something for him. He was going on a work trip to the countryside, for two weeks, and he needed somebody to take care of his cat."

Senzey smiled at the thought of it. A cat who needed a babysitter. A cat's job was to hunt for rats, not to live inside a house like a princess in a castle. But she had agreed to do it. Luke was a nice, polite guy who had asked for her help, and she would give it.

"So I stayed at his house while he was gone. The first time I stayed there he gave me a list of things to do," Senzey told Lizbeth. "Like feed pumpkin to the cat. Pumpkin! Do not forget to lock the door. Clean out the refrigerator if the electricity stays off. Make sure the windows are closed when it rains. The list was very long."

Lizbeth smiled. "He got that from me. Only way to keep things from flying in one ear and straight out the other, I always said."

"But he also told me to please eat his food, to use his air-conditioning, and his television and his internet. I know now that he was asking me to stay there more for me than for him. He had other people to watch his cat for him. He was so kind, that when he came back I cooked him a big Haitian dinner— *lambi, akra, pikliz*. He was very happy." Senzey readily drifted into her memories.

"Bless your heart," Lizbeth said.

Senzey told them how she had stayed in Luke's apartment many times after that, while he was traveling, how the two of them started spending more and more time together when he was home. How, after returning to Port-au-Prince from one long trip to Cap-Haïtien and back, he asked her to stay.

"And then he went back to Texas, and disappeared," she said, tears once again filling her eyes. "I wrote many emails, with no answer. And then I sent a letter."

"That letter did not reach my doorstep until eight months after Luke passed," Lizbeth said.

"I had to give it to another NGO worker to take back to the US to have it mailed, because there is no mail system here," Senzey said. "I didn't know how long it would take. But after I did not hear from Luke, I was like a zombie. Here I was, with his baby growing inside of me, and I thought he did not even care."

"You poor thing, you must have been devastated," Lizbeth said.

"Then one day, when I had only two months more to go, I met a man and woman while I was coming out of the clinic. They were very nice, sometimes taking me for something to eat, asking to do shopping for me and coming with me to appointments. They were like friends. Not even my own sister did what they did. There was nobody who had been that kind to me since Luke left."

Senzey remembered how she had told these people her story, how she was mad at Luke for leaving her like this, scared and alone and without a way to properly care for the baby.

"They talked a lot about how hard it was going to be for me to earn any money. The only job I knew was my work at the hotel, and they would never allow me to live there with a baby. So when they told me about a place nearby, where my baby would get a better start in life, where I could leave him until I could find a way to take care of him, I listened. They told me it was the best thing to do for my child."

"Then they offered me a little money. Usually, they said, some money is paid to a mother bringing her child to this place, to help her care for her other children who are still at home. Of course, I had no other children, but they told me that was okay, that I could use the money to get my own start."

When the baby was born, Senzey took one look into the eyes that were Luke's eyes, brushed her fingers across the same light, soft hair she'd caressed on Luke's head, and burst into tears. Then she kissed the baby goodbye. She used the money they gave her to get to Jacmel, and Martine.

"Well, all right then." Lizbeth looked around to the others for support. "Seems like there's only one thing for us to do." She placed her two palms firmly down on the table. "We've got to march right on over to that orphanage and get that baby back."

25

"It is not that easy." Mackenson's eyes were following Senzey as she headed to the restrooms just outside the coffeehouse's open back wall.

"What do you mean, not easy? Why not?" Lizbeth asked.

"I don't get it. Was that place an actual orphanage? Who were those people?" Charlie asked.

Mackenson hesitated before answering. "There are many mothers here who are in a hard situation."

"That doesn't answer my question," Charlie said.

"There are sometimes not many choices for a girl."

"Go on." Charlie took a sip of her coffee.

Mackenson shot a wary glance in Lizbeth's direction, and took a deep breath. "They call them 'baby-finders'. There are many of them here. They are people paid by the orphanages to convince women to give up their children."

"Why would they do that?" Bea snapped. "Why would they want to fill up orphanages with children who aren't orphans?"

"It is a business," Mackenson told them. "They keep children there, sometimes, to raise money from sponsors, but most of the money goes right into the pockets of the people running the orphanages."

"So they're just warehousing the children there?" Charlie asked.

"They do not always keep them there," Mackenson said.

"So they find them homes, adopt them out?" Lizbeth cocked her head.

Again he hesitated.

"Spit it out, Mackenson," she urged. "I need to hear this."

"Maybe sometimes they find them homes."

"So what else could happen?" Charlie pulled her chair closer to his.

"I have heard things," he said.

"What things?" Bea spoke up.

"Some of the children," he answered slowly, "the older ones, are sometimes sold to be *restaveks*. And some are sold to . . . others."

"You mean like traffickers?" Charlie asked loudly.

It was then that they noticed Senzey had returned. Mackenson wondered how long the girl had been standing nearby.

Senzey shook her head. Mackenson could see fear building in her eyes. "No, no, it is not like that. They told me I could have him back when I am ready. That Lukson will be there when I return for him."

Lizbeth reached an arm out to Senzey to gently guide her onto the seat next to her.

"They promised he would be taken care of," she insisted. "They showed me pictures. The children in this place are happy."

She looked to the others' faces, as if seeking assurance that this was true.

"It was the best choice, it was the only choice, until I can care for him myself," she said, tears returning to her eyes. "I am trying, but it has not yet worked as I hoped."

Senzey wiped her cheeks with the back of her arm. "I could not come back to see him for six months, they told me. It is too upsetting for the children when the mothers come, they said."

"Hogwash," Lizbeth said.

"Disgusting," Bea said.

"So," Senzey continued, "my plan was to go get him after six months. And now it is six months, and I still have not found a way to care for my baby." She lowered her gaze to the floor.

"But I can help." Lizbeth wrapped her arm around the girl's shoulder.

Senzey, still crying, did not look up.

Then Mackenson leaned in toward her, switching to Creole to try to calm the girl. "It is all right, mama. You did what you thought was right. So you gave your baby to the orphanage. Okay. Now you have some help. You do not have to be a victim. Go try to get him back. Before it is too late, and something happens that you will regret forever."

26

Senzey could not see her own toes dangling beneath the surface of the cloudy water. The pool of the Hotel Abernathy was empty of people, the lounge chairs piled high by the gate, spotted with mud from the last rain. She leaned back on her hands, stretching her palms flat against the rough concrete. She had never felt more confused in her life.

It had not been easy saying goodbye to Martine. "She is a good person," Senzey had told the others as they headed down the bumpy hill toward the road that would lead them back to Port-au-Prince. "She is always helping others. It is all that really matters for her. The money you pay Martine for her art"—she pointed toward the paintings piled high in the rear of Charlie's car—"she uses it to help many young women, to keep them out of trouble. You see how she lives, like a poor person. But she does not really have to live that way. It is her choice. And most of her time she spends showing the women how to make money by doing their own art, by making crafts or helping others who are making things to sell. For me, she is teaching me with my painting."

But any money Senzey could make from her art turned out not to be enough. She took other work in Jacmel whenever she could find it, in hotels and restaurants, but it was not often, and did not provide enough to make a difference. The six months she had given herself to find a solution had gone by, and she still could barely provide for herself, let alone a child. She was beginning to think she never would.

She kicked at the water, the splashing making a noise as if a child were playing around. It was good to be alone, to have some time to think. All that talk in the car had been enough to make her crazy.

"Lukson. What kind of a name is Lukson?" Lizbeth had asked, right in the middle of a very long story she had been telling about Luke. The woman never seemed to stop talking. "Do we call him "Lucky" for short?"

"It is from the name of Luke," Senzey told her.

"Here in Haiti, many people give their sons the name of their father," Mackenson explained.

"Oh, I get it," Lizbeth said. "Like you, right? Your father was Mack?"

"That is right," he replied.

"So, what, your son will be called 'Mackensonson'?" Bea chimed in. "And his son will be 'Mackensonsonson'?"

They had all started laughing. Senzey did not feel like laughing. But she smiled to be polite. Lizbeth seemed like a good woman, a kind woman. She reminded her so much of Luke that she could barely look at her. Senzey admired her determination. She understood that Lizbeth's offers to help were real, that they came from a good place in her heart. And she also understood how badly the woman wanted to get the baby, to hold him in her arms. Senzey felt that way herself.

But she was sure of one thing—she would not allow herself to become a burden to Luke's mother, a woman she had only known for one day. No matter what, she could not rely on another to do what she should be doing herself. She had already done that once, when she handed her baby to the couple from the orphanage. She would not do it again.

If only her father were here. He would know what to say, what to do. She thought about the last time she had seen him, when she kissed him goodbye that morning nine years ago as he left for the school where he taught. He had told her to be good, then laughed like he always did. He knew Senzey was not the daughter he needed to worry about.

That afternoon, she had left their home to shop for dinner when the ground started to rumble. Suddenly she was on her knees, grasping to hold on to the earth, which seemed to be falling away at her touch. People were yelling, crying for help. She began to crawl back toward the road to her house, but became lost in the thickening white cloud, and confused by the unfamiliar piles of concrete where a house or a shop should have stood. Senzey felt as though she was moving in circles. For a few minutes the ground would remain still, then it would rattle and shake again. People ran through the streets, covered in blood and dust, some missing hands or feet. Others lay still, their bodies crushed and broken.

It was hours later when she fell into the arms of her sister Darline, who confirmed what Senzey had already feared. Their house had crashed down, with their mother and the younger children still inside. They were all gone.

That night, and the night after, the two sisters slept in the street. Senzey remembered how oddly dark and silent it had been, the sky lit by candles and cooking fires, the hushed conversations and prayers, the gentle sobbing that never seemed to end.

Word finally got to them that their father had been found, crushed to death. They were told he had been trying to rescue some women trapped under the fallen walls of a nursing school. But there was no time to mourn the loss of their family. Senzey and Darline could only think about surviving.

On the third day after the earthquake, they went with some others from their neighborhood to an open field where people were camping together, sleeping under shelters made of sticks and blankets and pieces of clothing. Soon the rain came, drenching everything. Not long after, some *blans* arrived with tarps. Sometimes they came with food and water.

At first it was okay, everyone cooking and sharing what little they had, taking care of each other. But the camp grew quickly, oozing out like a stain across the pebbly land. Things began to change. People started stealing from each other, fighting with each other. The police would come and beat up everyone in their path. After a while the owner of the land wanted to take it back. People were given deadlines to leave, but nobody had money to go anywhere else. Senzey and her sister ended up staying there for three years.

Then they went to live in a small house in Cité Soleil that they shared with a guy who was Darline's boyfriend, along with his mother, his two brothers and their girlfriends, plus two cousins. There was not even enough room for all of them to sleep at the same time. Senzey tried to bring money to the household, sometimes selling charcoal, sometimes making packages of water to sell. She felt lucky when she finally got a job cleaning rooms at the Hotel le Président. It was far from her plan of becoming a teacher—to make her father proud—or her dream to be an artist, or maybe even both. But that did not seem to matter anymore.

Senzey scooped up a wasp that was struggling on the surface of the water, using a leaf to lift it out of harm's way and depositing it onto the warm concrete with a shake. She wondered what her father would think about her situation now. Would he think she had been foolish to let herself become pregnant with Luke's son? Would he understand that she had loved him? Would he be disappointed in her for abandoning Lukson, for leaving him behind instead of finding some way, any way, to take care of him herself?

Suddenly Senzey felt ashamed. What must Lizbeth and her friends think of her? There was no way they would understand her reasons, reasons that would look only like excuses to someone who did not live the life she had lived here, on this island on the edge of the world.

Senzey listened to the sounds of the evening traffic coming from the other side of the thick wall that separated the hotel from the street, grinding like gears on a machine that could not be stopped. The sun was low in the sky, its last rays peeking across the horizon. She watched until it disappeared, and then shivered, despite the warm, thick air that remained. She stood and pulled down the hem of her dress, wrapped her arms around herself, and squeezed. Tomorrow she would see her baby.

27

The familiar brew of mosquito repellant and cigarette smoke, the clatter of dishes and sweet fusion of languages made Bea feel right at home, back in her wicker chair on the veranda of the old hotel.

Stanley had greeted her like royalty when she and Charlie sat down for breakfast, delivering her coffee and mango juice without her even asking. She'd wanted to ask after Robert, but didn't dare run the risk of any more of Charlie's teasing. So she'd kept her mouth shut, listening for the sound of the Frenchman's sexy accent as they watched the sun start its climb into the sky.

Now Charlie was gone, off to find the orphanage with Lizbeth and Senzey. Personally, Bea was worn out from it all, exhausted from the trip to Jacmel, and wanting some time to rest. She'd just put down her crocheting and allowed her eyes to slip closed for a morning nap when she felt two strong hands come to rest on her shoulders.

"Bonjour, Madame Bea. How is everything with you this fine morning?"

She sat up and smoothed the front of her blouse. "Good morning, Robert. It's so nice to see you again."

"May I?" He pulled out a chair and sat. "And your visit to the beach, I trust it went well?"

Bea caught Robert up with the goings-on in Jacmel, and told him of the mission the other three ladies had set out on that morning. "I'm just praying they find that baby safe and sound," she told him. "And praying that Charlie will get back to finding her mother. And that's a lot of praying for someone who doesn't really believe much in prayers."

"Well then, I will add my prayers to yours." Bea could sense Robert leaning forward in his chair. "I have a surprise for you today, Madame Bea."

"And what might that be, Monsieur Robert?" she asked, a little smile playing at her lips.

"It is Mambo Michèle. I have spoken of you to her. And she would like to know you, as you would like to know her."

"That's marvelous, Robert!" Bea reached for his hand to give it a squeeze. "Can we meet her today? I have so many questions."

"She is coming this morning. We will wait for her here."

Now Bea was far too excited to nap. She sat by as patiently as she could while Robert worked, the click-clacking of his computer like the ticking of a clock. As had happened the first time, she felt the *mambo*'s presence before anyone spoke. It felt like a cool breeze was blowing across the veranda, when Bea knew that, in reality, the air had remained thick and still.

Robert and the *mambo* exchanged greetings in French. Bea could hear their two smacks, one kiss on each cheek, as the French are fond of doing. Then the woman sat. Bea could feel the energy coming from the *mambo*, like a bolt of lightning jumping from tower to tower. And, for once in her life, Bea found herself at a loss for words.

"I have told Mambo Michèle about your abilities," Robert prompted. "About how you communicated with my wife. She is most interested to hear about that."

Bea's sudden shyness caught her off guard. It was as though the mere presence of the *mambo* had her cowering like a scared rabbit. She imagined the woman large and majestic. "Me?" she said, her voice a tinny squeak. "Oh, it's not anything that special."

"Do not be so humble, Madame Bea," Robert urged. "What you do is very unique."

"No, really. A lot of folks could do it, if they wanted to. It's not like I'm a sorceress or priestess or anything."

"But you have been trained for this, am I correct?" The woman's voice came out deep and thick, like a heavy sauce poured from a pitcher.

"You speak English?" Bea asked.

"A little. I have family, in Miami. I go there sometimes."

"Nice place, Miami." What a stupid thing to say, Bea thought. What was it about this woman that threw her off base like this?

"And your training?" the woman repeated.

Bea shook her head. "No training."

Bea could have sworn she heard a little cluck from the *mambo*. She cleared her throat and continued. "Actually, I was born this way. I've known ever since I was a girl that there was something different about me."

"Different? In what way?" Robert asked.

"You don't really want to hear all this."

"But I do," Robert insisted.

Bea wished she had remembered to put on some lipstick that morning. "Well, for one thing," she answered, "I'd see shadows around corners. And sometimes I had dreams that were so vivid and complicated that I'd be shocked to wake up and find they weren't real. Believe me, I used to be so scared of the dark that I'd sleep fully clothed with all the lights on. Always."

Robert's laugh began to put her at ease.

"And after?" the *mambo* asked.

"So, later, I'd find myself picking up on people's feelings, their emotions, and would hear myself giving advice right and left. But I chalked that up to being a hairdresser. It's sort of a prerequisite of the trade. Then, the older I got, the more I began to think it was something bigger than that. After an aunt died, and started visiting me in my shop, I realized I had a gift."

"A hairdresser? You are a beautician?"

"Yes, I am," Bea answered, wondering if there wasn't a bit of judgment in the woman's words. A Virgo, no doubt about it. She patted the table around her, searching for her fan. "And you," she asked the *mambo*, "how did you come upon your gift?"

"I was trained to be a *mambo*." The woman placed the fan in Bea's hand. "And your religion," she asked, "how does it work?"

Bea laughed. "It's no religion. Quite the contrary, in fact. Lots of religious folks think what I do is heresy. Some say people like me are tricked by demons."

From her silence, the woman seemed to be thinking about it.

"Tell me," the *mambo* finally said. "Is there a purpose for what you do?"

The question got Bea's hackles up again. "Purpose?" she snapped. "Of course it has a purpose. Why else would I do it?"

Robert quickly stepped in. "What Madame Bea does is to help those who are grieving a loss, to bring them some peace. In

English it is called closure. *Clôture*. Her work can give answers to the questions left unanswered, the things left unsaid. It is like giving people the possibility for a second chance."

"That's beautifully put, Robert. Thank you."

"So that is all that you do? Talk with the dead?" the *mambo* asked.

"That's not enough?" How on earth did she end up in a smackdown with a *mambo*?

Robert laughed a little.

"And what about you?" Bea asked the woman. "What's your deal?"

"Deal?"

"How do you do your Vodou?"

The *mambo* didn't answer right away. Bea waited.

"You have to understand, Madame Bea, that the Haitians are very protective of their religion." Robert placed a glass of cold water in her hand.

"So they don't even talk about it? I see." Bea slumped back in her chair, disappointed, batting at the air half-heartedly with her fan.

"I do not 'do Vodou'. I serve the *loa*, the spirits," Mambo Michèle suddenly offered.

Bea sat up. "You're saying *you* don't believe in Vodou?"

"Vodou is a part of life, not something you believe in."

Bea leaned in toward the *mambo*. "So then, what do you do? Spells? Magic potions?"

"Yes—*wanga*, magic, is something people ask for."

"It can be done for love, money, health, work, protection, revenge—all sorts of reasons for many different problems," Robert added.

"Revenge?"

"It is a very practical system," he explained.

"Interesting."

Mambo Michèle continued with her reply. "Most people, they ask for a *leson*."

"Divinations, readings," Robert interpreted.

"Aha! So she talks to dead people too."

"It is the *loa* she contacts. The *loa* help resolve the issues, and prevent problems in the future. They are the ones who give the *mambo* the information to pass along."

"It all sounds very complicated."

"It is."

"But, think about it. It's really not all that different from what I do, right? We both listen to people's problems, and we both go to the spirits for guidance."

"Yes, that is true."

"And then we pass along all we've seen and heard, to help solve those problems. We're both healers, in a sense."

"*Guérisseuses*," Robert translated for Mambo Michèle, who seemed to contemplate the notion for a few minutes. Bea sat and listened to the birds cawing in the trees around them.

Then the *mambo* responded. "I would like for you to do something for me."

"Me?" What on earth could a woman with her powers need from Bea?

"I want to talk to somebody. To see how it works."

"Oh, I don't know—"

"It is my mother. She died many years ago, when I was a girl."

At first Bea panicked at the thought. She'd never tried to channel a person who probably didn't speak English. But then again, what the hell did she have to lose? The woman already seemed doubtful of her abilities. It would either work, or it wouldn't.

What Bea discovered, once she'd closed her eyes and opened her mind, was that the *mambo*'s mother was quite eager to connect with her daughter. And the messages came not in the words of any language, but rather in pictures and symbols and scenes, like a movie. She described what she saw to Mambo Michèle as best she could. The woman appeared in all white, in a full-length, lacy, tiered dress. She was beautiful, her dark skin glowing beneath a scarf wound tightly around her head. And she had the most wonderful thoughts to send along to her daughter.

As Bea finished, she could hear the familiar sound of a person in tears. It happened quite frequently after a reading. But, as was often the case, the tears were not coming from a place of distress or sadness. Mambo Michèle's mother had spoken only of her pride in her daughter, her delight that Michèle had chosen to carry on with the work her mother had done herself.

"Robert," Bea whispered, while they gave the *mambo* a moment to collect herself. "Do you think I might be able to get Mambo Michèle to give *me* a bit of help?"

"Go ahead," he urged. "Ask her."

The *mambo* sniffled daintily. "What is it you are looking for, Madame Bea?"

"Just a little advice. It seems as though my own powers might be slightly limited, compared to yours. I'd love to put some of that magic you have to work for my granddaughter, and for my friend."

"It would be an honor."

Bea felt a rush of gratitude, like the warmth from a cup of tea on a cold night. She leaned in toward the *mambo*, who she now pictured as looking exactly like the mother who had come through in her vision. "Thank you. That is truly kind of you." She pulled her chair up closer to the table. "Now," she began, "let me tell you what I'm looking for. First—"

Mambo Michèle interrupted before she could finish, calling out to Stanley for her tools—a candle and a glass of water.

Bea sat back in her wicker chair, her feet coming to rest on a cushioned stool, her face tipped into the breeze from the whirring fan above, and waited for the magic to happen.

28

The cluster of blonds caught Charlie's eye the minute she descended onto the veranda the next morning. Women on a church mission, no doubt about it, with their neat, low ponytails and flowery summer dresses, still crisp in the thickening air. Had they traveled to Haiti with their teenage children, dropping in for a couple of days to pound a few crooked nails into some sub-standard shack that could have been better constructed by the Haitians themselves? Or were they here delivering boatloads of clothing and shoes, used items that the locals sometimes called *Kennedys*, a charitable effort that only had the effect of taking the food right out of local merchants' mouths. Why buy something, when you can get it for free?

It was exactly what she and Robert had been talking about, over shots of rum, late into the night the evening before. The difference between do-gooders and doing good, he proposed, is knowing that you don't have all the answers. Better for people to give cash, or come down to Haiti themselves and spend their money, than to send things or do things that may not be needed or wanted. A little can go a long way in a country where most people survive on less than two dollars a day.

Of course, Charlie was once a part of that whole do-gooder world herself. She now cringed at the memories of her stepfather forcing his dogma on people that had been following their own traditions for generations. And now, her parents pretending to be saviors when all they were doing was exploiting others for their own benefit. How low could they go? she wondered.

Charlie felt a tiny hammer pounding at her head from the inside out. If only these people would leave already, she thought, hearing the voices of the women grow louder as their numbers increased. How many blonds does it take to do good, anyway? She had to laugh at her cranky self, more than a little hungover from the rum she and Robert had consumed after an exhausted Bea, a discouraged Lizbeth, and a silent Senzey had turned in for the night. They had not found the baby yesterday. At first they had not even been able to find the orphanage on the street Senzey had been told it was on, but instead had driven around in circles through a maze of traffic, Senzey peering through the car window for the building she'd been shown in pictures. She had been shown a whole album, she told them, with photos of *blans* bottle-feeding and cooing over tiny bundles of warmth, drawing pictures and playing ball with smiling toddlers. *Your child will be loved*, she was promised.

Hours went by before Senzey finally did spy a house that she said looked something like the one she'd been shown. Charlie veered off the street and onto the sidewalk to get a closer look. It was the one, Senzey insisted, but why did it look so quiet, like no one was there? Indeed, the windows were dark, the front door blocked by trash that had clearly piled up over some time. When they noticed the padlock, Senzey had cried out as if she were in pain. "They're gone," she wailed. "My baby is gone."

It had been a long day, and an even longer evening. Senzey had been using Charlie's phone to repeatedly dial the number she had for the couple that had convinced her to leave her baby with the orphanage, not wanting to believe that the number was no longer in use, as the message kept telling her. Lizbeth kept grumbling about damn baby-finders, despite Charlie's gentle kicks under the table. She tried to be encouraging, suggesting they all get some rest and regroup in the morning, when their minds would be clearer. But Lizbeth and Senzey must have stayed awake late in their shared room, as they had not yet appeared for breakfast. As for Charlie, her mind was not clear at all. Only Bea, who was up to something down below in the hotel garden, seemed to have any semblance of a plan, however crazy that plan might be.

The knock on the door of their hotel room had come early that morning, Charlie unlocking it sleepily to find a tall Haitian woman draped in ruffled white cotton, her head wrapped in a bright red turban, clunky beads strung around her neck like garlands on a Christmas tree, and a baby doll—the old-fashioned kind with a hard plastic face and eyes that opened and shut—in her hand. In the other hand was a dagger. Charlie rubbed her eyes and waited for the woman to identify herself.

"Madame Bea," the woman said instead, the words a command rather than a question.

Charlie turned to her grandmother, who, to her surprise, was already up and dressed, her head covered by a wide-brimmed straw hat, her arms ringed in Lizbeth's neon mosquito bracelets.

"Mambo Michèle," Bea said. "This is my granddaughter, Charlie. Charlie, meet Mambo Michèle."

Charlie stood by in her tank top and pajama bottoms and watched as the woman took her grandmother's elbow, and the two sauntered off together like a couple of old friends.

Now she peered through the white wooden railings, down toward the spot where Bea and the *mambo* seemed to be setting a table for something. What the hell were those two up to, anyway? Did she even want to know? Across from her, the church women were signing for their breakfast and gathering their purses. Charlie was grateful for the coming silence, for the chance to concentrate on developing a plan of action for Lizbeth and Senzey, hopefully before they woke up. But where to start? Charlie's only hope was that the orphanage had moved, and not simply disappeared. But even if that were true, how would she find it? It's not as though these places listed their addresses online, or had big neon signs out in front or anything.

She sipped her coffee and watched as the group of women joined hands for a prayer, like football players in a huddle before the big game. Then they got to work, taking trips up and down the hotel's staircase, marching back and forth from their rooms to a trio of vans waiting below, their arms heavy with bundles and bags and, Charlie noticed, plastic-wrapped mattresses small enough to fit in a crib. When she saw a carton of disposable diapers go by, she jumped up from her chair.

"Morning. How y'all doing?" she asked, borrowing a bit of Lizbeth's Texas accent to help pave the way.

"Hey there," one of the women answered, her eyes hidden behind a pair of giant sunglasses. "We're doing just fine. And you?"

"Super," Charlie answered back, her stomach still turning somersaults from the night before.

"Are you here with a group? The Belles of Mercy? Someone said they're in town."

Charlie shook her head. "Nope. No group."

The woman smiled and nodded, and started to turn away.

"Where y'all going?" Charlie asked.

"We're getting ready to visit some orphanages, to help out a bit."

"Seriously?" Charlie flashed her famous smile. "That's awesome." She could not believe her good luck.

The woman nodded, and continued toward the vans.

"Mind if I ask you a favor?" Charlie said, thinking as fast as she could through the haze left by the rum.

"What's that?"

"Could I maybe come along?"

The woman stopped, taking in Charlie's ripped cutoffs and baggy tee.

"I've been wanting to find something to do down here, some way to help. You know, with all this poverty and all? It's such a darn shame."

The woman hesitated, looking around as though she were seeking permission from the others.

"Charity's the name." Charlie stuck out her hand for a shake.

"Charity," the woman repeated. "My name's Kathleen. Well, Charity"—she shrugged—"I suppose we could always use another pair of hands."

Charlie ran down to where Bea and the *mambo* were spreading a bright red and blue cloth across a rickety table, as if readying for a picnic. There was no time to explain, or to ask them what was going on. She simply told Bea she'd be back later, and to please pass on the message to Senzey and Lizbeth to just sit tight.

Her first stop with the women was an eye-opener, but would turn out to be far from the most alarming of the half dozen so-called orphanages they visited that day. From the outside it looked not unlike the other buildings on the block, a squat structure standing behind a treeless front yard that had been concreted over, and seemed clean enough, despite the need for a paint job.

The other women marched into the place with broad smiles plastered across their faces, eager to spread some love to the boys and girls. They were met with an onslaught of skinny, raggedy children leaping through the air and into their arms, as if they'd known the women their entire lives. Charlie was stopped dead in her tracks by a pair of boys, no older than six, who'd each flung their arms tightly around one of her legs, a hunger in their eyes that went way beyond their obvious need for food.

She followed Kathleen's lead as she and the other women tried to comfort the children with caresses and soft words in a language they couldn't understand. She joined in as they blew bubbles and sang songs and chanted rhymes while a woman who seemed to be in charge, helped by a young boy, unloaded goods from the van. Charlie watched as the two of them carted it all down a dark hallway, past the children's eager eyes and grabby hands. Their donations weren't even a drop in a bucket in this place, she realized, as she took in the room's crumbling floors and bare cabinets, the children's hollow cheeks and dirty limbs. That is, she thought, remembering what Mackenson had told them, if those donations even make it to the kids. These children were obviously used to visits from strangers, from *blans* with love to spare. So where was the evidence of the toys and clothes and food that Charlie was certain had been gathered and carted down here before, by others?

They seemed to get the same reaction everywhere they went. Children desperate for attention, clawing for a hint of affection, who had to be pried from the necks and hands of the visiting women when it was time for them to move on to the next place. Charlie found herself a bit in awe of Kathleen and her crew, with their can-do attitudes and endless patience. They were so incredibly kind, their hearts certainly in the right place. But she had to wonder if a disruption of the sort they were causing— no doubt one of a series that went on regularly in places like this—might be doing more harm than good. People loving and leaving, over and over—what does that do to a child who's already been abandoned?

But it was the sheer neglect that Charlie came to witness that shook her to her core. Most of the facilities she saw that day weren't fit for barnyard animals. Metal cots stacked one upon the other in crowded bunkrooms, the rusty frames supporting thin, rotting foam mattresses, if any mattress at all. Crumbling concrete walls, scattered broken chairs, bins, and shelves empty of books or toys or crayons, devoid of anything at all that spoke of a child's presence. But the children were there, an army of underfed, unloved, discounted souls, in worn and dirty clothing, with spots and rashes splashed across their tiny bodies, thick, yellow snot running down their grubby faces. What kind of abuse did these poor babies suffer when no one was around to see or hear? And how many of them were like poor little Lukson, given up by parents who were still out there some-where, holding on to dreams for a better life than their own for their children?

Lukson. She'd hoped upon hope that by some miracle she'd find him that day, but realized very quickly that would not be the case. She'd heard babies' cries coming from back rooms, seen a couple of kids that might be near his age being passed around during their visits, but there was no way she'd be able to identify him, let alone talk anyone into letting a *blan* walk away with one of their wards. The best she could do was stick to her plan and take note of every location they stopped in. Tomorrow she'd come back with Senzey, and Lizbeth.

She prayed Lukson hadn't been stuck in one of these god-awful places, warehoused like a piece of discarded merchandise. But if he was, she would find him, and would, somehow, shout out his heartbreaking story for the whole world to hear.

29

Lizbeth was beginning to think they were all crazy. Crazy as bullbats, as they said back home. Maybe it was all the heat down here making everyone believe in things they shouldn't, she thought as she stood in the hotel's front garden under the blazing midday sun, perspiration trickling down her skin like hot rain. Finding this baby—how was that ever gonna happen? That locked-up, empty house didn't leave them any clues as to where he might be. What were they supposed to do, go door-to-door, putting their lives at risk poking around every dark corner of the damn city looking to find him?

And Charlie, Lizbeth thought—where was Charlie in all this? Trotting off to who knows where, minding everybody's business but her own. Lord knows Charlie's grandmother had been right, back before they all got tangled up in this heap of a mess. That girl should just stick to her own knitting.

But now Bea was the one who seemed to have gone truly off her rocker. Being a medium was one thing. Lizbeth might sort of understand how that worked. But *this*? This just did not sit right.

Lizbeth felt as though she was going to faint as she waited, surrounded by those god-awful penis statues staring at her. Beside her, Senzey appeared cool as a cucumber, not a drop of sweat to be seen on her smooth dark skin. She'd been quiet all morning, and seemed to be paying not much mind to whatever Bea and this Vodou priestess lady she seemed to have got herself mixed up with had up their sleeves. Lizbeth just wanted it to be over.

She would never let on to Senzey, but, truth be told, she was again tempted to just go back home. Back to Texas, back to her tidy, air-conditioned little house with the memories of Luke and her husband to keep her company. This whole thing was just too painful, one minute thinking it was all gonna work out fine, the next feeling like there was no hope at all. But that padlocked door the day before had been a sign, she was sure, telling her it was finally time to call it quits. No doubt about it. Bea wasn't the only woman in the world who had the gift of intuition. No sirree.

"Please, sit."

She turned to see Robert, who had kindly brought her a chair. "Why, thank you so much." She plopped her damp body down onto the seat. What a gentleman he was. Robert was followed by Stanley, who, bless his heart, was toting a wooden tray with five tall glasses of water.

"Do you have any idea what those two are up to?" she asked Robert. "I couldn't get a lick of information outta Bea."

"They are preparing to make an offering," he whispered. "To Èrzulie Dantòr."

Lizbeth watched as Bea and the large Haitian woman fussed over a hodgepodge of items sitting atop their table: candles and fine silver chains and loose cigarettes, a cup of black coffee and a bottle of crème de cacao, a baby doll flat on its back, its blue eyes vacant and unblinking, and an arsenal of very sharp knives. "Excuse me? A what? To who?"

"They are asking a favor of Èrzulie Dantòr. She is the *loa* called the Black Madonna, known to be the protector of women and children. And to ask her a favor, they must offer her something in return, to show respect."

"You have got to be kidding me."

"What you see on this altar are her favorite things."

"Knives and baby dolls?"

"She is a devoted mother, and a fierce protector."

Lizbeth pursed her lips and shook her head. She pictured her husband, Darryl, rolling in his grave. Dear God, what had she got herself into? This was not at all what she had signed up for.

"Look." Robert pointed to a framed picture on the table, propped up against a glass. "You will never see Dantòr without a child in her arms."

Lizbeth leaned in for a better look. "Or a knife, I guess," she said, eyeing the long dagger grasped firmly in the woman's hand. "What's with her face?" Under her jeweled crown, Èrzulie Dantòr had been painted with two parallel scars raked across each cheek.

"It is said those are from a fight, with her sister Èrzulie Fréda. Some believe it was her sister who ripped out her tongue."

"She has no tongue?"

Robert shook his head. "Other people say she used to be a slave, that her tongue was cut out when she tried to warn other slaves of danger. Dantòr does not speak. She can only make a clicking sound."

One day she's talking with the dead, the next praying for help from a violent spirit without a tongue—the folks back home would never believe it. Not that she'd ever mention it to them, anyhow.

"Ah," Robert said. "I see we are almost ready."

Stanley had returned, this time with a steaming pot that he placed in the center of the altar. Lizbeth turned to Robert for more explanation.

"Her favorite food," he whispered. "Sacrifices are often part of an offering. This was a pig. Now it is pork griot," he added.

Lizbeth cringed.

Robert went quiet as the *mambo* stepped back from the altar, her hulking presence commanding the attention of those around her. One by one, she held a match to the six white candles on the table and they ignited, their yellow flames unwavering in the motionless air. The *mambo* became still, her eyes closed, as if concentrating very hard on something. Then she began to talk. To Lizbeth, the tone of her voice sounded like she was carrying on a casual conversation with a friend. Despite it all being in a language neither one of them knew, Bea stood there nodding, as if she actually understood exactly what the *mambo* was saying. And Senzey, she stayed as stiff as one of those statues, her hands clasped together, her eyes riveted on the picture of the Black Madonna.

Then the *mambo* turned, hiked up her long skirt in her hands, and headed toward the stairs that led up to the veranda, leaving the altar, the candles still burning behind her.

"What? *That's it?*" Lizbeth asked. "All that fuss, and it's done?"

Robert laughed. "That is it. It doesn't take long to make a simple offering." He took her arm. "Now we eat. Pork griot for everyone." Together they followed Bea and the *mambo* up the stairs for lunch, Senzey trailing behind.

Lizbeth wrinkled her nose as shiny cubes of meat were ladled onto her plate. "So what, we just sit back and wait for it all to work itself out? That baby's gonna pop up right out of the blue?"

"Have a little faith, Lizbeth." Bea spread a napkin carefully across her lap. "And it's not just help with the baby we asked Èrzulie Dantòr for. We also sought assistance with Charlie and her mother. My daughter."

"Well, God bless her. If Mambo Michèle can make all that happen, I'll eat my hat."

"And what about eating your lunch?" Robert laughed. "It does not appeal to you?"

Lizbeth picked at the meat. "Spicy food doesn't always agree with me," she said, just a bit of a lie.

"If it is the sacrifice I mentioned that you are worried about, there is no need. The pork for today's offering came from the hotel freezer, I am sure."

Lizbeth breathed a sigh of relief.

"People often misunderstand the notion of animal sacrifice in the Vodou religion," he explained. "But in places where there are no supermarkets, no refrigeration, where do you think one finds the meat they need for their offerings? The same way they find meat for their own tables. But you should not worry, Lizbeth. The slaughter is done by a person trained as a butcher. And nothing goes to waste. Sometimes an offering to a spirit can feed a whole community."

Lizbeth's stomach growled with anticipation. Missing breakfast always made her a little nuts. Robert turned his attention to the *mambo*, and they began speaking together in French.

"Try it," Bea urged, spooning the thick sauce into her mouth. "It's quite tasty."

And it was. Tangy and just a tad spicy, the soft cubes of pork practically melted in her mouth, and in no time they were all eaten.

"Was that so frightening?" Robert asked with a wink at her empty plate.

"This part was fine," Lizbeth said, dabbing the corners of her mouth with a napkin. "It's that other malarkey, with the candles and the knives and all, that's got me all bothered. I'll be heading straight for hell, getting mixed up in mumbo-jumbo like that."

"It is nothing to be troubled about," Mambo Michèle said. "Èrzulie Dantòr asks little in return for her blessings. She is fiery, and she is tough, but she will do anything to help a child. If you need the courage to fight," the *mambo* continued, "she is the one to go to."

The *mambo* was looking at Senzey as she spoke. Lizbeth noticed the girl lowering her eyes to the table.

"Well, that's all fine and dandy. But we still don't have a clue about where to find that child. And Charlie is still about as welcome as a wet shoe up there on the mountain. So where on God's green earth does that leave us?"

The five of them sat spooning up the last of the griot, sipping their water, mopping their damp brows, the only sound coming from the squeaky fan above.

It was the *mambo* who finally spoke, and when she did, it was in a rush of Creole to Senzey. Lizbeth watched as Senzey stood and bolted from the table.

"What was that all about?"

Mambo Michèle shrugged her shoulders. "I was only trying to give her some encouragement. That is all. To tell her she is lucky to have support from people like you. And I told her a saying I heard many times from my mother, something I thought would be of help."

"What's that?" Lizbeth asked.

A delicious, cool breeze rolled across the table.

"Tete pa janm twò lou pou mèt li."

"And what does that mean?" Bea asked.

"Something like 'breasts are never too heavy for those who have them'."

Bea laughed. "Easy for them to say."

"What the heck?" Now Lizbeth was *sure* they had all gone nuts.

"I think," Robert said, "it is saying that one must always assume one's own responsibilities, even if it is a difficult thing to do."

30

When Charlie pulled up to the hotel, returning from the orphanages with the church women, the first thing she saw was Lizbeth practically tripping down the stairs toward her.

"Whoa there, careful," she said as the woman fell into her arms.

"She's gone, Charlie. Senzey's missing!"

"Hold on a sec. What's going on?"

"She was there at lunch with us, but now she's just up and disappeared!"

Charlie checked her watch. "Maybe she went to do an errand, or take a walk."

Lizbeth shook her head. "Nope. She took her things with her. That girl wasn't fixing to come back. How're we ever gonna find her?"

"Did she leave a note? Anything?"

Lizbeth fumbled with her pocket. "Just her little sketch-book." She handed the spiral-bound pad to Charlie. The pages were covered with pencil drawings, doodles, and half-finished renderings that were signs of some serious practice. Flipping through back to front, Charlie stopped. Looking up at her from the paper was a sweet portrait of Lizbeth, her eyes shining bright, and with a smile that couldn't help but cause Charlie to smile herself. On the page facing it was a drawing of a young man, with those same eyes, that exact same smile.

"It's gonna get dark out before you know it. I'm worried sick." Lizbeth's eyes shifted down the driveway toward the street.

"Senzey knows her way around. She'll be fine."

"But why wouldn't she tell us where she was off to?"

By nightfall, Charlie, too, began to worry. Of course Senzey knew how to take care of herself, but Lizbeth was a wreck. And Charlie feared that the longer they waited, the more difficult it might be to find her. That's when she turned to Mackenson for help. "Please ask around your neighborhood," she told him over the phone. "Find out if anyone has seen her."

It wasn't until around ten o'clock that Mackenson finally called back. He'd found Senzey walking, alone, in Cité Soleil. She was in a bad way.

Charlie ignored Mackenson's advice that she should wait until morning to come to his house. "It is not safe to be driving in this city at night," he insisted. "Not even just for a woman alone, but for anyone."

Once on the road, Charlie did start to have second thoughts. It was pitch dark, with no streetlights anywhere. The roads were deserted, save for the few spots where small crowds had gathered, for one reason or another. She drove slowly, leaning into the windshield, stopping frequently to check the directions Mackenson had provided along with a warning not to deviate one bit from what he told her.

Suddenly her headlights revealed a commotion in the street ahead. Charlie slowed even more as she approached, and saw that it was a policeman signaling her to keep moving. Behind him was his partner, standing over a body lying in the gutter, motionless.

She was relieved to find Mackenson waiting for her outside his house, waving her in with his lit cell phone as if she were a pilot taxiing on the tarmac. From what she could make out in the dark, most of the neighborhood leading to Mackenson's place was one of the most desperate she'd seen all week—shacks made from cardboard and metal, homes that looked like they were constructed out of scraps from the dump. But now Charlie found herself parked in front of a tidy cinderblock house, painted a cool green that reminded her of ice-cream.

Mackenson led her through a small concrete patio, and hesitated before opening the front door. "I have to tell you something before we go in. My job was not all that we lost in the earthquake."

It wasn't until Charlie was introduced to Mackenson's wife that she understood what he meant. In the darkness of the candlelit room the woman stood with her armpits resting on two crutches, her one leg planted firmly on the floor.

"This is my wife, Fabiola. Fabiola, *sa a se* Charlie."

The woman leaned on one crutch and held out her hand. Charlie felt a warmth in her handshake that seemed to come from deep in her soul.

Charlie took in the room around her. The walls were bare, save for a large, mahogany cross, and a clock that seemed to have stopped doing its job long ago. A looming credenza and a solid rectangular dining table with six matching chairs were the only furniture in the room, except for a chalkboard that stood in one corner, its surface curiously covered with numbers and sums.

"Where's Senzey?" she asked.

Mackenson pulled up a chair for Fabiola, and pointed toward one of the two sheer curtains that separated the room they were in from the rest of the small house. Charlie imagined there must be a kitchen through one of the doorways, and that the other led to a bedroom.

"She is finally resting. When I found her, it was like she was in a trance, just walking, her eyes not telling me anything. I asked her if something happened, but she wouldn't talk. I could see that she had been crying, because her face was stained with tears and dust. I brought her here, and she still wouldn't talk. Fabiola tried to give her some ginger tea, but she would not drink it."

"What could have happened to her?" Charlie wondered out loud.

Mackenson shook his head. "I don't know. Finally, Fabiola got her to lie down, to try to sleep."

"Thank you, Mackenson," Charlie said. "Thank you both."

Fabiola stood at the sound of a cry from behind the curtain, and returned to the room with a skinny young girl in a night-gown trailing behind her.

"You have kids?" Charlie asked, suddenly embarrassed by how little she knew of Mackenson's life.

"Yes. This is our daughter, Rozalie. And we are also raising the two sons of my cousin."

Charlie's eyes went to the chalkboard.

"I am teaching them what I can," Mackenson said.

Charlie noted a defensiveness in his tone. How could she not have known this, with all that talk about how parents didn't have the money for education. Never once had it occurred to her that Mackenson might be in that very situation.

"Maybe the next session," he added. "We are trying."

Charlie watched Mackenson take his wife's crutches and help her settle back into the chair, where the sleepy child hung her arms around her mother's neck and curled up onto her lap as if they were one.

"I found them."

Charlie looked up to see Senzey standing in the doorway. Her eyes were cold, her posture limp. The striped jersey dress she'd been wearing when they left Jacmel now looked soiled, and seemed to hang on her slender frame like a sack.

Charlie went to Senzey's side. "Who?" she asked as she led her to a chair. "Who did you find?"

"The people. The man and the woman who took my baby."

"The baby-finders?" Mackenson asked.

Senzey's words came out flat, as though squeezed of their feeling. "I walked all over looking for them, going first to the house where they lived in Cité Soleil, where they took me a few times. Nobody was there. Then I went to the places they used to take me. To the clinic, where they first met me outside. They were nowhere. Finally, I went back to the house, and waited in front, to see if they would come home. And they did."

"Where is he?" Charlie asked. "Where's Lukson?"

She watched as Senzey's gaze turned to the sleeping girl in Fabiola's lap. A tear began its path down her cheek as she spoke. "My baby—they told me—they think my baby did not survive."

31

The three women stood in the morning sunlight, waiting for the gates of the lime-green cinderblock building to open.

"What kind of a hospital is this, not open at night?" Lizbeth asked. "What, folks are supposed to need their help only by the light of day?"

Charlie could see that Lizbeth was having a hard time accepting this latest blow. She'd been all business when Charlie had arrived back at the hotel with Senzey, pouring herself into fussing over the girl, doing anything she could to try to avoid feeling the pain that must have come from hearing what Senzey had to say. She'd jumped at the chance to go with them to the hospital, to have a concrete task on which to focus.

It was Mackenson who had encouraged Charlie to take Senzey back to the place where the baby was born, to try to get the full story, to maybe find out where the child was buried, so that Senzey might at least be able to properly grieve. It is important, he insisted. After the earthquake, so many nameless bodies disappeared, carted away in trucks to be dumped into mass graves. People were still suffering from the loss as if it were yesterday. It should not have to be that way, this time, for her.

He had also explained to Charlie just how common the story the baby-finders had told Senzey was. The baby had only made it for two days, they said, never leaving the hospital. Babies dying soon after birth was not uncommon in Haiti, Mackenson told her.

Finally the doors to the hospital were opened. Once inside, Charlie saw Lizbeth's tight mask drop, her eyes falling on the stained mattresses of the gurneys lining the halls, the used syringes discarded into open bins, the floors spattered here and there with what she could only assume was dried blood. Lizbeth held her hand to her nose, to block out the stench of human waste that filled the place like a sour perfume.

Senzey looked haunted by being there. They followed her down a long hallway as she led them to the ward she remembered as the place where she'd given birth. She poked her head in the door and slowly looked around, as if she might find some trace of her lost child in the crowded room. Charlie peered over her shoulder, rolling her eyes at the irony of the plastic shower curtains embossed with beach scenes and palm trees that separated one little cubicle from the next.

She turned to see a woman dressed in white rushing down the hall toward them, alerted by the presence of the two *blans*. In a torrent of Creole she began to question Senzey. Charlie heard Senzey reply and recognized Lukson's name. The woman shook her head and continued down the hall. Charlie could sense the chaos building as the corridors filled with people. Senzey was stopping anyone and everyone who looked remotely official to ask about her baby. No one seemed to have an answer.

It wasn't until they were about to leave when Charlie noticed a young nurse do a double take at the sight of Senzey's face. Senzey seemed to do the same back at her. They stopped. They talked. Senzey's brow became wrinkled with confusion.

"What? What's going on?" Lizbeth asked, looking as though she were about to burst. "What's she saying to you?"

"She remembers me," Senzey said. "She remembers my drawings. And she remembers my baby. She was the one who stayed with me while he was being born. She held my hand, and she told me to give him a name. She says she would be surprised if Lukson did not make it. He was healthy and fine, just like I remember him, the last time she saw him. She says that maybe my baby is alive."

The car felt like it was filled with electricity as the three women sat, stuck in traffic worse than Charlie had ever seen it. It was all stop and go on the route through the city and back to the hotel, where they were headed to try to figure out their next move. She didn't dare risk a short cut, and instead chose to concentrate on the market stands and painted storefronts she'd come to rely on as landmarks to find her way around.

They turned left and crawled down a street Charlie thought she recognized from her outing with the church ladies. As they neared the low cinderblock building she remembered from their visit, traffic slowed nearly to a halt. Charlie noticed a flash of yellow in the rearview mirror. It was a truck, inching its way around her, pulling past them to come to a stop on the other side of the street. The traffic came to a standstill. She slid down in her seat.

"What? What is wrong?" Senzey asked, craning her neck to see for herself.

Charlie pointed to the truck, her stomach lurching as she spied the logo on the front passenger door. She truly thought she might be sick.

"So? It's a truck," Senzey said.

Through her window, Charlie could see the driver's-side door of the truck opening. She slouched even lower in the seat, waiting for those two pointy cowboy boots to cross the street toward them.

It wasn't until the approaching figure was practically up against her front bumper that Charlie realized who it was. On the face beneath the wide-brimmed hat the eyelids were a little puffier, the freckled skin a little more drawn, but there was no doubt about it. It was her mother. Her mother, who was rushing toward the door of the orphanage as if she owned the place, leading a small girl by the hand. Charlie felt as though she'd been spun around a million times.

And in a flash her mother was back, alone, flying across the street and into the yellow truck, its engine roaring to life.

Charlie sprang into action without thinking, cutting off the oncoming wall of traffic to a blast of honking horns, forcing an awkward U-turn as she jammed her way into the jumble of cars and motorbikes and tap taps heading the other way, to secure a spot two car-lengths behind her mother.

"What the heck are you doing?" Lizbeth asked, peering out from behind her fingers. "You're gonna get us killed!"

Charlie kept the yellow truck in her sight, riding the bumper of the Toyota directly in front of her to block anyone else from cutting in. The streets were teeming with pedestrians, making the going even slower as they darted in and out of the traffic. Charlie had no plan for what she was going to do once she caught up with her mother. All she knew is that she couldn't stop following her.

"Just bear with me," she asked of the others as she inched the car forward. "There's something I need to do. I'll explain later."

When the Toyota made a turn, Charlie found herself just one car-length away from her mother, a battered SUV sandwiched between them. Charlie felt as though the city was swelling around her, the crowd growing denser, the traffic closing in on all sides. She opened the window. The traffic had once again come to almost a complete stop. She closed her eyes for a quick moment, trying to ease the nausea that was building inside her. They flew open again when the car jerked with the movement of the bumper being tapped from behind.

"Watch it!" Lizbeth yelled.

But Charlie didn't react. Through the windshield she saw her mother edging her way around a tap tap and turning down a side street toward who knows where. Charlie rested her head on the steering wheel. They were boxed in, stuck in place, unable to move an inch.

"What is going on?" Lizbeth's voice was crackling with fear.

Charlie looked up to see a sea of pedestrians rushing toward them, motorbikes pivoting and heading back in the direction they had come, as if a tide had suddenly turned. Drivers were leaning out of the windows of their cars for a better view.

"I don't know." She rolled back the sunroof and stood on her seat. About forty yards ahead, she spied the problem. The intersection was littered with garbage piled high. Charlie watched a mob of young men running around, rolling tires into the mess.

Suddenly flames began shooting up like a fiery curtain, blocking the spectacle from view.

"What's that god-awful smell?" Lizbeth cried out.

Charlie sat down and closed the sunroof. "Rubber. They're burning tires."

"It is a demonstration. They are angry about the government taking money that was meant to help the people," Senzey explained.

"A riot!" Lizbeth gasped.

"Calm down, Lizbeth. It's only a little protest. They just want to be heard. Nobody's out to hurt anybody." Charlie shifted the car into reverse, following the lead of other drivers around her. They began backing up in a crazy dance, crawling backward toward escape, when a popping sound rang through the air.

"Now they're shooting!" Lizbeth crouched down on the seat behind Charlie.

"It is probably the police," Senzey said. "They come with rubber bullets, and tear gas, to chase the people away."

"Oh my Lord. Be careful! You're like two sitting ducks up there in front."

"We'll be fine, Lizbeth," Charlie said. She'd managed to point the car toward a side street, where there was at least a semblance of forward motion.

It seemed like hours before they arrived at the hotel, the route back a maze of wrong turns and dead ends, Lizbeth on edge, her eyes peeled for signs of another flare-up. But Charlie's mind remained focused, fixed on only one thing—the yellow truck, and her mother inside. What she didn't want to think about was another thing—what her mother was doing dragging that poor child into that wretched place.

32

"Are you feeling all right, Madame Bea?" Robert placed his cool hand on Bea's forearm.

She felt goose bumps from his touch. "Of course I am. Why do you ask?"

"I do not believe you've actually heard a word I've said." He laughed.

"Oh, I apologize, Robert. How rude of me. It's just that Charlie got in so late last night, and I'm dead tired." It was amazing how much the French loved to talk, she thought, with a yawn.

"You must tell her not to go out alone at night," the *mambo* said.

"She is right," Stanley added as he placed three glasses of rum punch on the table. *Just a little aperitif before lunch*, Robert had said when he ordered.

As tired as she was now, Bea had been happy to stay behind while the others took off for the hospital. If they'd listened to her, they could have saved themselves a trip. She knew that baby was alive.

"How dangerous can it be?" she asked. "Charlie grew up in the jungle, for god's sake. With killer ants and poisonous snakes and piranhas and worms that crawl under your skin. And with a stepfather who was worse than all of them put together."

"It is a different kind of danger," Robert said.

"I was sort of kidding. But seriously, what are people so afraid of?"

"It is probably no different from elsewhere," the *mambo* said. "There is crime everywhere, am I right? You just need to be aware, keep your eyes open."

"I can assure you, Charlie's eyes never close." Not like my own, Bea thought as she sipped her punch. She put down the glass and rested her head against the back of her chair. "This drink's about to turn me into a zombie."

"You should not say that around here," Robert teased.

"You're probably right," she laughed. "Zombies. Just another one of those crazy things people think goes on in places like this, right?"

"Well," Robert said after a beat, "not exactly."

Bea heard the *mambo* utter a dismissive little "shoop" in response, like she'd sucked in some air through the gaps in her teeth.

"What? You don't like to talk about zombies? I would think you'd know quite a bit about the topic," Bea said.

Robert laughed. "I think Mambo Michèle is probably tired of what everybody imagines, what everyone exaggerates about Haitian Vodou."

"They all think it is about dolls with pins, and bloody sacrifices," the *mambo* said.

"So there are no zombies?" Bea yawned again as the words left her mouth.

"I did not say that," the *mambo* responded.

"I think what Mambo Michèle is saying is that zombification is more of a—how do you say—cultural practice, than a Vodou practice."

"So there *are* zombies." Bea felt as though she were trying to keep up with a ping-pong game.

"It is just part of the way we do justice here," the *mambo* explained.

"So the *cops* turn people into zombies?"

Robert laughed. "Turning someone into a zombie is actually against the law, considered murder. But sometimes just the idea of the curse is enough to scare a person into behaving."

"To become a zombie is worse than death," the *mambo* added. "Here in Haiti, there is no punishment as horrible as the idea that a person can cause you to die and come back as a slave."

"Wait a minute." Now Bea felt wide awake. "You said 'sometimes', Robert. Does that mean there are times when a person actually *is* turned into a zombie?"

Robert hesitated with his answer to Bea. "So they say."

"And how's *that* supposed to work?"

"They steal the soul," the *mambo* said, as casually as someone explaining how a bicycle works, or how to core an apple.

"It is complicated, and something of a secret." Robert was clearly enjoying himself. "But imagine being drugged into a coma so deep that it looks like death, even to the doctors. Enough to be buried alive. Hours, or maybe even days after, you are dug up and revived with an antidote, but you are not the same as before. The poison has affected your body, and your brain, forever."

Bea shivered in the hot air.

"But you must understand, Madame Bea, that zombies are usually not innocent victims," he continued. "Their fate is most often revenge for ills they have caused in their community—like taking advantage of their neighbors, malicious gossiping, things that made them appear as though their good fortune was coming at the expense of others."

"Ha! Half my town would be zombies by now if that were the case."

All this zombie talk had Bea a bit jumpy. She reached for her rum punch. "Why aren't they back yet?" she groaned, her thoughts coming out aloud.

"Have patience," Mambo Michèle added. "Things take time. Things take work."

"So much for the magic," Bea said with a sigh.

"Do you know that the magical procedures of Vodou are known as *travay*?" the *mambo* barked back at her. "It means 'work'. That is because it is not just something you do, then wait for the miracles to happen. It is just a part of the effort. The Haitian people understand that if you want something in life, you have to work for it. The magic is a way to call on more hands to help."

"It is like what is on the Haitian flag," Robert chimed in. "The motto says, '*L'union fait la force*.'"

"Unity makes strength," Mambo Michèle translated. "That is what Haitian Vodou is about. A practice united in strength."

Bea nodded her understanding. Nevertheless, she sure wished a miracle would happen, or maybe even a couple of miracles.

"It is hard to lose someone you love," Robert said, breaking a silence that had come over the table.

"You mean Lizbeth? Or Senzey?"

"I see it on your face, Madame Bea," he said, his voice as warm as the midday air.

"It's Charlie I worry about, not me. I'm an old woman. I understand how these things happen, why people choose to do what they do. But Charlie, she's just a girl. And a girl needs her mother."

"Perhaps," he answered. "But we all yearn for what we have lost. Am I right, Madame Michèle?"

The *mambo*'s answer was drowned out by the clatter of footsteps hurrying up the stairs to the veranda.

"Welcome back, ladies," Robert said. Bea heard his chair scrape back on the floor below.

Lizbeth and Senzey responded in a jumble of words—*riot, hospital, baby, truck, fire, liars*—

"Whoa, whoa, whoa," Bea pleaded.

"The baby might be alive!" Lizbeth said, panting.

"I could have told you that." She was sure Lukson would have come through with Luke, during her reading, had he crossed over. But nobody had seemed to want to listen to what Bea had to say about that. "So where's Charlie?"

"Oh, she said to tell you." Lizbeth paused to catch her breath. "She went back on up the mountain, to see her mom."

33

A thousand scenarios were running through Charlie's mind as she drove back up the mountain, none of them good. In one, her stepfather runs her off with a shotgun. In another he laughs in her face. And in yet another, her mother simply ignores her presence, not even looking her in the eye. Charlie had no clue how she was going to handle the situation, could not even fathom what she really expected to gain from a confrontation. All she knew was that it had to be done.

Between the phony school and the sickening orphanages, Charlie had seen things that couldn't be unseen. Things that her mother, obviously, had a hand in. She was no innocent victim as her grandmother had suggested. She'd chosen to go down this crooked road with Jim. The two of them probably had a whole empire of scams working down here. She had to see this through—for herself, for Bea, for all those desperate people breaking their backs under the hot sun day in, day out, and for all the little Luksons who had no voice of their own.

She had reached the gates of Farming for Freedom before she realized how much ground she'd covered. The sun was setting, its rays reflecting in a perfect double rainbow. Charlie drove past the property and brought the Mitsubishi to a stop behind a thick grove of trees. She could detect no movement on the long driveway leading up over the hill toward the compound. Thankfully, her arrival seemed to have alerted no one. Charlie got out of the car and rested against the back bumper, thinking.

She was struggling to come up with her next move when she noticed the yellow truck coming down the driveway, toward the gate, toward the road, toward her. And this time it wasn't her mother behind the wheel, it was him.

Charlie crouched down behind her car and watched as her stepfather stopped and got out to open the gate. He paused and turned his head from one side to the other, as if sniffing her presence in the air. Charlie held her breath until he was back in his truck, passing through the open gate before speeding away. She then ran down the bumpy road, slipping through with seconds to spare before the gate swung shut. She stood to catch her breath, scanning the horizon for the guard, Eddy, with his soldier-boy rifle and ridiculous Ray-Bans, but there was not a soul in sight. The air was thick with smoke, the odor of burning charcoal telling her it must be close to dinnertime for the people who had no choice but to call this place home.

She forced herself forward, crossing the grounds with a will she knew could snap in two given the chance. Past the rotting Mapou stumps, past the decrepit shacks, the mud puddles and the trash piles, her strides lengthening at each turn.

When she reached the white picket fence she stopped. The glow from a lamp inside gave the house the look of a warm country cottage. She could almost imagine her mother baking cookies inside. Charlie held tight to the fantasy as she shakily navigated the stone path that led through the soft, green lawn and up to the door. She took a deep breath and raised her hand to knock.

The door swung open. "*Kisa li yé*—" Her mother stopped, seemingly mid-sentence. She looked as though she'd seen a ghost—pale, her arms trembling. Charlie feared the woman might faint. It crossed her mind that perhaps April was actually ill, that Bea's dream had been right after all.

"Charity?" April took a step closer.

Charlie couldn't speak.

Her mother's voice seemed to have abandoned her as well. "What's going on? Why are you here?" she finally asked. "Is something wrong? Are you all right?"

Charlie simply nodded.

"Is it Bea?"

Charlie noticed the dread suddenly clouding her mother's face. "Bea's fine."

"I don't understand. What are you—"

"We're both fine."

"Are you sure?" Her mother's faint eyebrows were raised toward the ceiling, her forehead pleated with wrinkles.

"I'm sure."

"Charity," she said, and repeated it again, as if saying the name out loud might make things feel more real. She reached out to touch Charlie's face. "It's really you."

Charlie jerked back a little, and watched as her mother's hand slowly dropped to her side.

"Why are you here, Charity? Tell me what's happening."

"Bea made me come. She came to Haiti with me. She thought there was something wrong with you," she said accusingly. Charlie's eyes scanned the room behind her mother, taking note of the well-polished furniture, the book-lined shelves, the bone china tea set on the table.

"Me?" Her mother seemed to melt with relief. "Why on earth—" She didn't finish the thought. "Oh, Charity," she said instead. "How I've missed you."

Charlie wanted to believe her. To surrender herself to her mother's words, to lose herself in the comfort of her embrace after so many years of feeling as abandoned as the children in the orphanages. But at the thought of those hungry faces, Charlie found her resolve stiffening.

"*Missed me?* You sure had a funny way of showing it. All those years, no phone calls, no letters, not even one stupid birthday card?"

"But Charity—"

"And my name isn't Charity anymore. It's Charlie. Plain old Charlie. Charity has never meant a thing to you, and obviously neither have I."

"But I did send you letters. Too many to count. I swear I did. And cards, every birthday, every Easter, every Christmas that I had to spend without you."

Charlie shook her head, refusing to believe her mother's lies.

"You never answered," her mother continued.

"You let me go!" Charlie shouted, suddenly unable to control herself. "You made a choice. *You chose Jim.*"

Her mother shrank away a little. "You don't understand, Charity."

"There is nothing to understand." Charlie bit back tears. "And all this." She pointed behind her. "This joke of a school. How could you?"

Her mother didn't respond.

"And I saw you at that place, that 'orphanage'. What's going on? What the hell are you and Jim up to?"

"You can't be here, Charity," her mother said, her voice suddenly panicked, her eyes wide with fear. "He'll be back. Soon. You need to leave."

"I'm not scared of Jim," Charlie said, desperately wanting to believe that was the truth.

"Leave, now," her mother begged. "I'll come to you. I'll explain everything tomorrow."

Charlie took a moment to really look at her mother, to see if there was a visible sign of why she had gone so wrong. But all she saw was a taller, younger version of Bea, her eyes deep and knowing, her silver-streaked, strawberry-blond hair and flowered dress worn loose and long, her ankles and wrists wrapped in beads and bangles whose purchase could have—and may have, Charlie liked to think—supported a few enterprising Haitians for months on end. Gone was the buttoned-up preacher's wife. In its place, she now realized, was a sort of 1960s hippie version of the mother she used to know. It made no sense.

"Explain it to me now, April," she demanded. Her mother stiffened at Charlie's calculated use of her name.

"Charity, please. You know what will happen if he finds you here."

"He's already found me here. I've spoken to him. He didn't tell you about our lovely reunion?" she sneered.

Again her mother looked horrified. "Charity—Charlie, *please*. Tomorrow. *I promise*. You'll hear everything."

Charlie took one last look at her mother. "I'll go," she said finally. "We're at the Abernathy. But don't worry. You don't need to make promises you won't keep." She turned away from the door and felt her mother's hand on her shoulder, the touch sending a jolt through her body. She resisted the urge to react, forcing herself to remain silent and still as her mother held on.

"I love you, Charity. I hope you have it in you to understand. I'll see you in the morning. Now go."

Charlie headed back down the stone path without a glance behind her, tears flowing furiously down her cheeks.

34

Bea had the ears of a bat. Or at least those of a good watchdog. So when Charlie tried to sneak in on tiptoe that night, she was wide awake in a flash, eager to hear everything her granddaughter had to say.

But Charlie did not want to talk. Bea knew better than to push the girl. So she bit her tongue and sat in silence as Charlie brushed her teeth and dressed for bed. *Goodnight, Bibi* was all she said. And *I love you*.

Bea had a tough time falling asleep, her imagination running wild with thoughts of what Charlie might have encountered up there on the mountain. If only she could see, Bea's eyes would have surely told her something. But she couldn't, and had only Charlie's silence to go by. And when her thoughts turned into dreams, things became even more disturbing. Zombies and werewolves; a raft full of babies, drifting out to sea; a church on fire; hissing snakes. These weren't the kind of dreams she'd share. Not with anyone. They were all so embarrassingly obvious, plucked straight from the headlines in her brain. Nothing for a psychic to crow about.

The sun was barely above the horizon when Bea started slowly down the stairs to the veranda the next morning, one hand gripping tight to the wobbly railing.

"Allow me to assist." Robert's rich, caramel voice drifted up toward her. "And how is everything this morning, Madame Bea? I trust that Charlie arrived back safely?" He helped her the rest of the way down and into a chair.

Bea nodded. "She's still asleep, which is not a good sign. She's an early riser by nature. The only time I ever see Charlie sleep past dawn is when she's upset. Didn't even stir at those damn roosters having a party under our window."

"Let me get you some coffee."

Bea sat back and dabbed at the perspiration beading on the sides of her nose. Robert was such a calming presence, like a hot bubble bath on a cold day, or a double Scotch after a hard one.

"I have added a little milk, just as you like it." He placed her hand gently on the side of the cup.

"Be careful, Robert. You're spoiling me."

"You deserve to be spoiled, do you not?"

Bea felt her face grow even warmer.

"You are a special woman, Bea. I have not met many like you in my life."

"Oh, please." She hid her face with her coffee.

"Truly, most women—how should I say—women of a certain age, they lose their shine. Yet you, dear Bea, you are lit up from somewhere deep inside."

"It's probably the mosquito spray I've got plastered all over myself." She shifted awkwardly in her seat.

"It is no joke. You are not a shy woman. Why are you so reluctant to accept a compliment?"

"I don't know, Robert. Maybe it's because I just don't know what to say."

"How about 'thank you'?"

"Well then, *merci beaucoup*, my friend. Compliment accepted."

"Do you know what the famous French writer Victor Hugo once said about compliments? He said, 'A compliment is something like a kiss through a veil.'"

Again Bea felt her face redden. "And do you know what the famous American comedienne Phyllis Diller had to say about it? 'You know you're old when someone compliments your alligator shoes, and you're barefoot.'"

Robert nearly spat out his coffee. "Oh, Bea. You are a delight. I am going to miss you when you go back home."

"Robert, I—"

"Ah, *mon dieu*."

"What is it?"

"It is uncanny."

"What? What's going on?" Bea repeated.

"There is a woman coming up the stairs, from the garden. A woman who looks remarkably like you, Madame Bea." He laughed. "The same walk, the same kind of dress—it's as if I'm seeing a ghost appear from years ago."

Bea heard the fading sound of a motorbike heading down the driveway as footsteps approached. From behind, two hands came to rest on her shoulders.

"Hello, Mom."

35

She hadn't meant to shock Bea like that, Charlie thought, as she grabbed a handful of napkins to help dry the old woman's tears. She'd never seen her grandmother really cry before. Maybe some sniffles at a sappy movie every once in a while, but never this. Bea had always been the toughest woman in the room. Now Charlie realized she should have given her grandmother some warning. And she would have, had she believed her mother would actually show up at the hotel.

"It's okay, Bibi. Calm down. I'm here now." She turned, squinting, toward her mother. "Look what you've done to her."

"But I—"

Charlie held out an arm as her mother stepped in to help. "Please, I've got this."

"I'll be all right, Charlie." Bea took the napkins into her shaking hands.

"I'm so sorry. I didn't mean it to happen this way," April said, wiping the tears from her own eyes.

"So what way *did* you mean for it to happen?" Bea asked with a sniffle. "All those years, not one single word from you, making your daughter feel so alone, so rejected, making me feel so, so—" Bea's words were lost in the bundle of napkins.

Charlie was speechless. All those times her grandmother had covered up for her own daughter, making excuses, telling Charlie that April loved her, that she was sure there had to be a rational explanation for everything, pretending, herself, to be fine about it all. She had never recognized how brokenhearted Bea truly was. She sat down next to her grandmother and wrapped a hand gently around her bony, trembling fingers.

Robert stood and slipped away, quietly intercepting Lizbeth and Senzey as they descended the stairs from their room, leading them to a table on the other side of the veranda. April cocked her head toward his empty chair, as if asking for permission to sit. Charlie nodded her assent.

Not trusting what she might say, Charlie waited out the silence. It was her mother who spoke first.

"Now, I know you both have questions," April began, sounding as if she were reciting a speech she'd rehearsed in her head for years. "And I understand that you both have lots of anger." She turned her moist eyes toward Charlie. "And you can lay all the blame you want on me. That's okay. All I ask for is one thing—that you give me the chance to talk."

Charlie sat back and folded her arms across her chest. Inside she felt as though she were going to break. Beside her, Bea was drying the wet lenses of her glasses with her scarf.

"First of all," April said, swallowing nervously before her next words. "I am sorry. Sorrier than either of you could ever imagine. There is never any excuse for a mother letting go of her child."

"*Letting go?* No, April. You didn't just let go. You abandoned the poor girl." Charlie noticed heads turn at the volume of her grandmother's voice. She cast her eyes downward.

"Charity, you have to understand, I did what I thought was best for you."

"Charlie," she hissed. "My name is *Charlie*."

"Charlie," her mother repeated.

"Were you thinking of what was best for her when you married that man?" Bea asked. "Were you thinking of what was best for her when you snatched her from everything she knew and loved, dragging her thousands of miles away? And what about after? Was it best for Charlie that you never wrote, never called, that you just disappeared into thin air?"

Charlie gently stroked Bea's forearm, as if trying to calm an anxious dog.

"But I *did* write," her mother protested. "You know I did."

"Never a word since this child landed back on my doorstep a decade ago."

April's eyebrows knitted together in confusion. "And what about you?"

Now it was Bea's turn to look confused.

"Maybe I should start at the beginning," April said.

"Maybe you'd better." Bea took a sip of water and sat back in her chair, placing the glass on the table with a small thud. Beyond the walls, the noise was intensifying, signaling yet another day of unrest on the streets.

Charlie's mother rubbed her forehead with her hands. "Okay, let's see if I can make some sense of this." She took a deep breath. "Once I left home, I knew pretty quickly that I'd made a mistake, marrying Jim, following him down there. But after the way you and I had said goodbye, I wasn't about to admit to that, wasn't about to come crawling home to my mama with my tail between my legs. I was determined to make things work, no matter what. Believe me, Jim's ugly side came out loud and clear down there, the way he strutted around as if he owned the place and everyone in it. I began to see the real Jim, the angry Jim, the controlling Jim. The jungle was hard on both of us, but I had Charlie." She turned to her daughter, her deep hazel eyes soft and, Charlie thought, very sad. "It didn't matter if I was in the jungle or on Mars, I had my girl, and that made life perfect."

Charlie felt the hard metal of Bea's rings dig into her skin as her grandmother grasped her hand under the table.

"Jim didn't have any of that," her mother continued. "All he had was me, and it seemed as though I was a daily disappointment to him. Nothing I did was right. I could see that he was having problems adjusting to his new post, and problems getting along with the people. I thought that maybe if I helped with that, things would get better for all of us. But it only seemed to make him angrier, more resentful of me."

She paused before continuing.

"Believe me, there were plenty of times I thought we should all leave. But I was too scared to even mention it to Jim. Besides, you were thriving down there, Charlie. I learned from you, watching how easily you connected with everyone, seeing how free you were, how easily you gave your love, how readily you received it back."

April smiled.

"Do you remember how quickly you learned the language? You used to rattle it off as if you were born to it. Everyone was so impressed. I had to scramble just to keep up with you, but I finally got it. Learning that language gave me freedom, Charlie, a place in a world Jim would never enter. Remember how furious he'd get? He made that rule about only speaking English at home? I think he was scared we were talking about him, right?" She laughed a little. "But you and I, we got out there and spoke with everyone. We learned what they wanted, what they needed. You and I were a team."

"Until we weren't," Charlie muttered under her breath. But her mother just kept talking, as if she'd been saving up a lifetime's worth of words for this day.

"Jim never did connect with anyone down there," she said. "He hated that everyone came to me, instead of him, with their problems. And the more alienated he felt, the more frustrated and angry he became. So—" She paused for a breath. "One day, I decided to confide in one of the other women, while I was on a sort of retreat—a training weekend for mission wives. I told her I was beginning to think that ours wasn't a good situation for Jim, that he didn't seem to be adjusting well. I shared with her my thoughts about how everything was taking a toll on our marriage, and how for the sake of the family perhaps it was best we all go back. *The adjustment to the jungle is hard on everyone*, is what she told me. That having a child and being newly married probably made it even tougher. That I needed to focus more on my husband, that it was my job to support him. To pray to God for direction. She made me feel selfish, and small."

She stopped for a moment, reaching up to scrape her messy hair back into the clip on top of her head.

"Toward the end of the retreat, I found myself admitting to her that I sometimes thought about leaving Jim. I thought she was my friend. But before I'd even returned to our compound, Jim had heard everything. The woman's husband had told him.

After that, I lost my freedom. Jim did his best to never let me out of his sight. I wasn't even allowed to communicate over the radio for our morning check-in with the missionary base."

"Oh, April." Bea groaned.

"I wanted to tell you, Mom. I really did. At that point, I *did* want to run back home and forget it had all happened. But I just couldn't bring myself to do it. I felt like such a failure. All the other missionaries, all the church people, they loved Jim, told me I was so blessed to have a man like that in my life. I couldn't figure out what was wrong with me. I'd been told that it was God's plan that we were to work side by side in the jungle. Who was I to say it wasn't? So, I just buried my thoughts and pressed on. I thought that if I tried harder, if I prayed more, if I read the Bible more, did my job to be the godly wife that Jim deserved, things would fall into place."

A vision flashed in Charlie's mind of her mother as a young woman, a tiny, tight smile fixed on her face like a mask.

"But what happened as you got older, Charlie, was that I began to see that my biggest job was going to be to protect you. You were the center of my universe. But to Jim, that was not what God had intended. You were starting to question him, to confront him. Every day you were becoming more like your Grandma Bea than like me. And I realized that even if I didn't have the strength to leave, you could. So I told Jim that maybe the time had come for you to go to school back in the States. But he wasn't about to follow any of my advice. So I 'agreed' to send you to the mission boarding school just a few hours away—making him think it was his own idea—to keep you out of harm's way.

"Then, just over a year later, you were back. And I felt like it was only a matter of time before things were going to truly blow up. I began stashing away a little money, whatever I could save out of my allowance, and started thinking about a plan."

Charlie ran her fingers through her bed-head hair. "So, let me get this straight. You purposefully let things get so bad that Jim would kick me out?"

"Everything was going from bad to worse no matter what I did. I just didn't think it would all happen so quickly. So when I saw the opportunity, I took it. There was no way I was going to watch you suffering for one more day under that man's roof."

Charlie would never be able to erase the images of that last day in the jungle from her mind. The thoughts were whirling around and around in her head. "But you said you'd follow. *You promised.* You should have come with me."

"If we'd both left, Jim would have come after us. He never would have stood for me disobeying him. And then, the longer I stayed with him, the harder—"

Bea reached for her water, and held out the glass in the direction of her daughter. Charlie could see by the look on her mother's face that she was just beginning to realize how blind Bea had become.

"It's hard to explain, Charlie," her grandmother said. "It's really not something you'd understand unless you've been there yourself. Trust me. I know."

Charlie's thoughts were stopped dead in their tracks. "*You,* Bibi?"

April's eyebrows were raised in confusion.

"Go on," Bea said.

"It was like I was under a spell," April continued, her eyes still on Bea. "Like I had no will of my own. I guess it was part awe, part fear. Then it turned into just plain fear." She paused to take a sip of water. "It's so complicated. Your mind gets all messed up when you're so isolated. I didn't dare speak to anyone about it, not after the last time. And Jim knew exactly how to wear me down, how to punish me. It was as though I were being held prisoner in a jail without bars. He kept telling me I was nothing without him, and after a while, I believed him." Her eyes bored into Charlie's. "You will never—I hope to God—know what it's like to be under the control of a man like that."

"Amen to that," Bea echoed.

"But that doesn't explain why you couldn't write," Charlie said.

"I swear, Charlie, I did write, every single day. It was the only way I could survive, I missed you so much," she said, her throat closing on the words as a fresh crop of tears filled her eyes. "I kept writing, even after I never heard back."

"That man was messing with the mail!" Bea yelped.

"And I *did* call, after we arrived here in Haiti. You have no idea how many times I dialed that phone, just to hear your voice on the other end. I just couldn't—"

"You mean you called and hung up on me?" Bea was incredulous. "Why the hell didn't you speak?"

"How could I? After Jim told me about that phone conversation he had with you, when he called to suggest a reconciliation, what was I supposed to do?"

Charlie noticed Bea's neck tense, her back straighten, the way it always did right before she lost it. "What phone conversation? What, exactly, did he tell you?"

"What you said to him. That I had clearly made my choices, and that you never wanted to hear from me again."

Bea reached out for her daughter's hand. "That call never happened. What an awful man he is. Even worse than I ever

240

imagined. I *never* stopped caring about you. Not for one damn second."

"You were right, Mom," she sobbed. "About everything."

Bea shook her head, her own tears spilling behind her glasses. "You don't need to—"

"I *do* need to. I understand now how heartbroken you were when I left, when I took Charity—I mean, Charlie—thousands of miles away."

"So why are you still with him?" Charlie asked. Her grandmother may have understood, but she still didn't.

"I know who he is, Charlie." Her mother wiped her eyes. "I've had to live with his sins every single day of my adult life. But it wasn't until about three years ago, when we got here to Haiti, that I began to feel like myself again. The country was so full of life, and there was so much to be done. I felt like I had a place here, like I might make a difference. It wasn't long before I got completely wrapped up in my work, and began to feel I was meant to be here. And, despite Jim, I still feel that way."

"But what he's doing, up there on the mountain? What about those people working their asses off at that so-called school? Living in filth like animals, being treated no better than slaves? What about them?"

"You can choose to believe me or not, but I swear I spend every ounce of energy I have righting that man's wrongs. I think of it as my redemption. I do what I can, when his back is turned. I bring those men and women food, give them whatever money I can hide away. I teach them to read, and make sure they know they have a right to be paid for a job, should they be able to find one. And I watch out for their children."

"Funny," Charlie said. "I didn't see any kids up there."

Her mom suddenly became quiet. "There aren't," she finally said. "Jim doesn't allow it."

"So what does he do with them?" Charlie asked, not sure she really wanted to hear the answer.

"He convinces their parents to send them away, for a better life. Or at least that's what he tells them."

"And that's what you were doing yesterday, with that child you were dragging around like a dog on a leash."

"What child?" April turned to Bea, as if she might know what Charlie meant.

"I saw you," Charlie said. "Remember? At the orphanage."

"Oh, you mean little Mirlande. I was rushing to get her back inside before the riots grew. I had taken her out to see a doctor."

Her mother slumped back in her chair, her gaze coming to rest on a spot somewhere beyond Charlie's shoulder. "It's horrible, what goes on in those places," she finally said. "These children never stand a chance. Here they are, supposed to be getting love and attention, a decent start in life, and all they're getting is used and abused. They're moneymakers, that's all they are. Part of a headcount or a photo opportunity used to get folks back home to send in their dollars. And when they grow up? When they're not so cute and adorable anymore? Out they go, either sold as what can only be called slaves, or put out in the streets to fend for themselves. It's a filthy business. And Jim—that man's hands are so dirty he'll never be able to scrub them clean."

"So he's involved in all this?"

Her mother nodded. "He works with a lot of the orphanages."

"And you?"

"I make the rounds of them whenever I can, to do whatever I can. I bring towels, medicine, formula. Whatever I can get my hands on without Jim knowing. The people at those places, they think Jim knows what I do, that he sends me. And even if he does know, what can he say? I'm just keeping his little goldmine going by keeping those kids clothed and fed, right?"

For just a minute, Charlie felt as though she'd suddenly traveled back twenty years, back to a time when her mother was the answer to everything she ever wanted or needed, back to the time when her mother's touch could extinguish even the sharpest pain, when her kiss could solve the darkest of problems.

"Mom," she said, snapping back to the moment, "I want you to meet someone."

36

From the other table, Lizbeth and Senzey had been craning their necks to get a glimpse of the drama unfolding across the veranda. Charlie gestured for them to come over.

"Mom," she said again as the two women neared. "These are my friends. Lizbeth and Senzey. Lizbeth and Senzey, this is my mother, April."

"I am so pleased to be making your acquaintance," Lizbeth gushed, taking April's hand and pumping it up and down with such force that Charlie thought her mother was going to fall out of her chair. "You have quite a daughter in Charlie. A real spitfire."

"Thank you. It's nice to meet you as well," her mother replied before turning to Senzey.

"I am Senzey," was all the girl said.

"Senzey and Lizbeth are trying to find out what happened to a baby," Charlie explained eagerly.

Her mother eyed the two women, confused.

"It's Senzey's baby. Lizbeth's son was the father." Charlie waited for her mother's response.

"You need to explain, dear," Bea prompted. "You see," she continued without giving Charlie the chance, "Senzey was talked into leaving her baby at an orphanage, with the promise that she could come back and get him, if and when she had the means, and the will. But there's some confusion about where that boy is."

"And if he—"

Senzey was interrupted by Lizbeth. "Be positive, Senzey. Remember what that nurse said."

April's caution was obvious as she answered, her eyes remaining on Senzey. "It's a tricky world, the orphanages here."

"Yes, but you said you know—" Charlie said.

"Hold on. I'm not saying I can't help, but we have to be careful. Let me make some calls."

"Calls?" Lizbeth said. "I'm sorry, I don't know about y'all, but in my way of thinking we oughta be out there banging down some doors."

"But it is impossible," Robert said as he joined them. "Do you hear what is going on out there?" He nodded toward the gates at the bottom of the hotel's driveway. The shouts and honking horns had become punctuated with sporadic popping gunfire, and the air had turned thick with the smell of burning rubber. "And from what I have heard, it will only become worse throughout the day."

"He's right," April said. "But I think I can at least start trying to track this baby down over the phone. I know a lot of people. Let me see what I can do." She turned to Senzey. "What is his name, and how old would he be now?"

"Lukson. Six months and five days," the woman answered in a heartbeat, her eyes cast downward toward the floor.

"And what does Lukson look like? Do you have any photos?"

She shook her head. "I have no photo. But I will never forget his face. He had a little bit of hair on his head, like his father's, soft and light. Light-skinned, and blue eyes." She pointed to Lizbeth. "Like his grandmother."

Charlie watched as her mother pulled a pair of reading glasses from her bag and began to furiously scroll through the contacts on her phone. Part of her wanted to grab the woman from behind and give her a huge hug, but it was the other part—the one that couldn't yet let go of the story she'd been telling herself for years—that kept her rooted to her chair.

The table became silent as April made her first call. Charlie could hear the forced charm behind her mother's words, spoken in Creole. She tried to figure out how the conversation was going from Senzey and Robert's reactions, but their faces weren't revealing a thing. The only thing she recognized was Lukson's name.

"I told him I was calling for Jim," April explained once the call was complete. "I said that he needed to locate a baby named Lukson, and told him his age, what he looked like. I said Jim had someone who had deep pockets, someone who had interest in the boy. I'm not sure he believed me. But anyway, he claimed to have no knowledge of Lukson."

They sat as April went through several more of these calls, one right after the other. The response was always the same. The discomfort around the table was growing thick, like the smoke spilling from the streets.

"Shall we move inside?" Robert suggested to Bea, including Senzey and Lizbeth in his invitation. "The air is perhaps a little fresher in there."

Charlie mouthed a silent "thank you" to him as the four of them rose from the table.

"It's risky, Charlie," April said after they were gone, finally putting down the phone. "Every call I make is going to raise suspicion. If that boy is as valuable as I think he is, with his light skin and blue eyes, whoever has him is going to do everything they can to keep him hidden. A lot of these folks know each other. And word travels fast." Her eyes darted toward the street, as if she could see what was happening through the thickness of the wall. "If these damn protests would just stop already . . . I feel like we're racing against the clock. They're going to start moving that kid around like a pawn on a chess board."

"But won't the riots keep 'them' from getting out there as well?"

"Probably. But somebody's bound to call Jim, if they haven't already. And once he gets his antennae up, who knows what will happen?"

"Maybe we should just get going sooner, rather than later, like Lizbeth said."

"Or maybe *I* should."

"Oh, no you don't," Charlie said. "You think I'm going to let you go so easily, after all I've been through?"

"I'm sorry, Charlie. I know it's not going to be easy for you to forgive me."

"Well, I'm certainly not ever going to forgive you if you go out there and get yourself killed."

Her mother closed her eyes and then opened them again, as if she had offered a quick, silent prayer of thanks. "Look," she said, taking Charlie's hand. "We're stuck here for the time being, so we'll have to take the chance and see what we can uncover with some more calls. It's a gamble, but it's better than just sitting around. I have a boatload of names and numbers in here." She held up her phone. "*Somebody* has to know where that child is. I'll just have to be as careful as I can not to raise any red flags."

And with that, April dived back into her pursuit. Charlie left the veranda to go inside and check on Bea and the others. Charlie spied a pitcher of rum punch in the center of their table. Robert winked in her direction.

"Any luck?" Lizbeth asked eagerly, her eyes red from the smoky air.

"Not yet." Charlie struggled to sound positive. "But she's still trying."

"Doesn't sound like things are getting any calmer out there." Bea waved an arm toward the front of the hotel.

"It probably sounds worse than it really is," Charlie said, just as a volley of gunfire erupted in the distance.

She went back outside to her mother.

"*Non. Wi. Li se pou Pastè Jim,*" was what April was saying, her nose wrinkling and her eyes scrunching closed, as if she were worried about the response her words might bring. "*Mèsi, mèsi.*" She slammed the phone down onto the table. "I think the word is out," she said. "The minute things get quiet, that baby is going to disappear into thin air, not that we even know yet where he's going to disappear from."

"Isn't there *anyone*? What about those baby-finders?"

April shook her head. "They're not about to give away anything. They were paid to do a job. And I'm sure they're not going to do anything to jeopardize their future employment."

"They should be arrested."

April snorted. "If only. Unfortunately, that's not the way things work around here." She turned her head to the sky beyond the wall, as if the answer might be found in the clouds. "Wait!"

She suddenly grabbed the phone. "There is a guy I haven't tried, a young volunteer who's been around a while. He bent my ear one day over how disgusted he was about the conditions of the orphanage he was working in. About how he was going to try to do something about it. I warned him how hard that might be but, of course, I encouraged him. I know he'll remember me. Let me try."

Charlie listened as April furiously poured Senzey's story out into the mouthpiece of her phone. Then she saw her mother break into a grin.

"He is? You're pretty sure? Uh-huh." She motioned to Charlie for a pen. Charlie ran in a flash to the front desk and back. "Okay. Thanks. I will. *Bonswa.* And be safe."

"Bingo," she said to Charlie. They rushed inside to the others to share their news.

"I can't guarantee it's him, but it's worth a shot, isn't it?" April seemed almost breathless.

"Yes!" A rare flash of hope crossed Senzey's face.

"It may not be easy," April added.

"Who needs easy?" Bea asked.

"These places can use all sorts of tricks when it comes down to making money."

"Don't think you can scare us off that easy, woman." Lizbeth stood and planted her hands onto her broad hips.

Charlie's eyes went wide. Gone was that Texan mouse they'd come across in Miami airport. In its place was a fiery tiger, as pushy as any self-respecting grandma had a right to be.

"Mark my words, y'all," she said as she focused her eyes on each of them, from one to the next. "We're gonna get that child back, come hell or high water."

37

The memory that came to Charlie was as vivid as a big-screen, high-definition movie. She was seated in a kitchen chair, her mother standing behind her trying to tame her unruly curls, when a tribeswoman showed up at their door.

"It is time," said the woman, who—like all the tribeswomen—looked to Charlie like a cat with whiskers, with sticks poking out of the piercings that ran along her lips. Another birth was about to occur in the village. Charlie's hair left half-combed, her mother grabbed her medical kit, and, with Charlie following behind, walked out the door.

It was a normal course of events in their household. Charlie's mother had taken it upon herself to attend all the births, and had recently started to bring Charlie, who was probably no more than nine years old at the time. *It will be good to have your help*, her mother had told her.

Charlie had been alarmed at first, hearing the sounds that emerged from the center of the communal round house, behind the wall of women, their painted bodies shielding the actual birth from view. But while the one giving birth screamed and wailed with pain, the others acted as though it were a party or a sporting match, shouting their encouragement and support as the baby was pushed from its mother's womb. Luckily, April usually stayed in the background, there in case of emergency only. Charlie would grasp tightly at her hand, her eyes half hidden behind her mother's arm. But it wasn't long before she became used to the ritual, fascinated by the way the baby would be roused by a gourd full of water being poured over its tiny body, and how the mother would suction its nose and mouth using her own mouth. April had taught her that the people of the jungle did not believe that a baby was a real person until someone, usually the grandmother or mother, gave it its first touch, sharing their spirit with the newborn and making it human. Charlie always held her breath at that part, having learned that if nobody picked up the baby quickly enough, there would be the possibility that an evil spirit—in an attempt to enter into the tribe's world—would jump into the infant's body.

On the particular day that Charlie was remembering, something else altogether happened. She heard the familiar shouts from the crowd as the baby emerged, and peeked around her mother for a sight of the child. Then she heard the newborn's cry. But the women protecting the birth from view hadn't budged. And instead of shouting out their encouragement, they seemed to be whispering among themselves, their eyes dark with concern. Then Charlie heard a second cry.

Her mother turned to her and told her to go home. *Tell Jim I'll be home soon*, she said. Charlie started to protest, until she saw the look in her mother's eyes.

The next part of the memory was hazier. That same night, she'd fallen asleep before her mother's return. She was woken by her stepfather's ranting, which wasn't unusual. Normally she'd just cover her head with a pillow and try to go back to sleep. But this time she could swear she was detecting the sound of a baby whimpering between Jim's shouts.

"It's none of our business," she heard him yell as his fist hit the kitchen table.

"It *is* our business, Jim. Every human life is our business."

Charlie remembered her surprise at the sound of April standing up to her husband. She also remembered waiting for the sound of the slap that was bound to follow. But this time her mother did not back down.

"Just because it's always been done this way doesn't mean it's right. You, of all people, should understand that, trying to get these folks to believe in what you do, instead of what their parents and grandparents and those before them have been taught."

"I'm not saying it's right," he bellowed. "I'm saying we cannot risk the anger of this community. You know how they feel about twins. I will be blamed for every single bad thing that happens in this place for as long as we're here."

"I am not letting this baby starve. Think about what the Lord would have to say about that, Jim, about me, about you, knowing that you have the blood of an innocent child on your hands, a child that has been left in the jungle to rot or be eaten alive."

Charlie did not sleep that night. She didn't remember how the argument ended, but she could still picture rising the next morning to the sight of her mother cooing over the tiniest creature she'd ever laid eyes on. It looked like a baby bird that had fallen out of the nest. She watched as her mother dipped a finger into a pot of warm milk, pressing it gently to the newborn's pale lips.

"You try with him," she said, standing so Charlie could take a seat next to the crate her mother had lined with soft blankets. Charlie was dying to ask what had happened, why this child was here, under their roof, instead of with his own mother. But April looked as though she were about to drop from exhaustion, so Charlie remained silent as she tried in vain to get the infant to open his tiny mouth.

"They think twins are a curse," her mother said, as if reading her mind. "So one is abandoned, for the sake of the community." Her mother began clearing the table of Jim's breakfast dishes as she spoke, her face clouded with sadness. "If a person tries to touch it, feed it, or help it in any way, they say that the spirits will cause trouble for the entire village—sickness, drought, death."

"How did he get here?" Charlie asked, stroking the infant's soft head with one finger.

"I waited outside the round house until after dark, when I saw his mother leaving. I followed her into the jungle. She didn't know."

Charlie recalled how she'd felt at that moment, picturing her mother bravely defying her own husband with her actions, risking the fury of the entire community to do what she knew was the right thing. But in the end, the baby didn't make it. April had spent days doing her best to nurture the infant, patiently trying to get him to eat, silencing his weak cries to hide his presence from the outside world. Charlie did what she could to help, taking a shift during the day so her mother could sleep. Jim, of course, knew what was happening, but his pride made him pretend the child didn't exist. When the baby died, it was only Charlie and her mother saying prayers beside the tiny grave tucked away under a tall palm tree deep in the jungle.

That was the mother Charlie saw sitting in the passenger seat beside her now, leading their little group through the narrow backstreets of Port-au-Prince with the confidence of a four-star general. Lizbeth and Senzey chattered nervously in the back seat, their voices tinged with apprehension.

It was a lucky break for all of them that Jim was away, having left that morning for some business in Les Cayes, about a four-hour drive from Port-au-Prince. Still, it wasn't until after sunset that they finally dared to leave the hotel. Though things appeared to be slightly calmer, some of the streets were still blocked. Things could flare up at any time, Robert had warned as he saw them off at the hotel. But April did not feel it would be wise to wait any longer.

They stood behind her as she knocked on the door, first gently rapping, then pounding harder with her fist. The door opened a couple of inches to reveal a pair of eyes peering out at them, then quickly closed. The women all looked to April.

"Just wait," she said, her gaze remaining fixed on the door.

And then the door opened again, this time wider. A thickset Haitian man in a short-sleeved shirt and creased linen pants greeted April. He seemed taken aback by her presence.

He checked his watch. "What are you doing here so late at night, Mrs. Clark, and in the middle of all this unrest?" he asked, his concern a thin veneer masking an obvious discomfort with the situation. "Is there something I can do for you?" His lips curled into a tight smile.

"I think maybe there is. May we come in?"

One look at the others behind her and the smile melted away. "Of course, of course."

The orphanage was quiet, the children who lived there no doubt already in bed. Charlie could see Lizbeth's shock at the sparseness of the place.

"I've been told that perhaps this woman's child is here," April said.

His eyes darted to Senzey. "I do not think I know this woman."

"Maybe not, but that doesn't mean her son isn't here."

He shrugged his shoulders.

"She left her child with a couple, a man and a woman, who were to bring him to an orphanage. She signed the papers. I think this is the place."

Now he shook his head.

"A baby. Six months old."

The man didn't budge.

"Lukson," Charlie said. "His name is Lukson."

"Perhaps he is being called another name now?" the man said, pulling at his collar, clearly becoming uneasy.

"You do have a couple of infants here, if I recall, don't you?" Charlie's mother asked.

"It is hard to know. Sometimes the children are moved around."

"You are the director of this orphanage, and you can't keep track of the children in your care?"

"So much trouble for one little *milat*," he muttered.

"So you *do* know who he is."

"I did not say that." He looked away. "It is just that I—"

"Well, if you do know where that *mulatto*, as you call him, is, it's best you tell me right now. You see, Pastor Jim wants the baby reunited with his mother." April pointed to Senzey. "Immediately."

The director's eyes rounded in surprise. "Is that so?"

"He sent me here himself." Charlie detected a quiver in her mother's voice.

The man stood looking at the four women, as if sizing them up in his head. His attention was broken by the sound of a soft thud through the wall behind him. He seemed to jump at the chance to get away. "You must excuse me for a minute. I need to make sure the staff has everything under control."

Charlie and her mother eyed each other nervously as he backed out of the room.

Senzey dropped down onto a wobbly wooden bench.

Lizbeth took the opportunity to poke around, checking behind curtains and sifting through shelves as though she might find Lukson hidden among the tin plates and cracked cups.

"He is lying," Senzey said. "I know he is lying. Just like those others were lying to me about Lukson being dead."

Lizbeth crammed one ear up against the wall, waving a hand at Senzey to be quiet.

"Why do they make it so difficult? I am his *mother*."

Lizbeth continued to snoop, her hand jiggling a doorknob. Charlie and April stayed in place, their eyes locked on the doorway through which the man had disappeared.

"How can they live with themselves?" Lizbeth ranted as she looked around the cold, spare room. "Having those children all shut up in a place like this."

It was then that the orphanage director returned. "Lukson. Yes, I remember now. A chubby baby, with light hair?"

"Where is he?" Senzey demanded, stepping so close to the man that their noses were practically touching.

"Your baby," he said, as he took a deep breath and folded his hands against his chest, "is gone. Congratulations, he has been adopted."

38

Bea struggled to keep up with the *mambo*'s pace, the hem of the long yellow skirt tripping her up and messing with her progress. She had been told to dress in bright colors—no black, no white. Modest, and, most importantly, clean. Worried that the wear she'd already placed on the clothes she'd brought down to Haiti might show, Bea was forced to raid Charlie's suitcase, knowing that the girl had not even touched any of the nicer things Bea had insisted she pack, instead hopping into her jeans and T-shirts each morning without a thought.

The walk wasn't far, but it was tricky, and the stray sounds of gunfire here and there weren't making it any easier. After weaving their way through what, to Bea, felt like a rat's maze, the *mambo* finally came to a stop. She handed Bea a piece of cloth, a red blur through the thick lenses of her glasses.

"It is a *moushwa*," Mambo Michèle explained. "A scarf, for your head."

Bea could feel the weight of an evening storm approaching. The *mambo* had warned her that they could very well be out all night, which was fine with Bea. An invitation to participate in an official Vodou service wasn't something that was bound to come twice in her lifetime. The brief note she'd left for Charlie and the others would have to suffice. She would explain the rest tomorrow.

After their offering to Èrzulie Dantòr a few days earlier, the *mambo* had mentioned to Bea that there was one other step they would need to take to make sure they would get the *loa*'s help. "Sometimes several different kinds of *travay* are required in difficult situations. You will come with me in two days. Just you, and nobody else. It is our secret."

Bea had almost forgotten, with the shock of April appearing on the veranda of the Abernathy that morning. They'd ended up spending a long day together at the hotel, a lucky consequence of the street demonstrations. But as April and the others were preparing to leave for the orphanage, the *mambo*'s invitation had come back to mind. Bea had told them to take care and wished them luck when they finally left, crossing paths with the *mambo* as she mounted the stairs.

"We are entering the *peristil*, our house of worship," Mambo Michèle now told her. "What you will find there will be almost like a party, a party to honor a group of spirits. You are meant to have fun, to enjoy yourself. I am hoping that Èrzulie Dantòr will appear, to speak with you. Did you bring the fruit?"

Bea nodded and patted her tote, which held the mangoes and papayas she'd managed to wangle from Stanley. The fruit was for the *loa*, an offering to the spirits. The *mambo* took Bea's arm and led her inside, where the chaotic signs of last-minute preparations signaled a late start—orders were being shouted out from all corners of the stuffy room, chairs dragged across the floor, the odor of garlic and onions permeating the air.

"Now we sit," the *mambo* said. "The *Priyè Ginen*, the prayers, will begin soon."

"But that is not possible," Senzey argued, her fiery eyes locked on the man standing across from her. "I did not sign anything saying you could give my baby away. I have the papers right here." She took them from her bag and shook them in his face. "That was not the agreement."

"I am sure you are wrong," the orphanage director insisted, before turning to Charlie's mom. "Maybe you can explain."

"No," April shook her head. "There is nothing for me to explain. That's your job. And, I might add, if you did adopt this baby out against his mother's wishes, it seems to me that it's something the police would be very interested in. Am I right?"

The man drew back in surprise. "Mrs. Clark, this is simply a misunderstanding, that is all. Perhaps you can come back tomorrow, just you and your husband, and we can talk."

"We can talk right now. Without my husband."

"We've got all night," Lizbeth piped in.

"We're all ears," Charlie added, taking her phone from her pocket to record a video, making a show of it for the orphanage director's sake.

"Now, where is that baby?" April demanded, squaring off in front of the man.

Bea sat before the altar with the rest of the congregation, her head bowed and her feet bare. The prayers began in what appeared to be

French, one word flowing into the next like a gentle wind blowing across the room, *Jésus . . . Sainte Marie, Mère de Dieu*, the call and response reminding her a bit of a gospel church back home. She closed her eyes through the dozens of verses, the chanting a sweet lullaby to her ears. Then the spoken prayers stopped, replaced by the sounds of a muted rattling, drummers tapping softly on their instruments, and a gentle clapping of hands.

The *mambo* leaned in to whisper in Bea's ear. "They are calling out to the spirits," she whispered. "Making way for them to arrive."

Bea listened as the voices lifted into song, the room filling with melodies that sounded old, and powerful. And then suddenly, as if someone had spun the dial, everything changed. The drumbeats grew louder, the applause sharper. The songs became faster and shifted in key, the call and response more frantic, the words ringing out in a language Bea had never heard.

"The children are sleeping. This is no time to talk. You must go, now!"

"I'll be happy to tend to those little ones while y'all have your discussion," Lizbeth offered, trying to push her way around the orphanage director's firmly rooted body toward the closed doors behind him.

"That will not be necessary," he said as he barred the way.

"Where are your records?" Charlie said. "We need to see who took that baby. And we're not leaving until we do."

"The records?" The man fumbled his words.

"Who has my boy?" Senzey yelled. "Lukson!" Her shouting blended with the crying of a woken child.

"I'll bet he is here," Charlie heard her mother say. "Right here, behind one of those doors." Charlie turned toward her, trying to figure out what she was up to. "That boy—" Her mother stepped closer to the man, until they were practically touching. "He must be quite valuable, for you to be going to all this trouble."

The man shook his head. "I do not know what you are talking about."

"Don't you dare treat me like a fool," April snapped. "I know damn well what goes on here, how those children are precious to you only as a way to line your own pockets. A boy like Lukson? He'd be worth ten times more than any of the others. That light hair and those blue eyes must work like a magnet to pull the money out of donors' wallets. How many sponsors has he attracted, can you tell me that? How many dollars has that baby earned for you?"

The man looked as though a boiling brew were rising up through his body, ready to explode right through his head.

"Let us see the children," Charlie's mother demanded. "Now."

The prayers were over, the chairs cleared away. "It is time to call to the *loa* to dance with us," the *mambo* explained. "If Èrzulie Dantòr comes, I will bring you to speak with her."

"But what do I say?"

"You tell her your problem. Ask her for what you want."

The sound of drums brought their conversation to a halt, followed by what seemed like a hundred rattles shaking in time to the beat.

"*Anonse o zanj nan dlo*," the voices rang out in song.

"And now we begin," said the *mambo*.

"I will call the police!" the man shouted as April pushed her way past him.

"*You* will call the police?" she laughed. "Go ahead and call them. And while you're at it, why don't you call the ambassador? Call the damn president! Bring them all on. I'm not the one with something to hide here."

Charlie and the others followed as April opened the door to the first bedroom, the smell of urine hitting them like a brick. In the darkness, Charlie could barely make out the tiny bodies lumped together in two and threes, on cots stacked up halfway to the ceiling. Senzey ran from bed to bed, peering at the piles of sleeping children who were all too big to be her own. One little girl, alarmed by the activity in the room, awoke with a start and began to whimper, holding her thin blanket close to her face. Charlie stayed behind for a few minutes as the others moved on to the next bedroom, gently stroking the child's hair until she fell back to sleep, just like her own mother used to do for her.

Out in the hallway, things were becoming more heated, as the orphanage director continued to threaten the women. "I have already called your husband," he shouted at April. "He has sent somebody to get you. They are on their way. He told me you have no right to be here."

The room itself seemed to have come alive, the walls throbbing with drumbeats growing faster and louder, the floor bouncing with the weight of dozens of pairs of feet pounding to the wild rhythms. Bea could not keep herself from joining in. It was as though she were being pulled by invisible hands, swept into the crowd of revelers who were happy to include her as one of their own.

She had no idea how long they'd been dancing, their bodies swaying and twirling back and forth to the melodies, Bea holding up her long skirt with one hand, while the other held fast to Mambo Michèle. At the *mambo*'s insistence, they'd paused a few times for something to eat and drink, for a chance for Bea to sit and allow her sweat to dry. But Bea had no interest in sitting still. This was one party she was not going to miss.

Faster and faster the beat accelerated, the rattles now producing one continuous purr, the songs thundering across the room. Suddenly Bea felt herself being pulled back by the *mambo*. Around her she heard gasps and a sympathetic clucking, the sounds of people witnessing another's ordeal.

"What's happening?" she shouted above the frenzy.

"It is a woman, she is jerking and falling."

"Is she okay?"

"We must leave her alone, to allow the spirit to enter."

Bea stood back, a swirling sea of color thrashing around her, her own heart keeping pace with the pulse of the room, the collective joy and energy an incredible force that seemed to be lifting her soul as high as the clouds. She stood swaying and clapping until she heard the *mambo* speak her name.

"Madame Bea, it is her. It is Èrzulie Dantòr. It is time."

Charlie saw her mother visibly pale at the director's words. And then, as if energized by some remote force, April roared back into action.

"Rights?" she screamed. "How can my husband talk about rights? Neither of you two crooks would know lawful from criminal. Now, where are the rest of the children?"

"There are no more children here. You have seen them all," the director insisted, standing up to her like a rooster with its chest puffed out.

"Well, you're going to have to prove that to me." She pointed to a pair of unopened doors behind him, at the end of the hall. "Who's going first? You, or me?"

Bea could sense the thick air of the encircling crowd. The drums kept up their driving rhythm; the songs continued to fill her ears. The *mambo* gently pushed her forward, then let go. Bea stood alone, the room pulsing around her. A sudden breath on her face signaled the *loa*'s presence. Bea felt two strong hands clamping over her own as she was led into a jerky dance, rocked from side to side by another's forceful command. A strange clicking arose from the person before her, a sound from deep in the back of the throat. In an instant both Bea's hands were above her head as she was spun in an awkward twirl that had her stumbling to the ground. And then it was over.

Bam! The door crashed in at the force of their feet. It had been locked. And the orphanage director had refused to open it. What were they supposed to do but kick it in, which they did with the strength of an army of four fueled by anger, determination, and the kind of love that comes from the bonds between woman and child. All it took was one peep from the baby in that room and the door came tumbling down. And there he was, as soft and precious as Senzey had described, his hair a silky halo, his blue eyes wide with surprise. Senzey grabbed him to her breast, looking as though she would never let go.

Lizbeth stood by with her mouth wide open. "Oh my Lord," she finally said, reaching out one finger to gently stroke the top of his tiny head. "Hello, my sweet baby." She turned to the others in awe. "He's the spitting image of his father."

Charlie saw tears begin to flow from both Lizbeth and Senzey, and felt her own eyes watering.

"We have to get out of here," her mother said. "Fast."

The orphanage director stood, speechless, his eyes glued to the broken door torn from its hinges.

"And you," April said, backing up as the others hustled toward the front door, "don't you think you're going to get away with a thing. I'll be back. And next time, I'm bringing every honest cop I can find who's not on your payroll, any government official who has the decency to do what's right, and we will shut this place down. And you and that fucking husband of mine, you are both going to go down with it. I guarantee it."

Charlie stopped outside the door, waiting for her mother to catch up. And when she did, the woman found herself wrapped up in the hug her daughter had been waiting ten years to give.

39

The sun had not yet risen when Bea showed up back at the hotel. By that time, Charlie and April had both given in to the allure of sleep, curled together on the wicker sofa beneath the veranda's broad eave, where they had camped out watching for a pair of headlights winding up the hotel driveway that would signal Bea's safe return.

Their own return to the hotel had caused quite a commotion, with the baby screaming from hunger, and a mad dash through the hotel in a futile search for a bottle. Stanley delivered a pot of warm milk to the table, and Senzey tried to feed Lukson with her finger. The baby, frustrated and starving, screamed even louder. Then Lizbeth took over, attempting to get him to take some milk from a cup, which ended with a soaked dishtowel and not much more. It was Robert who finally came up with the solution of a syringe from the hotel's first aid kit.

After the baby had calmed, the women retreated to their rooms, Lizabeth carrying a pile of soft, clean cloth napkins, courtesy of the hotel laundry, which would have to suffice for diapers until the next day. Comforted and sated, the baby was tucked up for the night on the mattress between his mother and grandmother, neither of whom were likely to take their eyes off of him for the sake of a night's sleep.

It was already late when Charlie and April found Bea's note, stuck in the doorjamb of the room Charlie shared with her grandmother. Charlie turned the key and flipped on the light, finding her grandmother's bed empty. April read Bea's message out loud.

"Off on a mission! Do not worry. All will be fine. Do not wait up. I am in good hands."

"What the hell?" Charlie hurriedly checked the bathroom, not wanting to really believe her grandmother was missing. "That's it? That's all she had to say?" Where could her grandmother have gone at this time of night? And in the middle of a riot? What was she thinking? Charlie rushed out the door and scurried down the covered walkway to Robert's room, her mother close behind.

"What is it?" he asked, his eyes heavy with sleep. "Is everything okay? Is it the baby?"

"It's my grandmother. Do you know where she is?" Charlie found herself shaking in the warm night air.

"Madame Bea? I assumed she was sleeping. She is not there?"

Charlie shook her head. "She left a note, but didn't say anything about where she was going."

Robert took in a deep breath. "That is strange." His eyes drifted up toward the full moon above. "But at least the city is quiet, for now." He placed his hand on Charlie's shoulder. "I am sure you are worried. If you would like, we can call the police, but I would not expect them to do much tonight. I suggest you be patient and wait. Bea will be back. I have a feeling I know what she is up to, and she will be kept safe. Try to be patient," he repeated.

Charlie's mother took her arm and led her back downstairs to the veranda. "He's right, you know." She sat and patted the cushion beside her.

Charlie sat, her gaze focused on the millions of stars that hung like a canopy across the sky.

"It never has been easy, living with your grandmother."

Charlie didn't need her mother to tell her that. How many times over the past year had she found herself the victim of Bea's stubbornness?

"She always seemed to be one step ahead of everyone else, her intuition telling her more about what was going on with me than I even knew myself."

Charlie had to laugh. "Must have been tough getting away with a lie."

"You have no idea," April said. "It was truly irritating, the candles and crystals all over the house, the herbs and the feathers, the smudging and the cleansing, the people coming and going, looking for a reading. It was so embarrassing for a young girl just trying to fit in. Honestly? I think it's what made me turn to the church, and to Jim. All that weirdness, that touchy-feely bull? I was sick of everyone talking all the time. I just wanted to get out there and *do*."

From the other side of the thick wall surrounding the hotel and its garden came the sounds of night in the city—the lone roar of a motorbike, the toot of a horn, voices echoing in anger.

"But you know?" her mother continued. "Now I'm actually glad I was raised the way I was. No matter how much I fought it, the things I learned from living with Bea must have crept in somehow when I wasn't paying attention."

"Like what?" Charlie asked.

"Well, like realizing that we need to be open to things beyond what we think we know, that the world is not to be looked at as just black and white."

"Seems so," Charlie agreed.

"And that everything, virtually everything, happens for a reason."

Charlie allowed her head to come to rest on her mother's shoulder.

"I hope you can find it in yourself to forgive me, Charlie." She wrapped her arm around her daughter. "I've made some terrible mistakes, ones that can't be erased. But you know, another thing Bea taught me is that the mistakes we make are what we learn from, they're the things that make us grow."

"We all make mistakes, Mom."

Her mother gave her shoulder a little squeeze.

"And right now, I've gotta say, I'm feeling pretty okay. Except, of course, for the fact that my blind-as-a-bat grandmother is missing on the streets of a strange city that's been erupting like a tinderbox, getting herself into who knows what kind of trouble and making me want to tear out my hair."

"Bea will be all right. She's what we used to call a real pisser," her mother continued. "Do they still use that phrase?"

"Never heard it, but I get it."

"I thought she would have slowed down by now. But apparently not."

"So you're not worried?"

"Bea knows who to trust. And who to not. She always has."

Around them the lights of the old hotel blinked off, leaving them in near darkness on the abandoned veranda.

"What are you going to do, Mom?"

"I don't know, baby. I just don't know."

"You can't go back to him, not now."

"No, I can't. But I can't run away, either. This is my home. I've never felt more at peace with myself than I do here. Another thing I learned from your grandmother is that we're all here for a purpose. And somehow mine seems to be linked with this island. It's hard to explain, but there's something about the spirit of these people, the way they can see humor in the face of such devastating adversity. *Dan ri danje*, they say. Teeth laugh at danger. I love that one. But to me, it's also the way they solve problems, the way they carry respect for their neighbors, and love for their families. I know it sounds crazy, to an outsider."

"It's not crazy, Mom. Not at all."

"And Haiti—it's a small spot on a small island. Jim knows too many people. There's nowhere for me to hide, even if I wanted to, which I don't."

They talked long into the night, trading memories of a happier past so long ago, sharing hopes and dreams of a future yet to come, the ghosts of the old hotel the only witnesses to their secrets.

"Can't an old blind woman get a place to sit anymore?"

Charlie and her mother woke to the sight of Bea and the woman who'd appeared at the door of her room a few mornings earlier—the woman with the dagger in her hand. Mambo Michèle. To Charlie, they both looked as though they'd been at a rave all night, Bea's hair pulled loose and flying wild with the dampness of the tropical air, the *mambo*'s makeup smeared, her eyes bright with excitement. And what was Bea doing wearing Charlie's skirt, its hem dark as if it had been dragged through the dirt?

"Where have you been?" Charlie asked, as though she were confronting a wayward teenager sneaking in after curfew.

"Just taking care of a few loose ends," Bea answered, like it was the most normal thing in the world for an old blind woman to be out on her own in a not-so-safe foreign city overnight. "So where's the baby? Can we see him?"

"How do you know—"

"Don't ask," her mother warned. "He's upstairs sleeping, with his mother and his grandmother. We've had quite a night."

"As have we," the *mambo* said. "You are a good woman, Madame Bea, and a lucky one." She turned to April. "And you as well, my dear. *You bon poul fè bon pitit.* A good hen hatches a good chick. And with that, it is time that I say goodnight." She placed her hands on Bea's shoulders, the two of them breaking into a little shimmy and a laugh that echoed out into the garden, where a rooster crowed to announce the appearance of the rising sun.

40

Charlie held the picture frame in her hands. "What were you guys all dressed up for?" she asked Bea. "You're in a big purple hat, Mom's got these weird boots on. She has to be about ten in this one." She placed the framed photo back on her mother's mantel.

"Probably one of our girls' nights out," Bea said, her ear cocked toward the front door.

"Your grandmother used to get me to crash parties with her, down at the women's club," April shouted from the bedroom, where she was hastily packing a few of her things.

Charlie continued to snoop, to get a quick peek at everything she hadn't noticed on her first visit to the home April shared with Jim up on the mountain.

"I will never forget the time you stood up and gave a toast at that Bar Mitzvah," April called out. Charlie could tell her mother was trying hard to keep the conversation light, for their sakes.

"That was before you became embarrassed by me. When you still allowed yourself to be seen in my presence," Bea called back.

"Well, you *were* pretty weird, Mom." April appeared in the doorframe, a pair of khakis draped over one arm. "What mother tells her daughter's best friend that she's about to suffer an unwelcome surprise? Seriously, Charlie. It was fifth grade, career day. I thought it would be pretty cool to have Mom come in and talk about hairdressing. When it was her turn to speak, she asked for a volunteer. I thought she was going to demonstrate braiding or something. But no. She pulls out her tarot deck and does a damn reading. I thought I was going to die."

Bea laughed. "Oh, come on, April. It wasn't my fault that she picked the Ten of Swords! And really, I wasn't that bad. Remember how I used to give you Christmas in August?"

"It's true. You did do that." April turned to Charlie. "Houdini, our Cocker Spaniel, had just died. Bea came up with the brilliant distraction of making it Christmas right then and there. We decorated the house, made cookies. The whole thing. It was so much fun we kept it up for years."

"We did that once in the jungle, don't you remember, Mom?"

"I do remember." April smiled wistfully, before her face hardened at the thought of the situation at hand. She quickly retreated to the bedroom to finish her packing.

"Are you almost done in there?" Bea called after her.

"Just about. We still have time." Charlie worried that April might be trying to convince herself as much as them. "It's seven hours minimum from Les Cayes, after he battles the traffic getting through the city. And it will be even longer, with the demonstrations."

They had debated the wisdom of going up the mountain that day. Charlie's mother was certain that Jim wouldn't have

273

started heading back to Farming for Freedom until daybreak at the earliest, even if he did catch wind of what they'd been up to in Port-au-Prince. The roads, she told them, were terrible. And there was no way Jim was going to put himself in danger by leaving while it was still dark. As angry as he might be, he was not that brave a man. So they agreed to leave the hotel as soon as possible, to get out of the city before the roads became jammed with protestors, and in plenty of time to get in and out of the house on the hill before Jim's return. Dissuading Bea from accompanying them was not an option. She insisted on at least setting foot in the place her daughter had lived for so many years.

Charlie ran her fingers over the familiar surface of a little carved jaguar that used to sit on their kitchen counter in the jungle. Out of the corner of her eye she could see Bea fidgeting nervously in her chair by the door.

"I just need to find a couple of things," April shouted from the bedroom. "Charlie? Quick, can you come in here and help me for a second?"

Charlie's eyes nearly popped out of her head when she saw the bundles of cash strewn across the quilted bedspread.

"What," her mother said, "you think I'm about to leave it all for him? Maybe it's dirty money now, but that doesn't mean it needs to stay that way. Just think of all the good we can do with this, Charlie."

"Holy shit."

"Help me, will you? I need to get up there on that shelf." April dragged out a small ladder that had been leaning against the wall inside the closet. Charlie opened it wide and held tight as her mother climbed to the top.

"Careful," she warned.

"I know there's something up here," her mother said as she rifled through a couple of boxes.

"What are you looking for? Shouldn't we be going already?"

"I'm hurrying."

"What's so important?"

"I need proof."

"Proof?"

"Evidence. Of where the money comes from. Jim is not going to get away with this."

The ladder wobbled as April reached to an even higher shelf. Charlie tightened her grip.

"Aha! Got it."

Suddenly there was the sound of a deep voice in the other room. They both froze.

"Hello, Jim," they heard Bea say loudly as their eyes locked onto each other's.

"What's that, *JIM*?" Bea asked, turning up the volume even more. "Speak up. My hearing's not so good these days."

"I said, long time no see," Jim boomed. Charlie felt sick at the familiar tone, the fake niceness that coated his words like a boxer's robe about to be tossed off for the fight.

"Likewise, Jim, likewise."

April silently lowered herself down the rungs one by one, carefully folding the document she'd managed to retrieve and sliding it into her pocket. She turned to Charlie with a shaky index finger held across her lips, and began to furiously stuff the cash from the bed into her bra and under the waistband of her pants, motioning for Charlie to do the same.

"Did you have a nice trip, Jim?" Bea yelled.

God bless Bibi. Charlie's heart pounded against her chest. Smart woman, stalling for time.

"I did, I did," he shouted back. Charlie could sense the explosion just seconds away.

"That's nice."

"Uh-huh," Jim answered, sounding distracted.

"Fruitful?" she asked.

"Yeah," he answered, quieter this time.

Charlie turned to her mother at the sound of his boots approaching the bedroom. April kicked the last bundle of money under the bed just as her husband's wiry frame filled the doorway.

Jim's eyes darted around the room, taking inventory. "So what's going on in here?" he said when his focus finally landed on April. "You planning a trip or something?" A tight-lipped smile snaked across his face.

Charlie had seen that smile before. She'd witnessed it plenty of times, the way he'd try to assert his control over a situation by pretending to be all nice, expecting everyone to bow down to his power, or else.

"I'm leaving, Jim," April said quietly.

Charlie noticed a flash of surprise in his eyes. "Really? You think that's what you're gonna do? Run off for a few days with these two?" Jim looked almost amused. Charlie knew better.

"I'm not just going for a few days."

Her stepfather took out a handkerchief and slowly wiped it across his sweaty face. "Now, let's not be rash, April. I know it must be a shock to come across her again." He thrust his chin toward Charlie. "And your mom. Of course it's got you a little worked up."

"I am not 'a little worked up', Jim." Charlie's mother grabbed her bag from the bed and slung the strap over her shoulder.

Jim had the look of a rat about to be trapped into a corner. Again his eyes scanned the room.

"Look," he said, "why don't we just sit down and have a talk about all this?" He reached for the strap.

April pulled back. "I'm going."

Charlie saw his shoulders stiffen as she followed her mother past Jim, through the doorway that led back into the front room. She could feel the clock ticking down.

"You can't leave, April," he said, his volume rising. "We both know that. God put us on this earth to do his work as a team. You turn against me, you're turning against Him."

April spun around to face him. "His work? You call this His work? If that's what you think, then you should go back and actually read that Bible you're always waving around like a weapon, using it to make yourself look like a big man who should be treated as a god himself. Well, you know what? You're not a big man—you're just a bad one. Back home, you'd be in prison by now. And with some luck, that's exactly what will happen here as well."

Jim was shaking his head violently back and forth, as though the gesture could erase her words. "Think about all those people you're gonna hurt, how many lives you're gonna destroy, April. This is something bigger than us. It's not about Bea, or Charity, or even me—"

"When has it ever not been about you?" April turned to lift Bea out of her chair, and started with her toward the front door, Jim close behind.

Charlie saw Jim's face turn purple. He moved to block the door.

"You're a selfish woman, April. Just like your damn daughter. The two of you," he hissed. "Sticking your goddamn noses in my business. Do you know how much trouble you've already caused me, with my associates? Do you?" he yelled.

"Get the hell out of my way," April said, trying to push past him. In an instant, Jim had her upper arm gripped in his clutch. She struggled to pull away, but Jim held fast.

"Get your hands off of her!" Bea yelled, waving her arms in Jim's direction.

Jim shoved April aside, bringing Bea down with her. Charlie leaped in to catch her grandmother, but was too late. The old woman's face collided with a thud against the corner of a small stone table.

"I'm okay," Bea insisted, struggling to get up from the floor. But from the look of the mark spreading under her eye like red wine on a tablecloth, Charlie knew she was not.

Jim took a step back as April and Charlie helped Bea up. April jammed the strap of her bag higher on her shoulder and threw open the door.

"Go ahead and leave!" Charlie heard him shout, after they were already twenty feet down the path. "See if I care."

The three women rushed toward their SUV as the door slammed behind them. Charlie fumbled to open the car, but froze, her heart stopping when she saw what Jim had done. The car was leaning toward her at an odd angle, resting on two flat tires, their metal rims grazing the earth below.

"Shit, shit, shit!" She kicked at the dirt.

"Oh no," her mother moaned.

"What's happening?" Bea asked, her voice weak and trembling.

A sudden movement over Bea's shoulder kept Charlie from answering. April spun around as Charlie jumped in to shield her grandmother.

The guard, Eddy, stood silently by the side of the house, the blinding sun bouncing off the lenses of his dark glasses, his rifle by his side.

"Here," he said in a loud whisper, before tossing something small and shiny to Charlie's mother.

She held up a pair of keys.

Eddy pointed his chin toward the canary yellow truck parked behind the crippled SUV. "Quick, Madame April," he urged. "Now go." And then he disappeared.

41

Six weeks later

Even with her aching back and throbbing knees, and hands so chapped they looked like red leather, Lizbeth was as happy as a hog in mud. The soapy tiled floor was finally coming clean. Her next job would be to measure the windows for curtains.

She could hear Senzey's voice coming from the next room. She had to hand it to the girl. It seemed like once she got an idea in her head, there was no stopping her. *Fanm Ansanm* was set to open in just four days.

At first Lizbeth had been crushed that Senzey had no interest in getting herself to Texas with the baby. April had warned them about how tough it might be, what with the new immigration restrictions and all. But Senzey didn't seem to even want to try.

"I am sure Texas is a very nice place," Senzey had told her. "Luke talked so much about it. And someday I would like to see it, and would like very much for my son to see it as well. But Haiti is my home. I do not want to leave."

Lizbeth had felt as though she'd been kicked in the gut by a mule. She'd had the whole thing pictured in her head. Little Lukson all set up in a crib in Luke's old room, with some new wallpaper and a thick, soft rug, maybe one of those lights that make the ceiling look like a starry night sky. And she'd imagined Senzey spending her days in the backyard painting at an easel, like a real van Gogh. Maybe even teaching some art classes down at the local community center.

But Senzey had other ideas. *Fanm Ansanm* came from what she had seen Martine doing down in Jacmel. Senzey was hellbent on doing something to help women, other mothers, to keep them from making the kind of choice she'd been forced to make. And the only way to do that, she said, was to teach them skills that would allow them to earn their own money. Lizbeth loved the name she chose. *Fanm Ansanm.* Women Together.

Things quickly fell into place. Mackenson's brother, the one who was a priest, had an empty building that was a part of his church. Some Germans had been planning to start a project there the year before, but for one reason or another it never happened. So Mackenson convinced his brother to turn over the space to Senzey. It was plenty big enough for all the classrooms and the day care, and also for the little shops or workrooms they'd need someday to help the women start their businesses. And it had a huge kitchen. But still, money would be needed to run the place, to buy materials, and to help support the women while they learned, so they could afford to feed their families.

That's when Lizbeth stepped in. She bet on the fact that those church folks back home wouldn't know what hit them once she got her hands on their wallets. They wanted to help?

She'd show them what help was. She knew those people's intentions were right. She just needed to show them how to start thinking with their heads instead of their hearts.

One quick trip back to Texas, and she'd been proven right. The dollars had started flying down to Haiti faster than a sneeze through a screen door.

"I've seen a few people down here trying to do similar things," April had cautioned Senzey. "Like the woman who started up the project where they make jewelry. Nice idea, and beautiful stuff. I think they're doing well, but I've heard they have more women than they can handle lining up to get hired."

"But this is different," Senzey had insisted. "I want to give women skills that they can use on their own. That way we can keep taking in others to help."

So now the plan was to start by growing fruits and vegetables, the way they did it down here, on rooftops, in old tires. They would sell their organic produce to restaurants. They'd also try canning their own sauces and jams to be put up for sale. They hoped to get into teaching some cooking, so some women might be able to, one day, start their own little restaurants. Mackenson's wife, Fabiola, would be of help there, with her experience as a cook. And Lizbeth had hauled her big old sewing machine down from Texas, with the thought of sharing some of her own skills.

April, bless her heart, had also volunteered to chip in. Lizbeth would never forget the look on Charlie's face when her mother said she was planning on staying behind once she and Bea went back home to California.

They'd all been gathered around a table on the hotel's veranda, a bottle of rum between them, Bea sporting a shiner as purple as the milkweed that grew wild back home. *You shoulda seen the other guy*, is what she'd said to Robert when he expressed his concern.

After Senzey had finished telling them about the plan that had been cooking in her brain, Lizbeth surprised them with her own decision to remain in Haiti.

"You're staying?" Charlie asked, her eyes wide.

"I think you've had one too many *kleren*, Texas Grandma," Bea added, with a laugh.

"Well, maybe I have imbibed just a bit too much, but even so, I'm as serious as a dog with a rib-eye. You think I'm gonna leave behind the only family I have? That I'm not gonna stick around to see this baby take his first steps, say his first words? What am I going to do up there in Texas, rattling around that empty house all by myself? Besides, who's gonna help Senzey out with all this if I'm not around? My big old Texas mouth is gonna come in right handy around here."

"Seems like that makes four of us staying behind," April said.

Her words seemed to fall on Charlie hard. "But—"

"I told you, Charlie. Haiti is home to me. You think you had trouble adjusting to life in California? Imagine me trying to make that work, after all these years away. Senzey's project is perfect for me, exactly the kind of thing I think should be happening down here. I can be a huge help to her and Lizbeth. Besides, I have some unfinished business to attend to."

Lizbeth didn't know how she and Senzey would have ever got along without April, the way she knew how things worked in Haiti. The woman was a downright genius when it came to negotiating. She'd even managed, lickety-split, to find a place for all of them to live. Lukson was, by default, the man of the household, living like a little prince among Lizbeth, Senzey and April in a rented three-bedroom apartment in the suburb of

Pétion-Ville. The fancy part of town, as Charlie's mother put it, where the diplomats and foreigners and businessmen of Port-au-Prince lived high atop the frenzy of the city, cocooned in their gated estates. Theirs was not a mansion, by any means, but it was a nice place with plenty of room for a child to grow.

Senzey had big plans for *Fanm Ansanm*. While they waited for their first harvest, Mambo Michèle would be conducting a class in manufacturing herbal soaps and ceremonial candles. She had asked April to consider teaching a little hairdressing. And eventually, she said, they'd be hiring an instructor for a class in basic business management.

Lizbeth stood and stretched her back. Her afternoon naps were ancient history by now, with her being so busy and all. But that was fine by her, especially after hearing the Haitian proverb Mambo Michèle had scared her with once, after she'd caught Lizbeth letting out a big yawn: *Sleep is death's younger brother*, the woman had warned. That had woken Lizbeth up right then and there.

Through the doorway she saw Senzey ushering in yet another candidate, one more in the tide of young mamas just looking to help their families survive. This girl had two little ones hanging onto her skirt, both of them barely old enough to walk. Twins, Lizbeth thought. She could only imagine how hard it might be for Senzey to turn away any of these women. Word of mouth was traveling fast. They sure had their work cut out for them.

Up on the roof, she could hear April and Mackenson banging around, getting everything all cleaned up to make space for the garden. Must be hot as blue blazes up there, she imagined. Lord knows it was an oven inside, despite the open windows. How Senzey stood it, shuffling all those women in and out and fussing over Lukson without losing a drop of sweat, was beyond her. She supposed it was something she'd have to get used to, just like everything else around here.

Who would have dreamed she'd ever be living in a place like this? She certainly wouldn't have, that's for damn sure. But she had to admit, it truly had grown on her—those smiles that were more real than any you'd find on a Texan face, those streets bursting with color and chock-full of life no matter what the time of day, that sweet, juicy fruit that tasted like it had just been plucked straight from the tree. Even those crazy rainstorms that seemed to explode from above made her tingle all over.

Lizbeth stood at the window watching cotton-ball clouds drifting across the baby blue sky. Beautiful. "If only Luke were here to see all this," she sighed.

She looked up to see Senzey in the doorway, a motionless Lukson draped over one shoulder. The girl silently passed the sleeping child to her, where he snuggled in against her arms as if they were the edges of a warm cradle.

Lizbeth felt the warmth of tears rolling down her cheeks. The baby's eyes fluttered open, and his little pink lips bowed into a sleepy smile at the familiar sight of his grandmother's face.

42

Charlie squeezed past the life-size statue of Èrzulie Fréda to get to the foils, the jagged edges of the sculpture's tin crown catching on her sweater as she did. "Damn it, Bea. Did you have to choose something so big?"

"That thing is kind of creepy, if you ask me," Doreen said from her chair in front of the mirror.

"She's not creepy," Bea said. "She's the Vodou spirit of love."

"If you say so." Doreen had walked into the Bea's Hive salon looking like a zebra, thanks to the boxed at-home dye-job she'd succumbed to during Charlie's stay in Haiti. When it came to their hair, it seemed like the women of Carmel had zero patience. She was still doing damage control on those who had sought help elsewhere during her absence. Charlie had been booked solid since her return, and she was exhausted.

Bea, however, was in her element, spending her days entertaining the salon's endlessly revolving audience with her tales. Each time Charlie heard them, the stories became more dramatic—the search for the baby sounding like an action movie, the *mambo* becoming a mythical sorceress, Robert a matinée idol.

"Why don't you show Doreen your love letters—I mean, your postcards," Charlie teased. Robert was traveling through the States—Louisiana, North Carolina, Brooklyn—continuing his research on various Vodou practices. There was talk of him possibly coming to San Francisco to look into the life of a Vodou princess who lived there more than one hundred years ago.

"Mind your own business, Charlie. You know I don't think of Robert in that way."

"Uh-huh," Charlie said.

Doreen laughed.

"But I will show you the pictures of our baby," Bea offered. "Have I shown you those yet?"

Charlie loved how Bea had claimed part ownership of Lukson, acting every bit the long-distance grandmother as Lizbeth was in person down in Haiti. She and Lizbeth spoke daily, marveling over each little thing that child did. You'd think he was the first baby they'd ever been around, the way they went on and on.

Charlie and her mother also spoke daily. She could hear the excitement bubbling through in each conversation. For the first time in April's life, she claimed, she could actually see that she might make a difference, a real difference that was more than just a band-aid or a fool's errand. And each time they spoke, Charlie and her mother both made a promise to visit, their conversations ending with *I love you*, a signoff that once again felt as natural as a simple *goodbye*.

And Jim? April had finally managed to pull the rug out from under him, exposing him to his backers for what he was.

The travesty on the mountain was closing for good, a huge chunk of Jim's money being distributed as back pay among those who had suffered from his tyranny. She was still working on the orphanage racket, a difficult feat in a country that was used to turning a blind eye to those sorts of situations. Yet she was confident that, with time, and a bit more rabble-rousing, she'd be able to make some headway. For now, Jim had been rendered fairly harmless. She had no doubt he would eventually pop up with another scheme, in another place. That was who he was. But in the meantime, among both the church community back home and the underbelly of Port-au-Prince, he was about as welcome as a skunk at a lawn party, as Lizbeth would say.

"Have I told you about the zombies?" Bea asked Doreen. "They're real, you know."

Charlie cleared her throat loudly.

"Well, sort of," her grandmother added. "But they do know how to bring people back from the dead down there."

"You're scaring Doreen, Bea. Enough with the zombie talk."

"You're no fun, Charlie. Oh, and, by the way, don't forget to put some lowlights in her highlights, and cut off the over-bleached stuff."

"Yes, Queen Bea." Charlie shook her head. Her grandmother would never learn to let go of the reins of this place. No matter how hard Charlie tried, nothing would ever change at Bea's Hive. Even her attempts at decluttering had been thwarted. It wasn't just Èrzulie Fréda looming over the salon. It was also the mass of Martine's paintings, which had cost Charlie a fortune to frame in Carmel. Now they were crammed into every spare space along the salon's four walls, the glittering women watching over Charlie with their soulful eyes as she worked. Whatever bare, flat surface was left in the salon had also been claimed by the candles and bowls and cups, the red silk flowers and blue beads, the two baby dolls with eyes that opened and shut—Bea was planning on putting together an altar for Èrzulie Dantòr soon, she'd told Charlie.

Until then, her grandmother's prized possession from their trip—a gift from the *mambo*—remained folded, right there on the shelf next to the towels. The traditional Vodou flag would be draped right above the altar, somewhere convenient for Bea to run her hands over the thousands of tiny sequins and beads that depicted the *loa* in all her glory. There Bea would draw upon the magic of her friend Mambo Michèle and the power of Èrzulie Dantòr to do her stuff. In the meantime, she was using her own magic—the magic of her mouth—to bully their clients into chipping in for the Bea's Hive Salon Scholarship Fund, money that went straight toward sending Mackenson's daughter and her two cousins to school.

Despite her enthusiasm for hanging around the salon to entertain people with her stories, Bea had been busier than ever with her own clients, spending hours each day on the other side of the door. Charlie didn't know what the hell was going on back in Bea's little "office" behind the kitchen, what she and her devotees were talking about. She wasn't sure she even wanted to know.

For the most part, Charlie was happy to be home. She was honestly warming to what she did, helping people feel good about themselves, both inside and out, when she added her therapist hat to her hairdresser's toolbox. But that old restlessness, that yearning to walk among cultures other than her own, had been stirred up by the trip to Haiti. It was the freedom one feels in the unfamiliar, that space to listen to your own words, that constant challenge to your perceptions of the world, and of yourself. To Charlie, that was her comfort zone.

That's why this time, after the bell over the salon door rang for the last time that afternoon, and Bea turned to her, took off her glasses, leaned forward, and uttered those five familiar words, Charlie had to smile.

"Charlie," her grandmother said. "I've had a dream."

Acknowledgements

I am thrilled to share *Island on the Edge of the World* with you, my readers. This is my sixth book, and I have loved the process of writing and researching every one of them because each time I learned something more about cultures and people. I also love writing the acknowledgments, because, while writing a book may appear to be a solo act, it is not. This leads me to thank the most amazing, most gifted writer in the universe, Ellen Kaye. Let me tell you a bit about our relationship. She is the backbone to my books, my friend, my travel buddy and research partner. She is the hardest-working and most dedicated and most talented person I know, and I love working with her. Wonder what our work relationship is like? Think the odd couple. (I'll let you guess who's who.) She makes sense of my chaos. She helps me get the story out of my head. I admit it takes an enormous amount of time and energy to sort through some of the clutter in my brain.

Thank God she has a wonderful, patient husband in Andy Besch, who says, "Go for it, Ellen. I'll walk the dog and cook dinner while you go off again to the ends of the earth with Deb." Ellen, can you believe this is the fourth book we have worked on together? I also have to thank Tillie (the dog) for loaning her to me.

Beverley Cousins, you are an amazing editor. You dig in first and push hard. I am forever thankful for your notes, even when I grumble. I know now to trust your clarity of vision and the gift you bring to my stories. I am so grateful to you and your entire team at Penguin Random House. And I have such gratitude to Maddie West, my editor at Little, Brown UK and Sphere Fiction, for her constant faith in me. I love how you take time to conspire with us about all the whirling stories in my head. Thank you both so much for believing in me.

The ringmaster in all of this is Marly Rusoff, my agent and friend. I often think back to our first conversation, fifteen years ago, when I called you from Afghanistan. Imagine! We've already managed six books together. I adore you and your partner Mihai (Michael) Radulescu. Marly, thank you for helping see my stories reach a global platform, but most of all thank you for believing in that crazy hairdresser from Michigan who thought she had a book in her.

Lizzy Kremer, thank you for being my agent for the UK and Australia. You have always been a champion for my books. Being on your team is the best, and I am very grateful.

Noah and Zachary Lentz, thank you for being the loving sons you are. I draw inspiration from both of you. The fun—and periodically unpredictable—life that we lived was sometimes a blessing, and, a few times, not so much. For this book I drew from some of our complicated times as a family to help bring the story to life. I am so proud of the men you have become, despite having a mother who often lacked a good husband radar. Just like in the book, boys, we made it through and came out on top. You will both recognize the truth in the stories. I love you so much.

My daughters-in-law are amazing. Martha Villasana Lentz and Aretha Lentz, thank you for giving me the best gifts in the world—loving my sons, and giving me such beautiful grand-babies. I could never have dreamed that I could love so much.

Denis Asahara, what can I say? I am pretty sure I said, in the acknowledgments for the last book, that you make me crazy, and that still holds true today. I love you and thank you for always being supportive of my adventuresome spirit and creative side. I love that you enjoy the grandbabies as much as I do. I never knew that finding a low-maintenance man was possible until I met you. You make me so happy. I want to grow old with you.

Serena Evans Beeks, I am not sure I have ever met anyone so genuinely kind as you are. You showed me the beauty in all things Haitian, from the people to the art to the countryside. You taught me the mistakes we often make when trying to help poor nations. You took me from seeing, "Oh, those poor people" to "Oh, those beautiful, amazing, resourceful people." Thank you for showing me the real Haiti, and for teaching me how to listen to what Haitians are actually saying. You make such a difference in the lives of Haitian people. They are so fortunate to have you in their lives, as I know you feel you are to have them in yours.

I love missionaries. I grew up in the church, played church as a kid with my stuffed animals as my congregation, and really thought I would be a missionary when I grew up. Missionaries have always been a part of my life. My world became a better place when Tom and Teresa Elkins stepped into Tippy Toes for haircuts. I don't think they had any idea that I was adopting them as my family when we met, but I did. I love your wisdom and kindness and how you shared your incredible and complicated stories about mission life. You opened up the world of third-culture kids to me, both the good and the difficult side. Tom, your jungle stories always made me laugh, and Teresa, my family appreciates you for teaching me how to bake pies. You indeed have become family to me.

Katie Moore and Rachel Chapman, when I listened again to the recording of our conversation about living in the jungles of Venezuela, I was amazed, entertained, and shocked, all at the same time. Katie, you are a natural storyteller, and I hope that someday you'll turn your stories into a book. Rachel, the accounts of your life growing up moved and touched me deeply. You both are an inspiration for all things good.

Lynne Olmstead, I came to you as a stranger, asking you to share with me your life growing up, and then raising a family, in the middle of the Amazon. I could not have brought life to this story without your help. Your dedication to and love for the Yanomami people is beautiful and pure. Thank you for being raw and real with me about tribal life.

Thank you, Debbie Anderson, for giving me insight to the psychic stuff. You were so kind to offer your assistance. In speaking with those who have passed to the other side, you made it sound so easy. Like talking about the weather! You are a natural teacher and speaker, and helped me see things from a different point of view.

Karen Kinne, forever my best friend. I love how I can always send you something to read or hash out a character over the phone. Thank you for being such a beautiful part of my life.

Ingrid Ostick, how many times did you read the manuscript? It is so lovely to have someone to chat with about the characters as if they were real people. They feel real to me, and I can tell they felt real to you. Thank you for always being a good reader, and thank you for letting me explain intricate plots when I am having a hard time sorting things out. But the biggest perk is the friendship that we've developed.

Linda Bine, thank you for once again lending your exacting eyes to this endeavor. Your logical editor's brain has been invaluable when it comes to smoothing out a story that can, at times, become as messy as a tangled head of hair.

My family is from the southern part of the United States, but I was born a Yankee who never developed a true ear for their accent; mine would have gone a bit too "Hew-Haw" without guidance from Wendy Buford Clark and Kathy Murphy, who contributed so much to Lizbeth's Texan "Southern with a twist" accent. Thank you both.

Thanks to the many people who hosted and took care of us in Haiti—from the rental car agents at the airport to the hotel owners and staff to the outstanding cooks whose meals we ate, and so many more people who welcomed us so hospitably. A special shout-out to Herns Celestin, Charlotte Charles, Fabienne Jean, and Sonson and Fanicia Vitorin. Please note that for the good in the people and places depicted in this book, I was able to draw directly from our friends and experiences. For the bad, I had to use my imagination.

Thank you Haiti for being the most remarkable, complicated place that I have experienced in a long time. You are beautiful, and so misunderstood. My hope with this book is that people can experience Haiti the same way I did.

I would be a terrible grandma if I didn't thank all my grandbabies. Luna, Kai, Silas, Italya, Derek, Didier. You inspired this story for me. I would travel to the ends of the earth to make sure each and every one of you remain in my life, close enough for me to wrap my arms around you. The love of a grandmother will always move mountains.

I am always grateful to my clients at Tippy Toes salon for listening to my endless stories while I am trying to work out a plot. You all—or as we would say in the South, y'all—are really important to me, and I honestly could not do any of this without the support from all the beautiful people who walk in and out of the door at Tippy Toes every day.

I would love to thank my always faithful and loyal writing partner, Polly—my cat. We have written five books together. Thanks for being so faithfully furry and sweet, and always loving.

Lastly, thank you to my beautiful city of Mazatlán, Mexico. You opened your arms and let me in. I love this city. It fills my life with joy, happiness, and inspiration. Gracias.

How you can help Haiti

There are more than 35,000 NGOs in Haiti at last count, with no system for evaluating or overseeing their work. When deciding whether you wish to support a charity, consider the following:

- Does this effort increase Haitians' capacities for managing their own future?
- Are there Haitians involved in the management of the agency?
- Is the project moving toward sustainability?
- Is the administrative overhead low or zero?
- Is this effort providing employment for Haitians?
- Is it driven by the needs and goals of Haitians, and not by donors' wishes?

Here are a handful of organizations worth checking out:

Parents and children

Lumos

www.wearelumos.org

Dedicated to ending the institutionalization of children around the world, rescuing them from orphanages and reuniting them with their families. Working to effect change in education, health, and social care systems toward this goal.

Papillon

www.papillon-enterprise.com

Creates jobs for parents who are in need of income to support their children. Exports and markets Haitian artisan goods.

Healthcare/health education

Partners in Health

www.pih.org

Builds and strengthens health systems in communities of need.

Haiti Nursing Foundation

www.haitinursing.org

Supports advancement of quality nursing education.

Children's Medical Mission of Haiti

www.cmmh.org

Provides educational opportunities and life skills training to children with disabilities.

Education

Partnership Program, Episcopal Diocese of Haiti

www.episcopalschools.org/naes-community/ways-to-connect/
partnership-programs

Many denominations have outreach projects in Haiti. The
Episcopal School Partnership Program is focused on school part-
nerships in rural communities. Contact schools@LADiocese.org.

For A Reason

www.FARforareason.org

Provides tuition for motivated students who might otherwise be
at risk of having to leave school.

Agronomy

Zanmi Agrikol: Partners in Agriculture

www.partnersinag.org

Provides training for agronomists, producing fortified medical-
grade peanut mixture to combat malnutrition in infants and
children. Offers family sustainability programs to improve
families' crop production and incomes.

Miscellaneous

Restavek Freedom

www.restavekfreedom.org

An effort to end child slavery in Haiti.

Beyond Borders

www.beyondborders.net

Working to end child slavery and prevent violence against
women and girls in Haiti.

Work

www.dowork.org

Job preparation, training, and placement. Holds the annual Run Across Haiti, a coast-to-coast run with the purpose of creating dialogue, jobs, and income from tourism.

SOIL

www.oursoil.org

Provides sustainable methods of dealing with sewage, transforming wastes into resources.

Want to explore Haiti?

Expedition Ayiti

www.expeditionayiti.org

Promotes intercultural understanding via guided hikes through the beautiful Haitian countryside. Overnights are homestays, with 80 percent of hikers' fees directed to the host communities to be put toward a project of the community's choosing.

About the author

Deborah Rodriguez is the author of the international bestsellers *The Little Coffee Shop of Kabul*, *Return to the Little Coffee Shop of Kabul* and *The Zanzibar Wife*. She has also written two memoirs: *The Kabul Beauty School*, about her life in Afghanistan, and *The House on Carnaval Street*, on her experiences following her return to America. She spent five years teaching and later directing the Kabul Beauty School, the first modern beauty academy and training salon in Afghanistan.

Deborah also owned the Oasis Salon and the Cabul Coffee House, and is the founder of the nonprofit organization Oasis Rescue, which aims to teach women in post-conflict and disaster-stricken areas the art of hairdressing.

She lives in Mazatlán, Mexico, where she owns Tippy Toes salon and spa.

Reading group questions

1. What were your impressions of Haiti before you read this book?

2. Did your impressions about Haiti and/or the Haitian people change after reading the book?

3. Was there anything about Haiti in this book that you found surprising?

4. What did you find most interesting about the Haitian culture?

5. Would you be interested in traveling to Haiti?

6. Have you ever been involved in charitable causes? How effective do you think your efforts were?

7. If you were involved in a group dedicated to helping those in need in other countries, what would your suggested approach be?

8. Have you ever had experience with a psychic medium? If so, what was it like?

9. Do you know anyone who grew up, like Charlie, as a third-culture kid, raised in a culture other than their parents' or the one listed on their passport? How did that affect them, both positively and negatively?

10. Do you confide in your hairdresser in ways you don't with your friends? Does she/he know more about you than others might?

Some delicious Haitian dishes to share

By Georges Laguerre of Tigeorges Kafé, Miami, Florida

Akra
This fried dish is frequently served by sidewalk vendors in the evening. "*Fritay!*"

    3 to 4 malanga or taro roots
    ½ small onion
    1 green onion
    3 garlic cloves, peeled
    ½ green bell pepper
    ½ hot pepper
    1 egg
    1 tsp salt
    ¼ tsp black pepper
    a deep frying pan and enough frying oil to fill it halfway

1. Peel and grate the malanga or taro

2. Finely chop the onion, green onion, garlic, bell pepper and hot pepper

3. Combine all the grated and chopped ingredients and mix evenly

4. Add the salt, pepper and egg, and mix to form a batter

5. Heat the oil and test it with a small amount of batter—when it is hot enough, the oil will start to bubble when the batter is added

6. Divide the batter with a knife, a spoon or a fork, depending on the shape that you want to fry. Add the portions to the oil and fry until golden brown, about 5 minutes

Serve and eat straightaway—after 20 minutes, the flavor is no longer the same.

Pork Griot

Sometimes spelled "grillot" or "griyo". A Haitian favorite.

up to 5 lbs (2.25 kg) pork shoulder
3 sour oranges
1 hot pepper (habanero)
2 tsp salt
¼ tsp black peppercorns
1 oz (2 tbsp) white wine vinegar
5 to 10 cloves, depending on preference

1. The secret is not to wash the meat. Dice the pork shoulder into squares 2–3″ (5–7 cm) in size. If you are in a Haitian community, the butcher will know how to cut the meat for you

2. Peel the oranges, retaining the peel, and then extract the juice, ensuring there are no seeds or skin in the juice

3. Rub the diced meat with the skin of the oranges

4. In a mortar and pestle, crush the hot pepper, salt, peppercorns and cloves

5. Add the pork, spices, vinegar and sour orange juice to a heavy aluminum pot with a lid. Cook on a high heat for 30 minutes

6. Pour the contents out of the pot into a baking pan and put it in the oven to caramelize the meat. Keep an eye on the meat, turning it occasionally. It will only take a few minutes to reach a nice glaze.

Pikliz

Every house in Haiti has a jar of pikliz (pronounced 'pick-lees') in the kitchen. Haitians do not eat without pikliz.

1 lb (500 g) cabbage
1 lb (500 g) carrots
¼ lb (120 g) French green beans
3 hot peppers (habanero)
2 sour oranges
2 tsp salt

1. Shred the cabbage

2. Grate the carrots

3. Trim the beans, and cut into 1″ (2 cm) pieces

4. Wearing a glove, dice the peppers as small as you can

5. Juice the oranges, ensuring there are no seeds or pulp

6. Wearing gloves again, combine all the ingredients in a bowl. Simple!

Pain Patate

Traditionally a breakfast food for Haitians, today pain patate can sometimes be found as a dessert at events and restaurants. It is back-breaking work for the cook, as one has to grate all of the ingredients manually.

1 whole dried coconut
3 lbs (1.5 kg) white sweet potato
5 lbs (2.5 kg) bananas, very ripe
1 lb (500 g) ginger
1 key lime, very green
1 can (12 fl. oz/395 g) evaporated milk
1 can (12 fl. oz/395 g) condensed milk
1 can (12 fl. oz/395 g) coconut milk
1 lb (500 g) softened butter
½ cup brown sugar
1 oz (2 tbsp) pure vanilla extract
2 bay leaves

1. Crack the coconut and grate the flesh

2. Peel and grate the sweet potato

3. Mash the bananas

4. Peel and grate the ginger

5. Zest the key lime

6. Mix all the remaining ingredients and pour into a heavy aluminum pot

7. Cook for 30 minutes over a low heat, stirring occasionally with a wooden spoon

8. Then the mixture is ready to bake. Put the dough into a pan to be baked for one hour at 350 degrees Fahrenheit (180 degrees Celsius)

Allow the pain patate to cool before serving. It is best consumed the next day.

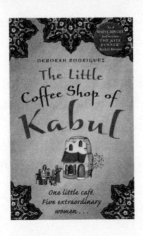

One little café. Five extraordinary women...

In a little coffee shop in one of the most dangerous places on Earth, five very different women come together.

Sunny, the proud proprietor, who needs an ingenious plan—and fast—to keep her café and customers safe...

Yazmina, a young pregnant woman stolen from her remote village and now abandoned on Kabul's violent streets...

Candace, a wealthy American who has finally left her husband for her Afghan lover, the enigmatic Wakil...

Isabel, a determined journalist with a secret that might keep her from the biggest story of her life...

And **Halajan**, the sixty-year-old den mother, whose long-hidden love affair breaks all the rules.

As these five discover there's more to one another than meets the eye, they form a unique bond that will forever change their lives and the lives of many others.

Six women, on opposite sides of the Earth,
yet forever joined by a café in Kabul.

Sunny, its former proprietor and the new owner of the
Screaming Peacock Vineyard in the Pacific Northwest.
But can she handle the challenges of life on her own?

Yazmina, the young mother who now runs the café,
until a terrifying event strikes at the heart of
her family, and business . . .

Layla and **Kat,** two Afghan teenagers in America, both
at war with the cultures that shaped them . . .

Zara, a young woman about to be forced into a marriage with
a man she despises, with devastating consequences for all . . .

These five women are about to learn what **Halajan,**
Yazmina's rebellious mother-in-law, has known all along:
that when the world as you know it disappears, you find
a new way to survive . . .

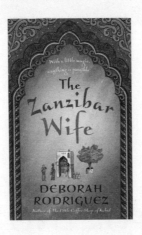

Oman. The ancient land of frankincense, windswept deserts, craggy mountaintops and turquoise seas. A place where tales of evil spirits and eerie phenomena abound. Into this magical nation come three remarkable women, each facing a crossroad in her life.

Rachel, a troubled American war photographer who is struggling to shed the trauma of her career for a simpler, gentler life. Now she has once again picked up her camera and is headed to Oman to cover a quite different story—for a glossy travel magazine.

Ariana Khan, a bubbly British woman struggling to keep up with the glitz of Dubai and ready to give up on love. She has rashly volunteered as Rachel's "fixer", a job she's never heard of in a country she knows nothing about.

And **Miza**, a young woman living far from her beloved homeland of Zanzibar. As the second wife of Tariq, an Omani man, she remains a secret from his terrifying "other" wife, Maryam. Until one day, when Tariq fails to come home . . .

As the three women journey together across this weird and wonderful land, they are forced to confront their darkest fears and their deepest wishes. Because here in Oman, things aren't always what they appear to be . . .

WIN!
A SPA DAY FOR TWO

One lucky winner will win a spa day for themselves and a friend including a treatment each and refreshments. We will also cover up to £100 travel expenses.

To enter please go to:
http://bit.ly/IslandSpaComp

Ts and Cs apply, visit the URL
above for more details